Chapter 1
The Body at the Bell

Ice stalagmites hung from the guttering and windowsills; white patches of frost clung to red brick walls like a fungus; there was stillness, only created by the icy chill of a cold January day in London. Puffs of white clouds formed as pedestrians, huddled in their warm coats, exhaled. No wind disturbed the clouds as they formed and slowly drifted away the cold stillness hugged the shoppers like a shroud. Sirens shouted their noisy movement across the city as the rush hour ended and early shoppers meandered through the icy streets in earnest, trying to stay indoors, be it at home or inside the centrally heated shops. Of all the sirens in the city; there were none louder than the unmarked police car Inspector Alker rode in to a new murder scene. A female her throat cut and she had been laid out naked, was all the information he had at this point. The police doctor was already at the scene with the uniformed officers who had first attended. Alker would be the last of the officials to arrive at the scene.

"Fucking cold this morning Sir," Sergeant Green said by way of casual conversation.

"Are you intellectually challenged Sergeant," Alker asked in his usual calm, collected way?

"No Sir."

"Well then there is no need for expletives, you are a Sergeant in the murder squad at Scotland Yard, we see some nasty, ugly things, but you will never hear me swear, except in extreme circumstances, and never in front of a lady. We need to show some decorum to gain the respect of the public. Keep your cursing for the public bar of your local."

"Sorry Sir."

"Are you afraid that the body might get up and leave, Sergeant?"

"No Sir."

"Panda cars race to the scene of a crime, we hurry, unless we are in pursuit; by the time we get there, the criminals will already have fled. Our job is to collect and collate evidence and pursue the criminal following the evidence trail. There are no criminals at the scene who are about to run, and there is no-one's life to save, she is already dead. So let's try and get there without killing anyone else," Alker said without looking at his new Sergeant, starring out the front window of the car, relaxed, and in control.

"Yes Sir, sorry Sir," Sergeant Green said contritely, his first morning with Inspector Alker and already he had made two mistakes, not a good start.

Inspector Alker had risen through the ranks, following in his father's footsteps, and exceeded his father's rise to sergeant. John felt that the recent surge of common place swearing was unacceptable, this was because of his strict Victorian upbringing, values he wouldn't shake. John Alker was more accustomed to the values of his parent's, which he considered a more socially acceptable standard; therefore he had also adopted those values.

John, stood at five foot nine and a quarter inches tall, in his stocking feet, he was just tall enough to join the police force. John would barely make the requisite height now, as pulled the collar of his overcoat up and huddled, into the coat to protect him from the cold. A steadfast, logical, even pedantic approach to solving crime had earned him the nick name of the Ferret, always digging into the files and finding that small, sometimes insignificant piece of evidence that led him to solving the crime. John would read the files over and over, looking at the evidence; and asking what appeared to be inane questions, were his trademarks, but his methods solved the highest number of crimes; a record of which he was justifiably proud.

Slowly the sun's rays began to illuminate the dark sky, pushing back the half-light of winter's dawn, to allow a bitterly cold but sunny day to emerge. The heat from the sun's rays were still too weak to lift the temperature more than a few degrees, may be to freezing point. Snow had been forecast for later in the day, Alker was dubious about that; it was too cold to snow.

Green pulled up outside the Bell pub, not the screeching halt associated with the police series shown on television, that was for flash and show, but a steady slow and stop. He had already been in trouble for swearing and speeding, and didn't want to create another mistake knowing that the Inspectors attitude was that the dead body wasn't going anywhere, and would wait an extra few moments. Alker got out of the car and surveyed the area; he took in the surroundings before entering the building. Assessing and collating all aspects, creating a mental picture of the area, entrances, exits and ease of entry and exit from the area, street positions and the lighting.

The Bell pub was an old Victorian building; a remnant of a much more elegant period where style and elegance went hand in hand, unlike the monoliths of today. Its red brick facia was dirty from age but still made Alker's heart pound as he looked up the three story building; architecture was a hobby for which he had little time now as an Inspector, the style and ornamentation of the facia shouted the pride of the builders, and stylish designs that modern buildings lacked. The pub was in a rundown area near the docks, and had long needed a face lift to remove the grime of decades of smoke filled air.

Nearby some of the buildings were being demolished to make way for more modern office blocks, concrete monoliths lacking the style and flair of the Bell. Centrally heated and double glazed but soulless blocks. Alker pondered whether the concrete office blocks would ever be viewed with the same admiration as the pub he now studied; its polished brick entrance inviting you to enter.

Alker and Green showed their warrant cards to the officer on the door who nodded in acknowledgement to them. Inside more officers were standing waiting for an order, Alker took in the room, it was a large room, with a high ceiling; Alker was pleased to see the wood and plaster carvings and moulding that decorated the ceiling still in place, a feature that was so popular in that period and indicative of the age of the building. It had been built as a hotel near the docks for the weary traveller, and as a watering hole for the local residents and the dock workers. The bedrooms long disused, there was no need for them today, there were much better establishments with their antiseptic decor and centrally heated rooms, functional but uninspiring, close by, to facilitate the reps or business men of today staying overnight.

Sat at a table was a lean man, ashen white and shaking; he looked down as he wrung his hands in a distraught way, he was obviously in shock.

"Detective Inspector Alker and Detective Sergeant Green from Scotland Yard, it must have been a terrible shock for you finding the body, would you like to see a doctor," Alker said as he introduced himself and Green?

"No, thank you; I, I, sorry," he said and jumped up making for the toilets, his hand over his mouth.

"That's the fourth time Sir, I don't think there is anything left to bring up," the constable close by said, as another constable followed the man to the toilets.

Alker took another look round and told the officer that he would question the man later, then made for the door to his right where there were several comings and goings; he followed the corridor out into the rear yard.

Extensions to the buildings either side blocked the sides of the yard in completely leaving just the rear gated wall which he noted with interest in that it had broken glass on top and barbed wire over that which extended all across the wall and gate.

"Interesting wouldn't you say; no access from the sides and I wouldn't like to tackle that wall and gate, let alone carrying a dead body over my shoulder. What do you say Green?"

"No Sir I wouldn't, especially seeing as the ground has a layer of ice on it, both sides of the gate, from swilling the yard down yesterday,"

"Well spotted Sergeant, no foot hold for a ladder, interesting, and no-one recalls anyone carrying a dead body through the bar, and you'd think they would, wouldn't you?" Alker's dry sense of humour broke the tension between them.

"Yes Sir, especially a naked woman, you'd think they would notice that," Green replied trying to help ease the tension.

The scene before them was that of the body of a woman in her early twenties, laid out purposely with her arms slightly away from her sides, and her legs spread slightly. It was obvious that she had been positioned like that for a reason. She had blonde hair, an attractive face, with an aquiline nose, full lips and high cheek bones. She was slim and had a flat tummy and well defined breasts, her skin was terribly pallid, almost white. At a glance, Alker could tell that she had looked after herself physically from the tone of the skin and muscles.

"She looks in good shape muscular, definitely not fat," Alker said by way of a question?

"Yes, she was fit enough, looked after herself, not excessively muscular but well defined," the man next to Alker said.

The man next to Alker was the police surgeon; he was older than Alker and more rotund. High blood pressure made his cheeks bright red which made it appear that he was permanently blushing.

"Time of death," Alker asked not expecting a definite time?

"Hard to tell Inspector, the normal rate of loss of body heat has been accelerated by the sub-zero temperatures of last night. At this point, it will only be a guess, and that is all it ever may be, but between say eleven last night and four o'clock this morning. Death was caused by, and again until after the autopsy I can't be definite, as you will appreciate; but from the size and depth of the gash in her throat it appears obvious. The cut was left to right starting just below the left ear, severing the carotid artery and trachea. A sharp blade from the cleanness of the cut, a scalpel perhaps, and I would say that the perpetrator had a steady hand there are no jagged edges as it was pulled through the skin. More than that will have to wait till after the autopsy."

"She looks very pale, almost white," Sergeant Green asked?

"Sorry, yes she was bled out, these marks on her ankles," he said pointing to the ridges on both ankles, "those I think, as I said these are just informed guesses, are from hanging her upside down to allow her to bleed out. Now I must go I will try and have the autopsy report on your desk by the day after tomorrow."

"Ok, thank you, sooner if possible I don't have much to go on," Alker said, still looking at the body with interest.

Alker stood by the body and every now and then turned to survey the area; as if working out some puzzle, digesting a fact or suggestion, before moving on to the next fact. Green stood near the door and watched him with interest trying to work out what he was thinking, how his mind was working.

Green was pleased when he was told that he was to report to Inspector Alker that morning, having just been appointed to Detective Sergeant. A week ago he was working in another division as a Sergeant having applied a few times for the transfer to the murder squad. A much needed week's holiday and then he was to join Alker as his Sergeant. Now he began to wonder, as he watched Alker digest the gruesome scene in what he presumed was infinite detail. What there was to see, what was he missing that Alker was seeing? A body in a yard that was so secure you couldn't get into it, except through the bar. Yet there she was laid out in a way that made you realise that it was a sexually orientated murder. What was he missing, Alker obviously from the time he was spending watching had gained far more information about the scene, the murderer, and the victim, than he had, but what?

"Sergeant we'll speak to the landlord now, have you got all the information you can from the scene," Alker asked him?

"Yes Sir," was Green's reply, but he wasn't sure what the Inspector had meant and decided that to agree was the best course of action, for now. Andrew was on a steep learning curve; he was learning how his new Inspector worked and the methods he used.

Entering the pub Alker walked slowly, looking around as he made his way along the corridor. He had already noted the two doors off the corridor, one to the toilets and the other to the kitchen; he opened both doors to be sure. Alker looked inside the rooms, and made a quick survey of the room before he closed the door again. From a quick visual survey, he was able to create a plan of the room, noting the points of access and egress, not just the doors the windows were also noted and any other means of access.

"I need to ask you some questions, how are you feeling now, more settled," Alker asked calm and with sincerity trying to put the landlord at ease?

"Yes, thank you, my stomach is calming down; it was such a shock, I mean, she, well you saw," he replied putting his hand to his mouth, as if he was about to vomit again.

"I know you have already told the constable all about finding her, but I need to ask again for my records, so what is your name?"

"Bob, sorry Robert Bell, and I am the owner, a pools win."

"Does anyone else work here?"

"Just my chef, a barmaid, and the cleaner, she works every other day. I bought it because I like pubs and decided that I may as well make money from er, my er, hobby, like."

"Who was working last night, and what time did you close?"

"Mondays I am on my own, it's too quiet to bring staff in, we get a, dozen or so locals, that's all we serve. The chef worked the morning as usual, we do a lot of lunches for the office staff we have around here, and we get the odd meeting, reps and the like. But at night, well there aren't many houses left now, all gone, this redevelopment, soon I'll be gone as well, they reckon a year at the most then this beautiful old building will make way for a block of flats, criminal."

Alker didn't say anything but agreed with Bob's sentiments.

"And closing time, this is a murder enquiry I am not interested in whether or not you did an extra hour or so, but I do need to know the time you cleared the bar and locked up, it's very important."

"Elev," Bob looked at Alker who was watching Bob's eyes, Bob noticed and corrected himself, "no, ok, I allowed a couple of regulars to stay in for a few, it was nearer midnight when I finally locked up."

Bob sat there looking at his hands during the interview, watching as he wrung his hands. Alker realised that it wasn't the fear of being found out, it was to do with finding the body he was still in shock. Alker guessed that the gaping hole in her throat showing all the blood vessels devoid of blood and the muscles now exposed in all their glory or gory detail, had far more to do with his demeanour, than a fear of being caught. Accustomed as he was to seeing dead bodies, without the blood they took on a totally different aura, he wouldn't admit it, but it turned his stomach, a gaping wound and no blood, it just wasn't natural in some way.

"You mentioned staff; how many do you have and when do they work?"

"Margaret is the cleaner she comes in on Mondays, Wednesdays, Fridays and Saturdays, ten till three, she is the chef's wife, he comes in, sorry Harry; he works Monday to Friday mornings, and Friday and Saturday nights. Bettina, she is the bar maid and works Friday to Sunday night only, she is a secretary at one of the local offices. She needed some money last Christmas and asked if I wanted help," he shrugged his shoulders, "I offered her a job temporary, and she is still with me, lovely girl."

"Do any of the staff have the keys to the pub?"

"No need; I am up every morning at seven thirty and let Margaret in when she is working; when Harry comes, she is here as am I, usually, and Bettina arrives when I am open at night and leaves when I close so no."

"Do they have access to the keys?"

"Not really, there is no need I get up and bottle up as I did this morning then I take the skip outside and unlike this morning," Bob stopped, he looked down at his hands as he fought another wave of nausea, he took a few deep breaths, before continuing, "I empty the bottles into the crates ready to go back to the brewery, so the back door is unlocked from then till I close, I made sure the gate was secure so that I could leave the back door unlocked. I unlock the front door as needed, when

I need to go to the bank, it is when both Harry and Margaret are both in; so I don't need to leave the keys, and at night, I am usually on my own, so I lock up."

"Have you ever seen the dead woman before this morning?"

"No Inspector I haven't, and believe me, I would remember a pretty woman like she was."

"Thank you Mr Bell, we may need to ask you some more questions, are you sure you don't want us to call a doctor for you?"

"Sure, thank you, Harry will be here, in a few minutes."

"You won't be able to go into the yard until we have finished out there, are you expecting any deliveries," Green said as John Alker buried himself in his over-coat pulling the collar up in readiness, against the cold outside?

"Ok, we get a delivery tomorrow, and no-one will need to go outside until the chef empties the bins later this afternoon about three, but if need be that can be left till tomorrow," Bob replied, still shaking as he held out his hand to shake the one John Alker offered.

"Come on get the car open Sergeant I'm freezing," John said as he stood waiting for Green to open the car.

They left the scene and headed back to Scotland Yard, Green drove in silence John appeared to be collating the information so Green avoided small talk.

"Sergeant, tell me what theories you derived from the scene?"

"Female, a sexual crime, er, m, male perp?"

"Sergeant what on earth is a perp," Alker demanded annoyed?

"It's perpetrator, just an abbreviation Sir," Green answered uneasily.

"Can you use that term in court? I presume it is an American slang term?"

"It is Sir, and no it cannot be used in court, sorry, male perpetrator, there isn't much to go on Sir."

"Not bad but we learned far more than those tit bits, correct male perpetra-tor, who felt comfortable, he wasn't in a hurry, he felt secure, so the crime was com-mitted somewhere that he knows, and that he knows he will not be disturbed. How long does it take to drain a body of blood, wash it, dry it, plus she had a thick, long head of hair, and then brush and comb it into a simple style?"

"According to my wife about three to four hours Sir, for just her hair," Green said partly as a joke.

"So, we also know that he is well educated, the crime was planned and ex-ecuted whilst the perpetrator felt safe. Far more than you noticed, then there is the scene; a layer of frost on the ice yet no foot prints prior to the arrival of the constables; so if we can determine when the frost was laid, we have a time prior to which the body was placed there, and hopefully the earliest time of death from the doctor, narrowing the time limitations. He was right handed as the doctor said. The cut was from the left ear down and across, a right handed cut, he had a steady hand,

and she didn't move the cut was clean. So we can also assume some sort of drug was used to sedate her. That leaves us with the placement of the body, intriguing, to say the least. The main suspect has to be the landlord, and we will interview him again, but I don't believe that he committed the crime, so how did the body get there; it couldn't have come through the public bar? That leaves us with the gate; well someone would have to be pretty determined to place the body in that particular place; to go to all the trouble and effort to leave it there. Has Robert Bell any enemies that would do such a dastardly thing, leave a dead woman like that, but that is for the next interview. For now what do you recommend as our next course of action?"

"Look into missing persons, but it might be too early for her to have been reported yet, a piece in the local newspapers 'HAVE YOU SEEN THIS WOMAN', and television."

'Good, yes but not local, let's go nationwide from the start. Also, open up a link with Interpol this guy has gone to a lot of trouble to disguise who she is; I doubt that she is a local girl; that would be too easy for us to follow up on."

For the rest, of the journey to Scotland Yard they sat in silence, Green taking in all the information and realising just how much can be gleaned from the scene; he was not new to police work having also gone through the ranks to Sergeant, but he kicked himself for not realising and spotting all that Alker had. Green put it down to nerves, being his first day with Inspector Alker, and vowed not to make that mistake again.

Chapter 2
Time Passes

The winter turned into spring, and all Alker and Green had found out was the same, as when they had examined the body and scene of crime on the first morning.

The doctor had a toxicology report done, which was usual in these cases, it revealed that there was a drug in her system, even though the body had been drained of blood some residual blood and body fluids remained in the organs, and there was enough for it to be analysed. The drug was not in use, nor was it being tested by a drug manufacturer. It wasn't a sedentary drug, which John found interesting, it contained the female hormone oestrogen, and was probably the pill or used to prevent pregnancy, but was not one of the ones recommended by the Family Planning Association. Another interesting factor was that she didn't have an appendix, it is not unusual for it to have been removed, it no-longer served the purpose it was intended for, but there was no scar; this fact was also noteworthy, it had been removed surgically, yet the scaring associated with its removal was not there. John made a note, how could the appendix have been removed without cutting her open, most unusual.

The follow up interview with Bob Bell had lasted two and a half hours; it ranged from basic questions to a grilling. With John and Andy acting as good cop and bad cop, for the interview, they were both satisfied that he knew nothing more; the interview revealed nothing they didn't already know. When Bob was questioned about any enemies, he said that he was not aware of any that might do a nasty trick like that.

John and Andy had spent a few nights in the Bell talking to the locals, arranging to interview them at their homes, one or two known criminals were taken down to the station to be interviewed, in the hopes that they would be able to give John and Andrew a lead. The consensus of opinion with Bob's customers just revealed that he was a good landlord and a generous person; no-one could identify the woman or give an explanation for her being there. All of the possible suspects they interviewed at the police station had solid alibis.

The uniform division conducted a house to house but again that revealed nothing, they had no name, or reason for her death or for her being placed in the pub yard, except that the crime was a sexually orientated crime.

Newspaper stories, television exposure, and Interpol all drew blanks, she just didn't exist, no family missing a very pretty young woman, no husband, boyfriend, children, uncles or aunties, no-one called the office, and she was buried as Jane Doe, a nobody.

The summer was a good one, hot and sticky and still no new information on the Body at the Bell, autumn, winter, nineteen sixty two turned into nineteen sixty three, then four and five and the Body at the Bell went further and further back in the files, along with other unsolved crimes, the perfect crime, no evidence, no clues, nothing.

As the years rolled on, Alker was promoted to Chief Inspector, and Green to Inspector, now a solid team, well in tune with how each other worked and thought. Every year on the anniversary of the Body at the Bell case Alker would spend time with Green reviewing that particular case, even though each month Alker would review the case personally. It had become his nemesis, a parasite; that had burrowed deep into his soul. John believed that there was no such thing as the perfect crime, every criminal made a mistake, there was always something, some clue, which would lead him eventually to the perpetrator. What was it, what was he missing?

"John, as you will be aware, there will soon be a vacancy for a Superintendent, and I would like you to apply for it. It's a good promotion and one you deserve, no-one has ever matched your success and arrest record, although that young sergeant you had in the early sixties nearly piped you last year. You taught him too well," the Chief Superintendent said laughing at his own joke.

"Thank you Sir, but I am a policeman, not a politician, I'd prefer to leave politics to the people who do it best, and I'll just catch criminals, if you don't mind?"

"Grand opportunity, bigger pension as well, think about it over the weekend, talk to Jane about it, let me know on Monday. Well my golf bags are waiting for me, I can just get nine in before it goes dark. I can't hold the offer for long John, Monday," he said and got up to leave, John shook his hand and smiled at him as he took John's hand gripping it firmly adding sincerity to the conversation.

"I will talk to Jane, but I think she will understand when I turn the offer down, even here as Chief Inspector I miss the challenges of the street. I am a policeman like my dad before me, but I thank you most sincerely, for the praise and confidence you have placed in me by offering me the post," John said graciously.

"Your loss, see you Monday," he said not accepting John's rejection and leaving the door of the offer open, and left John's office.

John was as he had said a policeman, a person that hunted and caught criminals. As the years had passed the constraints on the force had become tighter and tighter, money had become a factor, a crucial factor now in solving crimes; some crimes weren't investigated because the chances of catching the criminal were none existent. An officer would call at a break in when he was passing, possibly an hour or two later, but it was mainly for show; to pretend that the crime was being investigated. The officer would collect evidence so that if by chance the criminal were caught, whilst they were in the execution of another crime, then they could also be charged with the original offence as well, but finding the criminal from the evidence of that first crime alone, the police stood no chance.

In the early part of the spring of nineteen seventy two, John and Jane decided to buy a house in the country somewhere for them to retire to. Tired of the city life and the fumes from car exhausts, no real greenery for them, it would also allow Jane to pursue her hobby of gardening. She had green fingers and every plant she had put in the ground, had grown. Fresh vegetables from her small vegetable plot were always welcome when ready for the table; an array of flowers bloomed all year round, or so it seemed, from snowdrops in winter, bluebells in the spring and daffodils, to a stunning display of all kinds of flowers all through the summer and into the autumn. Jane wanted a bigger garden she wanted apple trees and pear trees, fresh fruit bushes so the summer house as they called it, had one prerequisite, it must have a large garden. To accommodate their friends they also decided that it must have at least three bedrooms, so that their friends could come and stay enjoying the country side as much as they did.

"Jane, are you sure about this, I mean at our time of life taking on another mortgage," John quizzed her one morning at breakfast?

"John dear, our time of life: you are only forty five, I am just forty two, so you will only be sixty five when it is paid off, and with our savings for the deposit and a twenty year mortgage, we won't miss the money, and our mortgage is so small these days; pro rata. Plus there is that savings plan about to mature, and we owe so little on this house, and it would be an investment. A run down old cottage in the country won't cost that much, if it does then we won't buy it, but at least let us look," Jane had pleaded with him, and she had got her way?

That weekend they set out, Jane had listed several properties for them to look at, ranging from a two bedroom cottage set in one acre of gardens.

"Planning permission may not be that easy to get, it could also be a listed building, so we had better watch out for those points," John had offered not trying to put her off the property, but being his usual cautious self.

At the other end of the scale, was a four bedroom parsonage set in large gardens next to the village graveyard, in need of repair.

John's only comment on that was that the work may exceed their budget, to which Jane had replied that he was a pessimist, hugged him and kissed him, smiling at his cautiousness.

It was the end of the month, and John as usual had called in his team to a meeting to discuss their cases. Following the meeting, John always went down into the old files looking into any cases he had not solved, but the Body at the Bell was the most important one. This case had become his nemesis it irritated him no end that here was the perfect crime. There was only supposition and clues, literally no evidence at all, and that was what had got to him, it was too perfect.

As he had told Jane he would do, he left the office early and arrived home in time for them to have an early evening meal on the road, so that they could view the first property at six, about a two hour drive from their home on the outskirts of London.

As they pulled up, Jane was the first to say, "no too small, and the garden is a wilderness of weeds. Sixty thousand, for that, they must be mad," she had said angrily?

"There are a lot of people in our position, and the locals are cashing in on the boom of buying country cottages as holiday homes," John had informed her calmly.

"Well, not from us, they're not," she replied, still angry at the overpriced cottage.

"Mr and Mrs Alker I'm Tony Drew from the estate agents, well worth the money don't you think, you could do a lot with this property."

"Like pull it down and start again, sorry we wasted our time," Jane chastised him.

"You won't get a property of this size for anything less; the values have gone through the roof lately, unless it's in need of major repairs; then by the end of repairing it, and all the aggravation it wouldn't be any cheaper," the estate agent said, not allowing them to put him off his stride.

"We won't be buying then; I don't mind paying for something, but I will not be ripped off by a speculator," Jane had the last word, his beaming smile dropped into a stunned look as they got back in the car and drove away..

The rest of the weekend went somewhat similar, overpriced, too much repair needed the garden too small, there was always an objection a flaw in the property, and it seemed to be Jane who was doing the rejecting. This pleased John because it didn't seem as though he was being awkward. Back to work on Monday and a new month his detection rate had fallen last month, due mainly to cost constraints, unable to field the officers he wanted to, or use the forensic team as much as he desired, tests were too expensive for the crime being investigated. He now had to justify every penny he spent, and it was getting to him.

For the next three weekends, they toured the country looking at country properties and had just about given up when they took a wrong turn and by chance turned into a village they hadn't visited previously.

"I know it's a bit farther than we agreed, but I'd like to see the village now we are here, and it is on our way home," Jane had argued.

John had agreed; they were still very much in love, and he liked to please her, just as she always did her best, to please, him. Twenty one years of married life and still very much in love, Jane had not been able to have children, and she passed all her matronly and parental love onto John. They had their arguments but never allowed them to come between them, always finding a solution, even if it meant one of them giving in and allowing the other to have their way. John joked about it saying that he had allowed her to have her own way the last time and Jane would normally agree and concede the argument or visa verse.

"John, stop," Jane had shouted as they entered the village!

John pulled up abruptly, shocked by the sudden yell, and looked at the for sale sign. He made a note of the telephone number, and then drove round to the other side of the village green; the property faced on to the green and he presumed that the pub on the other side was the only pub in the town.

John pulled up in front of the coaching house, and they got out; the ground was carpeted with the gold's and yellows of the autumnal leaves that now lay wet from the rain and soggy under foot, yet very picturesque in their own way, like a mosaic of dead and dying leaves, gold, amber, orange tints, all underfoot, like a carpet.

"Do you know of a hotel we can stay at for tonight," John asked in the bar.

"We have rooms, if you would like to see one, I can show you," the barman told him.

John and Jane followed the barman upstairs and into an old fashioned room with a low ceiling and flowery wall paper, dated, but the bed looked extremely comfortable and the room was clean. John enquired how much and took the room, he then asked about the house for sale. The barman told them that it was the old Vicarage, a new one had been built between here and the next village they now shared a vicar with the next village, the old Vicarage was up for sale, but needed a lot of work doing to it, damp and rewiring were but two items. John thanked him, and they unpacked then went down to use the public telephone on Jane's insistence.

"Wiring, damp, a fortune dear; but it is a lovely village and so unspoiled perhaps there is another less ram shackled house here dear," John had said with a smile, knowing that she was going to at least view the house. Her mind was already made up on that point, and John knew that there was no point in arguing with her. He also realised that they would make an offer and then it would be up to him to dissuade Jane, or barter with the estate agent agreeing a price subject to estimates for the repairs.

Chapter 3
Reporters Visit

"Tony this is for you; 'Vicarage disappears, is it Aliens?' a reporter called over laughing.

"Ok, ok, so I like Sci Fi, they do exist you know, we may never meet them, but out of all the billions of stars with planets do you honestly think that we are the only planet with life on it," he replied, annoyed at the inference.

"Not as we know it Jim," someone called back.

"Let me see the story, hum, interesting. It says here that a whole section of the vicarage has disappeared from a gas explosion, it was vaporised, gone; that is so, well never, come on, I ask you? There would be bits all over the village, yet there isn't a piece of brick anywhere. Hey, and if you think that aliens will have travelled all that way through the universe; light years of travel, just to take a bit of an old Vicarage, you can piss off. They would take it all; if that was what they wanted, for some obscure reason, why a vicarage? Aliens able to traverse the universe would be too advanced to miss their target, if that is what it was. I'll bet its military a new weapon or something like that, and they cocked it up and can't admit it."

"Has nobody got a story to write, come on, we have a deadline to meet where's the copies," the editor shouted at them.

"Boss, can I see you," Tony asked, he hated to admit it in front of his critics, but he was getting excited about the story, could it be aliens, he doubted it, but he wanted to see?

"Bring your piece in with you."

"Ok, boss its ready."

"Nice to see someone's been working around here," the editor said cryptically.

Tony went into the editor's office and handed him the piece he had written for the following day's paper, the editor read it and then looked at him.

"You want something; I can use this piece, anything else?"

"Yes boss, I'd like to go and check on this explosion, it seems odd to me. I'd like to."

"Hold it; we are a local evening paper; we do not investigate things a hundred miles away, so forget it. If you want to go, do it in your own time, ok."

"Yes boss, I am due a week's holiday can I book it for next week then?"

"No, too short notice, next month, perhaps, now piss off, and write the piece about the dog hooked on coke."

"Ok, the first is on a Sunday so I will take that week, I will put it in writing to you ok?"

"Get out of here," the editor smiled as he told Tony to leave.

"Sure boss, I'll leave my holiday application in your in tray."

Tony ducked as the empty tin ash tray flew past him hitting the door jam, just missing his head as he left the editor's office.

The next two weeks seemed to drag for Tony as he waited impatiently for his holiday to begin. He had several times tried to get the editor to allow him to do the investigation on office time, but he was adamant that it wasn't their kind of story and that he should try and get the magazine he ghost wrote for to finance the trip. Tony had smiled knowing that had it been a newspaper he would not have been allowed to work there, but because it was all Sci Fi and paranormal the editor had turned a blind eye to his moon lighting.

"A book boss, just think, I have done some research already, and almost a quarter of the house has disappeared, nothing, obliterated, kaput, gone, from a gas explosion! Bollocks," he had argued at one point, but to no avail he would just have to sweat it out till his holiday.

Tony loaded his car checking that he had all he needed for the trip, note pads, he took three with him just to be sure, pens half a dozen, mobile phone battery fully charged, plus a spare battery, in case he needed to verify points, a camera, film, tape recorder, laptop, oh and some clothes, to Tony at this point they were not essentials but his note pads etcetera were.

It took over two hours for him to drive to the village slowing down as he entered; the article said that the house was on the road leading into the village. The strands of bright yellow and black tape had alerted him to the property, he stopped in front of it, taking in the style and noting the lack of debris, and as yet nothing was missing the house looked intact. The explosion had removed part of the rear of the building; it was the right hand corner that had been vaporised.

Slowly he moved off, and booked into the only hotel in town an oldie worldly coaching house, low ceilings and exposed beams, blackened from centuries of exposure to smoke and grime, when the only heating was from a large open fire.

"Evening Sir; can I help you," the rotund landlord said, in his usual calm greeting, hoping for another guest?

"Yes, I'd like a room please, for say three days maybe longer?"

"Twenty nine fifty per night Sir, including breakfast, we will be serving dinner from seven if you wish to book a table?"

"Yes please say eight if that's ok?"

"Fine Sir, its booked, dinner for eight o' clock and a room, breakfast is from seven till nine, will you please fill in the register?"

"Great, I'm not an early riser; it'll probably get nine before I come down."

"Let's make it nine thirty then, unless we get another guest, I'll show you to your room."

Tony took his time he wanted to befriend the people; slowly, slowly catch a monkey, after all the reporters, the questions, the prying into the victim's character, how well he was liked, and the unwanted inferences, the villagers would not take too kindly to another round of questions.

Tony felt as though he had travelled back in time, the village had not changed in centuries, there were no new buildings. He would have guessed that the newest building would probably be two to three hundred years old. Stone built, some had thatched roofs and others stone slates, small windows, and low ceilings. It was as if he had stepped back in time to medieval times or earlier.

The village consisted of a couple of dozen cottages, a church, a local store, which also served as the post office, and the pub come hotel where he was now. As he looked out of the window, he could see seventy per cent of the village. The main road, little more than a country lane ran from his left to right, to cross roads, the road the pub was situated on, ran from the right hand lane from the cross roads, round to a point a few feet from the vicarage coming out facing the church. The village church was more of a chapel with a grave yard; it was just large enough to accommodate the small village community.

The vicarage was on the road he had entered by, he then turned right at the cross roads, and then first right again, on to the lane running between the top road and the road he had entered by surrounding the village green making it triangular in shape. The Sycamore trees on the pub side of the green, were now coming into leaf, the rest of the green was flat and grassed. No village pond in the centre that was on the outskirts, just out of sight, straight through the cross roads from the direction he had come. He compared the map left in the bedroom by the landlord to what he had seen, and got his bearings. The map listed places of special interest; there was a large country estate not far from the village, and the site of the village stocks was marked, along with the place where the gallows had been situated.

Tony put his face to the window and could just see the absent bedroom, so he picked up his binoculars and used them to see more clearly. He noted the clean cut of the brickwork, half joists protruding out into thin air with floor boards and also cut clean still attached. A central light hung down into what he presumed was the kitchen, judging by the oak wall and floor mounted cupboards, looking like new, without a scratch on them.

"You would need an angle grinder to cut the bricks so clean," he thought as he tried to see better, and resolved to take a closer look in the morning, it was almost time for dinner.

Tony went down to dinner and chatted with the waitress, in a friendly manner; he didn't want to push his luck, he decided just to chat, being friendly as a holiday maker would be; then it was into the bar for a few drinks with the locals.

He ordered his pint of bitter and sat on a chair in a corner; the entrance was to his right and to his left was the wall next to the bar. He looked around the room at the ornaments, all with a country side flavour as were the pictures, also all of country scenes except the one right above his head; this was a poem, hand written in script.

> *When is today tomorrow,*
> *Yesterday, today?*
> *When is tomorrow today*
> *Yesterday, tomorrow?*

"Excuse me Sir, but Billy will be upset if you sit there," the barman said when he returned from the kitchen, after taking a bar food order in, for a couple who had been looking at the menu when he entered.

"Oh sorry, I didn't realise that the seat was taken," Tony said puzzled.

"No, it isn't, it's just that, well, that table is special, and we don't want to upset," he stopped mid-sentence as an elderly man entered.

He stopped leaning heavily on his walking stick and looked at Tony, it was a quizzical look, not angry or annoyed, just questioning.

Billy was well into his seventies by the look of him, and half Cripple, Tony presumed, with arthritis. He was about five four in height, but as he leaned heavily on his walking stick and bent over, it was hard to be sure; wizened and haggard from years of working outdoors. There were laughter lines around his eyes, yet his face was pained and sorrowful. He had brown eyes that sparkled, yet there was a deep sadness etched into them. His tanned skin matched his brown eyes, and a full crop of curly white hair covered his head, it was cut short. His clothes old but clean and tidy, his shoes had a shine reminiscent of the years Tony had spent in the army, true spit and polish, one in which you could see your face.

"Taint my chair," he said in a broad accent.

"I'll move if you wish, I'm here for a break from work, just a few days sorry," Tony said, making to get up, yet hoping that the old man would tell him to stay, the ice had already been broken.

"Naw, tha con stay lad," he said.

"Well in that case let me buy you a drink, please, whatever he drinks please," Tony said to the barman? Who brought over half a pint of bitter for Billy and placed it on the table in front of him.

"Up from London are you, come to see the show, well you're too late, it's all over now," Billy said, his voice etched with anger and sorrow?

"That is what brought me here I admit it, but it was more, the views in the paper of the village; it looks so untouched and reminiscent of days long gone, peaceful, like that poem, beautiful script, who wrote it, do you know?"

"Aye, it were a friend of mine, a very dear friend of mine, he wrote it."

"Is it about the village, I mean it is today, yet I feel as though I have gone back in time to yesterday, it's prophetic?"

"I don't know what that means, but it isn't about this village, no."

"Yet it sums up what I feel at this moment, as I said it's as if I have travelled back in time to a genteel era. I can imagine a coach and horses pulling up outside here, and weary travellers getting off to spend the night here at this coaching house. What is it about then?"

"I can't tell you, my friend wrote it," Billy said and drifted of back to when they were together remembering when he first saw it.

"He didn't tell you what the verse meant then?"

"Oh yes, he told me, but I can't tell you."

"Perhaps if you tell me then I might be able to explain it to you so that you will understand it, who wrote it, was he a poet, a writer?"

"Naw, a Chief Inspector, retired like, he lived in the, sorry," there was tremendous pride in his voice when he spoke at the start of the sentence, then it trailed off as if he had said something he shouldn't have; a tear formed and he wiped it away, saying, "Bit of dirt."

"Look I'm going to be honest with you, but first another round I think," Tony said as a question?

"We always had rum and black at this time, seeing as I was ex-navy, and if he hadn't joined the police, he was going into the navy," Billy said now smiling as he remembered their habits.

"Rum and black it is then," Tony said getting up and going to the bar.

Tony had picked that table because it had a view of the whole room, and he had watched as locals came and went, noting their looks of disdain as they saw him alone at first, but now more so with Billy.

"You a reporter," one asked when he ordered the drinks?

"Yes, I am, but I'm on holiday why," Tony replied?

"Billy was a good friend of John's, and he is old, and John's death has had a bad effect on him, we don't want him upset anymore," he said bluntly, ensuring Tony got the message.

"I have no wish to, I actually am enjoying his company, he seems an interesting guy to me, ex-navy you know; I bet he was at sea in the last war, enlisted under age probably," Tony said smiling to ensure that his message was also understood.

He wasn't about to walk away from the person who knew John better than anyone else, therefore, what happened. Tony had guessed what the missing part of the sentence was that John had lived at the vicarage.

Tony paid for their drinks and joined Billy, "Tell you that I'm mental did they?"

"No, just asked me where I was from," Tony lied.

"And you said you were going to be honest with me. I learned a lot from John about telling when people were being honest."

"I am; OK yes, he said that John's death had affected you, but I told him that I was enjoying your company, and I am, so forget him. I am a reporter mainly for an evening newspaper, but I also write for a Sci Fi magazine. The guys at the office laugh at me, but I don't believe that we are the only beings in the universe. I don't believe that we will ever make contact with another species, another life form, but I am positive that they exist. As far as space travel is concerned we are now, let me see, er, think of it like this. We are prehistoric man who is trying to walk to America, which is the speed at which we travel in space, we are too slow. The nearest star to earth is about five light years away; light travels at one thousand eight hundred miles per second for round figures. So you multiply one, eight, zero, zero by sixty, then by sixty again for the speed per hour, then by twenty four, then by three hundred and sixty five, to give you the distance light travels in one light year, then by five for the distance to the nearest sun or star. See what I mean; can you imagine the daunting task of walking and swimming to America? It is like us going to Alpha Centura the nearest star; there are actually three suns or stars in that system."

"I don't quite follow you, but I, well it wasn't aliens if that's what you are thinking," Billy said categorically.

"No, if they made it this far, then they would have taken the whole house, not just a bit of it and why a house of all things? They would be too technologically advanced to make a mistake like that. No, it could be as someone mentioned, a new weapon, but I doubt that as well."

Billy looked into Tony's eyes assessing him; he took a drink from his glass, draining the glass and put it down firmly. Tony didn't say anything he just got up went to the bar and ordered another round. Billy watched as he went to the bar, trying to decide if he could trust Tony or not; Billy also tried to work out if Tony was being straight with him. Billy had been in the bar when the reporters had laughed at him. Billy had heard the reporters talking about him; calling him a silly old fool, and that had hurt him, but he also wanted desperately for the truth to come out; his main concern at the moment was if this guy was going to make fun of him, or not.

Tony returned to the table and placed the drink in front of Billy.

"I have heard all kinds of tales, some of them so ridiculous that they had to be true; exaggerated yes, stranger than fiction yes, but there has to be a basis of truth in them. I have heard tales that would turn your hair white, excuse the pun, and never once have I laughed at the story teller, or called them foolish, some have an explanation some remain unexplained. No Billy I will not laugh at you, I don't have to believe you, but I will not laugh at you."

"That was honest enough, you're right you don't have to believe me, but I will not be telling lies. If, I decide to confide in you, I will let you know tomorrow night, I need to think about it," Billy said, drained his glass and got up, now walking less steadily than when he entered from the amount of alcohol he had consumed.

"I will be here, thank you for the company, I have enjoyed talking to you," Tony got up and went to the bar and ordered another drink.

He sensed that he was not welcome by the locals; it wasn't so bad that you could cut the air with a knife, but it was there all the same, so he drank his rum and black and went to bed. The fact that he was uncomfortable was not his main concern, the truth was. He was now more determined to talk to Billy, he was sure that there was a story here, and he wanted it, he was also confident that it was the truth.

Next morning after breakfast he left the hotel and walked about the village stopping at the church and viewing the graveyard it had been kept well, it was neat and tidy, the villagers obviously cared about their ancestors, but there were broken head stones, ravaged with the passing of time, carved names no-longer readable, as the sandstone headstones had been worn down. Some were in stronger stone; granite and polished marble, the gold lettering worn off with time, but the names were still just visible. As he wandered round he saw some as old as the fifteenth century then a newish one, inscribed with 'In loving memory of a dear wife and friend,' the name was Jane Alker, above it was the one he was now particularly interested in, 'Reunited John Alker with his loving wife.'

Tony made a mental note as he heard footsteps behind him, his wife had died first, a good three years before him why, natural or illness, he wondered.

"Still nosing about, there isn't a story here you might as well be on your way. This village has lost a dear friend, and we don't want you lot digging into his past, trying to find some dirt to sully his good name, not that we would ever believe there is any, he was just a decent man, and we mourn his loss to us."

Tony looked at the man speaking to him; he was taller than Tony and heavily built a manual worker from the size and musculature of his body, a thick set man in his forties Tony guessed.

"A hobby of mine, did you know that some of these stones date back to the fifteenth century?"

"Some of them date back to the thirteen hundreds, and seeing as I am the grave digger and keep the records, I know which ones they are, but there is no writing left on them for you to read, so you are wasting your time here," he said the last bit with emphasis.

Tony took the hint and made his way towards the gate, but as he followed the side path to the main path he noticed a headstone with no inscription just a name and date in a corner, away from the main area, he noted it but didn't try to take a closer look just left.

After his walk around the village noting places of interest, not that there were that many that he didn't already know about, he went for lunch, then after lunch went across to the old Vicarage to look at the damage.

He ducked under the tape and went around to the back where the section of the house was missing. On his pad, he sketched the outline of the house and marked off the area missing, he also made notes.

1. No burn marks from an explosion?
2. No debris?
3. All edges cut clean no jagged bits?
4. A clean cut to all the Joists?
5. Internal fixtures and fittings all cut clean, no damage to ones still in place?
6. No broken windows?
7. Plates on the far side of kitchen still displayed in cupboard!!!!

Seven points that told him there was no explosion, so what had happened here? And why had the authorities and villagers hidden the truth?

Chapter 4
Corruption

Alan Winston was a studious boy exceedingly intelligent, having passed his eleven plus at nine and was now studying for his 'O' level GCSE at fourteen he had a keen interest in the sciences, particularly in physics, and the relatively new branch of Quantum Physics. He was a lonely boy; he was a year younger than the rest of the class he was in, but, a full year older in his abilities. Whilst the rest of the fourteen year old boys, were busy chasing the girls, after they had completed their homework, he continued to read about and digest books on physics and related sciences. His parents were quite wealthy his father ran a grocery business, and his mother, when not looking after the house, worked in the shop, but the majority of his class were from working class families and didn't have the finances his family had, just another reason for them to bully him and torment him.

"Hey four eyes, you got me pregnant," Sandra one of the girls in his class, said to him as he was leaving one evening in the winter of nineteen sixty two.

Her face was set as she spoke to him; he felt the fear, the nervousness of being bullied; three of her friends stood by her, verbal bullying, or was this the start of them physically attacking him, any excuse to hit him, push him around.

"Y, y, y, you are wrong," he stuttered, fearful that she might hit him again, as she had done on several occasions in the past, for no reason.

"Listen shit face, you fucked me, and now I am pregnant, so what are you going to do about it, hey?"

"B, but I, I didn't, leave me alone, that's not funny," Alan said nervously.

Sandra was fifteen almost sixteen and not from a good family, it was well known that her father got drunk when he got paid, and they had little money to spare for his drinking. She wasn't the best looking girl in the class, but she was well liked by the boys because of her liberal attitude towards having sex with them. Alan couldn't think of anyone apart from him who hadn't had sex with her, or so they had bragged about to him, as a tease, he just wasn't interested in her, or any of the girls in his class; she was common, a slut.

"When I tell my dad that you are the father of the child; he will be round your house and demanding that you pay for the upkeep of the child. Let's face it, I wouldn't marry a fink like you, but you can afford to keep the bastard," she told him in no uncertain terms.

"But, but I haven't had sex with you h, how can it be mine," Alan protested?

"Prove it, I say that it is yours, and you can't prove different can you, arse ache, so your dad will have to cough up won't he, now piss off," she said vehemently and pushed him in the shoulder knocking him onto the floor.

That evening Alan was nervous, his mother asked him what was wrong, but he said that there was nothing. He didn't know whether Sandra was telling the truth or not. Was she pregnant, or was it just another torment; another jibe at him, to make him uncomfortable, if it was; then it was working? He was more than nervous he was terrified. That evening he ate very little worried in case she did indeed intend on blaming him for her pregnancy. He sat at the dinner table and pushed his food around until it annoyed his mother, who told him off for messing with his food. He couldn't eat his stomach churned and churned, as the anguish grew and grew, until he thought he would vomit. What if she was telling the truth and she was pregnant, and was going to blame him so that his family would have to keep the bastard? How could he prove that it wasn't him; she had a baby inside her as her proof, what did he have? A blood test could prove that it wasn't his child, but only by the blood group. If, the baby's blood group was different to his, it would prove that he wasn't the biological father; but the test was not conclusive. The test wouldn't prove that the baby was his child if the child had the same blood group, because other people had the same blood grouping. Unfortunately for him, his was a common blood group so the likelihood of the baby's blood being his group was anything but slim. What if the child had the same blood as him? As the evening turned into night time he was convinced that any blood test would prove that he was the father, because his blood was one of the most common ones, and the more he thought about it the more he became convinced.

His father answered the knock at the door; it was close to ten o'clock when the thumping began.

"Yes," his father said angrily at the force used on the door, when he opened it.

"Your fucking son has got my Sandra pregnant, and I want to know what you're going to do about it," the man demanded.

"You had better come in," Alan heard his father say.

Alan was listening by his bedroom door to the conversation, waiting anxiously until his father told him to come downstairs.

"Alan this man says that you have had sex with his daughter," his father asked him?

"You fucked my Sandra, and I want to know what you're going to do about it. You'll have to pay for the bastard's upbringing," the man said aggressively.

"I, I didn't," was all Alan could say, he was too afraid to argue.

"You fucking liar, she's up the spout, and you made her that way, she told me," her father demanded, taking a threatening step towards Alan, who backed up.

"This is my house, and I would appreciate it if you would control your language, if my son got Sandra pregnant then he will have to marry her, so there is no need for threatening behaviour," Alan's father said forcefully, being correct and standing by his old fashioned values.

Alan looked at his dad, not a small man by any means, but not an aggressor like the man he faced, now standing between Alan and the man defending his son.

"Are you calling my Sandra a liar, she has the proof in her belly," he demanded, squaring up to Alan's dad.

"I think you had better leave; I will contact my solicitor in the morning to work out a plan what is your address?"

"Mister la-di-da no need, I know yours, and I will be back with Sandra, she can live here till she's had the bastard you can fucking keep her."

"You are throwing your daughter out," his dad said incredulously?

"You keep her, or I call the cops, he is under age," the man said, pointing at Alan.

"So is your daughter, now, please leave or, I will call the police," Alan's dad said emphasising the 'I'.

"Fuck you," he said angrily and punched Alan's dad, who had been caught off guard, in the face, bursting his nose, and then left storming out.

Alan's mum rang the police and a squad car soon pulled up outside, but too late to catch Sandra's dad, he was well away when he heard Alan's mum on the phone.

"Well, well, well we appear to have a problem here don't we son. Underage sex, she gets pregnant, no wonder her dad was in a bad temper. What do you have to say for yourself then," the policeman said looking down his nose at Alan?

"I, I, di, I didn't do it honest." Alan said almost in tears and shaking his head, as the policeman looked at him inquiringly, Alan knew that the officer didn't believe him.

"Done sex education at school, wanted to give it a try, well now you know the results, don't you?"

"B, But I didn't have sex with her," Alan pleaded.

"I am not going to arrest you for under age sex, don't let it happen again. I think the responsibility of bring up a child will be punishment enough. You have let your family down you do realise that don't you, and such a loving and nice family, as well. Well I'll be off I know the man and I will visit him and again not arrest him, but tell him to keep away until your solicitor has been in touch, or I will arrest him, OK Sir?"

Alan's father, who was still holing a bloody handkerchief to his nose, thanked the officer and showed him out then turned to Alan, and sent him to his room in disgrace.

The next three months were hell for Alan; Sandra made it common knowledge that he was the father, he walked around with his head down ashamed. The other children in his class taunted Alan, making fun of him. The teachers that once were friendly towards him now kept him at arm's length, except the science teacher who still saw him as a highly intelligent boy, and worthy of better things, he was perhaps also the only teacher who believed Alan, knowing what his values and aspirations were.

University was now a problem he would have a wife and child to support; therefore probably he would not be able to go, this would ruin his life, and Sandra was the cause. The last thing he wanted to do was work in his father's grocery business, he wanted to be a scientist, and she had ruined it for him, and he hated her for it, to the degree that he was avoiding any contact with the girls socially now, just studying.

His father's solicitor drew up a contract, stating that they would pay a set sum each month until the baby was born, once it was born they would continue to pay enough to keep the baby until Alan was old enough to marry Sandra, then he would keep them from his wages working in his father's shop. Alan buried himself in his books, he studied harder than ever before trying to block out the hell he now lived. The sudden lack of prospects, a life, as he put it, sucking up to people instead of creating, investigating, solving the problems of the universe, where we came from, and in time probably, not his lifetime, but where we were going as a civilisation and culture.

Their solicitor managed to make sure that Sandra did not live at their home, but stayed with her parents, and they contributed to the upkeep of the house in exchange. This was a relief to Alan, but it meant that he now had to work in his dad's shop on Saturday, and Sunday to earn the money they sent to Sandra's father.

It was late in that spring when Sandra with a new boyfriend had gone off on his motor bike, he took a corner too quickly and they both came off killing them both. Alan was pleased, as far as he was concerned she deserved to die, she had ruined his life, bringing disgrace to his family, and to him personally.

"Dad, can we have a blood test done on the baby, that will prove to you that it wasn't mine, please," Alan had pleaded?

"No, you should be pleased that you don't have to be lumbered with that tart, I am sure it was her who made you do it, she seduced you, so no I won't ask her parents to allow us to have a blood test done. What's happened has happened, and there is nothing you can do about it now, except get back to your studying and make something of yourself."

"But dad she brought shame to our family and to me, I have lived in hell since that night, and that is the only way to prove that I was not the father," he had pleaded but to no avail, his dad was adamant that the episode was over and finished.

"For all their nastiness and deviousness, they have just lost a daughter, and I cannot in all conscience ask them to allow us to take a blood sample that would be expecting too much. So leave it at that," his dad had said closing the conversation.

That did not bring his shame to an end; he was taunted and tormented all the following year about how lucky he was to have escaped. When the baby would have been born some of the pupils called him daddy just to make his life even more unbearable.

Following excellent grades he managed to pass his exams with ease, which helped get him a place at Manchester University, where he studied physics, gaining a Master's degree before going on to get his doctorate.

Several years later Alan's parents were driving home from the shop when a motor bike skidded and his dad swerved to avoid hitting the bike, hit black ice and then a tree killing both of them. Alan got an anonymous letter saying that it was poetic justice, and a pity he wasn't in the car.

Chapter 5
Story Time

Tony had dinner in the pub bar, a burger and chips with a pint, and then sat and watched as the bar filled up with the locals. His encounter with the grave digger, made him wonder, was there more to this story than he had originally thought? The grave digger's entrance in the bar, and the sinister stare he gave Tony made him all the more curious. He had been in tight situations before, and although he didn't relish the idea of taking the grave digger on, he was not about to be run off by him either.

It was darts and dominoes tonight, and the bar was filled with locals, the members of the other team, and their supporters. Soon there wasn't a seat to be had, except at the table where Tony sat. Dirty looks were aimed in his direction as if he had banned everyone else from sitting on the vacant chairs at his table. Tony watched with interest as the contest began

The Black Bull, his pub, won the first two games, and then lost the next two to The Crown the visiting pub. The dominoes were going a similar way; the two teams were evenly matched. There was total silence as the final game began, nerves jangled, and the concentration on the faces of the contestants was fixed. Five 'o' one was the game finishing on double top, followed by an outer bull then an inner bull, The Crown reached the outer bull first, the Black Bull caught up with them with the next two darts, this dart could win the contest, but he missed. The Crown now had three darts at the bull, before the Black Bull had another chance. He missed with the first dart hitting the outer bull, the dart now blocked the inner bull, and he missed with the next two darts, but only just. There were sighs of relief from the Black Bull, and anguish from The Crown as the last dart hit the metal of the inner bull. Sullenly he walked up to the dart board and removed his darts. He had thrown their chance away, Tony was impressed by the accuracy, even with the inner bull obscured he had managed to hit the metal and only just missed the inner bull, but what mattered to the Black Bull was that he had missed. The grave digger walked up to the line and composed himself, both teams stopped breathing as the excitement grew, even the dominoes players stopped to watch, all eyes were on the grave digger. Beads of sweat formed on his forehead, he had to hit the bull. They had started the match so the opposing team would have the same number of darts to win or draw the match; he needed to hit the bull with the first arrow.

Tony was concentrating so much on the match that he missed Billy's entrance and only spotted him as he sat down quietly; sliding onto the chair so as not to scrape the legs on the floor; the air was electric. Tony nodded to Billy in greeting, not daring to break the player's concentration, by making a noise.

The grave digger drew his arm back and aimed, he brought his arm forward as if testing his accuracy, then back and let the dart fly. The sigh was deafening as it hit the metal of the inner bull and fell on the floor, millimetres from winning, he again drew his arm back and aimed then let it fly, and he hit the inner bull, a massive cheer went up, and it was smiles all round. That had put The Crown under even greater pressure than he had been under, with just two darts, a middle bull with one dart to win, and if he missed the second one to draw the game and contest. Their contestant approached the line and composed himself. Tony had never realised just how competitive these matches were; as far as he was concerned, it was just a bit of fun, but to these guys it was as if the contests were for the world championships. His first dart did the same as the grave digger's hitting the wire and bouncing out onto the floor. Now the pressure was really on him, he had to hit the inner bull to draw. Tony looked at Billy who was now engrossed in the final throw, he had missed most of the games, but this was the final throw and could win the Black Bull the match. Billy may have noticed Tony looking at him, but if he did he didn't show that he was, watching with keen interest the contestant at the line.

The contestant composed himself someone shouted, "Go on Jimmy," to the disapproval of everyone else in the bar at the disturbance. He drew his arm back and aimed, someone else coughed one of their team; he dropped his arm again and waited, composing himself, then lifted his arm and drew it back. The dart flew straight and true clipping the inner bull wire and ending up in the outer bull. Game over the Black Bull had won by one dart; the bar erupted in cheers, and commiserations for the losers.

"Billy you can't smoke that in here sorry," the barman said as he brought Billy's half pint to the table.

"Me pipes not lit, just full of tobacco, I am not smoking it. Can't a guy have any pleasures these days? What's a pint without a smoke?"

"I agree, but the law is the law; if you want to light it, you'll have to go outside like everyone else, sorry," the barman said apologetically.

"He's right Billy, I'm sorry, but they could get a fine if a policeman entered. Would you like to sit outside; it's a nice evening?" Tony offered.

"Naw, I won't light it, but what can I point with if I haven't got me pipe," Billy said smiling waving the pipe around like a pointer?

"I didn't realise just how seriously they took these matches," Tony said starting a conversation.

"We are through to the county semi-finals this was always going to be a serious match. See those trophies?"

Tony looked in the direction Billy's pipe was pointing; there were three silver cups on the shelf the middle one raised slightly, the Black Bull had won it two years in succession, and the other two had three years stamped on them.

"We get to keep them, we won the county championships three years in a row to win each one of them, and if we win this year we get to keep the middle one, as well. If we lose then it will break an eight year run of winning the contest, some record," Billy said proudly, he was silent as he took a deep breath holding back another tear, "John got the team together, and we have done very well until."

"You are now through to the county championships, so you are still doing very well."

"Yes but, ok, I don't want to tell you this bit of the story, and then that bit. I will tell you all the story, at once, or nothing," Billy said draining his glass, Tony ordered another round.

"Not to be too blunt, but have you decided, I promise I will not make fun of you, no matter how ridiculous the story may seem. I had a quick look at the house the only conclusion I can come to is that it was not an explosion of any kind. No charring of the bricks from the flame, cut so clean that you would have to use a Stilsaw, not a plate broken. There was no explosion, and aliens who travel several light years to get here, would not take just a bit of a house."

"Aye, you're right, I suppose, can we say tomorrow at ten o'clock, at my house, two doors up from the pub, but I may change me mind between now and then, so do I have your word you will not bother me if I say I won't tell you?"

"You have my word," Tony said with sincerity.

Billy was a creature of habit; he had his usual two halves then two rum and blacks and then walked unsteadily home leaning heavily on his walking stick. Tony wondered how come he didn't fall when he moved the stick; he seemed so dependent on it so much for the support. He watched as the wizened old man made his way out of the bar, the seat to his trousers were now getting baggy and shiny from years of wear. His shoes old and battered yet still had a good shine to them. Tony was pleased with himself, he had an interview with Billy, mocked by reporters and probably some of the villagers, yet also lovingly protected by the villagers, from harm. 'We can call the old bugger an idiot but don't anyone else try it,' sort of attitude.

Next morning, Tony waited till five to ten then left the pub and went to Billy's house; he knocked on the door and waited. It took Billy so long to open the door he wondered if Billy had changed his mind. Finally, the door opened, and Billy looked at him still trying to assess Tony, who now stood holding his laptop and tape recorder.

32

"Well you look ready for a story, I suppose I can take a chance, come in," Billy said nervously.

"I hope you don't mind if I record the story, it will stop me needing to ask you to slow down or repeat anything?"

Billy opened the door wide and gestured inviting Tony to come in; he closed the door quietly and led the way into the front room. Billy moved towards the chair in the corner facing the door his back to the window and motioned Tony to take the settee, with a coffee table in front of it. The room was a small one, just enough room for the two piece suite, coffee table, and television on a stand with the stereo underneath, now playing some gentle melodies.

"Do you need a plug for the tape recorder?"

"If you don't mind, I have a spare battery, but both of them will only last a few hours, three to four, is it a long story?"

"Longer than that, use the one under the telly," Billy indicated where the socket was Tony plugged in the tape recorder.

"Cup of coffee, you Londoners drink a lot of that, don't you?"

"Yes they do tend to, but I come from the north up Manchester way and drink tea if."

"Civilised," Billy cut in, "tea is a British drink, I'll make us a cup whilst you get set up, it's all these bloody foreigners in London that made them drink so much coffee."

Billy got up and left the room; Tony smiled as he looked round at the decor, jaded with age, but again considering Billy was elderly, and living alone, he kept the place clean, unlike some of the people Tony had, had to deal with of Billy's advanced years.

It wasn't long before Billy came back with a tea tray, two cups, sugar bowl, tea pot, water pot, and a milk jug.

"You should have said I would have brought that for you," Tony said with concern.

"Fooled you as well, I use the stick to keep them happy, well it usually gets me one free drink a night, the pension doesn't go that far these days," he said with a smile.

"Don't worry your secret is safe with me, milk and no sugar please?"

Billy poured the teas then sat down handing Tony a cup.

"Where to begin, hum, I think at the oldest part John. He were born in 1928, his dad were a policeman, and that was all he ever wanted to be, a copper like his dad. He was five foot nine, but when he applied he stretched himself another quarter of an inch and was accepted. He worked hard and by the time he was thirty six he was an Inspector at Scotland Yard catching murderers and nasty villains.

He married a stunner, she was gorgeous, and a couple of inches smaller than him, but all the right proportions, everything in the right place as it were. And clever, she was a teacher, infants, unfortunately, they couldn't have children. I think it was something wrong with Jane, I overheard her saying that she had been for treatment one night when I was visiting. Today they would do something, but back then no chance. Anyway, she worked hard as well and became the headmistress of the infant's school. Then in nineteen sixty two it was a freezing day, and he had just met his new sergeant, John's first day after his promotion to Inspector, and they were called out to a body; a woman.

She had been laid out ceremonial like, her legs apart and her arms at an angle to her body. Her throat had been cut, and all the blood drained from her body. The doctor couldn't give an accurate time of death, because there was no blood left in her body, the killer had drained it all out; and the temperature that night had been freezing, minus four. It became known as the Body at the Bell.

She wasn't reported missing, and there were no clues as to where she had come from or who had killed her. It played on Johns mind something awful, he didn't believe that there could ever be the perfect crime; but there she was, starring him in the face, the perfect crime.

In nineteen sixty eight, John and Jane decided to buy a country house, they spent four years before finding the vicarage, they fell in love with it, and they bought the old Vicarage. They both continued to work, and came up here at weekends, the vicarage needed a lot doing to it, but John and Jane found the time and energy, to join in with the work, anyway I'm getting ahead of myself. They'd been here for a month or so; it was late spring, some of the local lads were working on the house. John, was in the garden that's, when I met him, for the first time."

Chapter 6

Intervening Years

"John was busy digging up the front lawn, and turning it, as told to by Jane, who was the gardener really, and he took his instructions from her. A scruffy looking chap walked up to the wall and leaned on it, he hung his coat over the wall, that was me."

He watched for a few moments then cocked his head to one side and tutted shaking his head as he made the sound.

"Are you having a laugh," John had said after a moment or two.

"Well if someone doesn't tell you, you'll not be fit for work tomorrow, bad back, aching, won't be able to stand up," the scruffy man had said.

"Suppose you can do better," John said stopping and leaning on the spade he was using?

"Oh, you're doing a grand job, but your poor back, I bet it's aching now after only half an hour or so."

John though about what he had said, and had to agree that his back was hurting, he put it down to using muscles he hardly ever used, "What if it is?"

"Well do the job proper like and use the right muscles and it won't."

"An expert on this subject are we," John said cheekily?

"Taint for me, to tell you what to do, but I do hate to see someone making a job harder than it needs to be."

"Ok, then show me, come on, you show me where I am going wrong."

"We need to agree a fee for me to teach you, I mean there's years of experience gone into what I know."

"Pound an hour, cash, and a pint after the front has been dug over."

"Pound hey, mek it two pints,"

"You drive a hard bargain, ok two pints, but after the front garden has been dug over."

"Deal, see, you are using your back muscles, don't, use your leg muscles, they are stronger, and you won't tire as easy, watch me."

"You make it look so easy, what's your name, mines John, John Alker."

"Billy, Billy Langtree, it rhymes with Lilly," Billy said with a smile.

"Named after the film star were you?"

"Maybe, who knows?"

They dug the front garden and broke the soil up ready for it to be seeded and planted, then they went to the pub for a few pints, it was the start of a close relationship.

On most Sunday evenings, John and Jane went home, so that they were ready for work on the Monday morning. Jane at this point was still teaching and now a deputy headmistress. Jane understood when John told her that he was turning down the job of Superintendent because she also didn't want the headmistress's job but later on she took it for a few years, she wanted to teach just as he wanted to be a policeman, catching criminals. He did apply for and got the job of Chief Inspector that was in nineteen seventy a few months before they bought the house.

Each weekend John and Jane went down to the house and painted or did some work in the garden, always with Billy's help. He became an invaluable help, not only in the work, but also he kept an eye on the builders during the week. Billy would check up daily on the builder's progress, if he wasn't happy with the work, he would ring John. Billy would have already given the builders a piece of his mind.

As they became more settled, spending every available minute of their free time there, things began to move forward. John helped organise the return of the Morris dancers to the village, Jane badgered the local farm community to put on a gymkhana and start a pony club. They pushed people into getting a fete, for the village, and as each element got going it brought more and more visitors to the little village. The road was a mess, potholed and a poor surface. John rang the local council and complained in no uncertain terms, using his interview skills and applying pressure on the local council, a week later the road had been resurfaced, and the faulty lights mended. They became as much a part of the village as if they had been born there.

It was in nineteen seventy eight when the Body at the Bell resurfaced; John was in his office; Green was now an Inspector and still with John and their sergeant was a woman Lynda Summers.

Lynda had joined them a few years previously as a DC and had been promoted, she was slim and attractive, rich auburn hair that hung down to her shoulders wavy but not curly, high cheek bones and eyes as green as emeralds, her figure was well proportioned. Her colleagues considered her a right cutie, cheeky as hell, but nice with it, John had found her a capable officer who wasn't afraid to push buttons to get results, and they worked well together.

Billy got up and made more tea for them, puffing on his pipe as he talked, which had made him thirsty, so he said, talking did that to him. Tony noticed the burn marks from the fallen ash from his pipe on the chair Billy sat in and the carpet around that chair.

"Well, it was nineteen seventy eight, the spring when Lynda came into John's office, he as usual was delving into an old file, the Body at the Bell file sat on his desk always, she knocked and entered," Billy continued.

"Sir, the Body at the Bell file can I see it," she asked, quite distant, something was wrong, and John knew it, and handed her the file

"Well Lynda what is it, you look as though you have lost a pound and found a penny?"

"This has just come through, I could have sworn," she paused, studying the photo and comparing it with the one in her hand, "Sir, is that the same woman or not, ignoring what we already know?"

"Lynda how can we ignore what we know, let me see."

Lynda handed the photo to John, and he gazed down at it, he didn't speak for a few moments checking and double checking the photo against the one in his file.

"Apart from the fact that we know that this woman died in nineteen sixty two, it is the same woman, where did this come from?"

"She has been reported as a missing person, one Sadie Jones, but the likeness is so perfect, she could and probably is related, and about the right age for her to be the woman's daughter say, but didn't you say that she was buried as a Jane Doe, no-one claimed the body?"

"Yes, we never traced a relative which was very unusual, even Interpol couldn't trace anyone. Where did it come from?"

"Manchester Sir."

"Manchester, hum, not really worth a trip is it," John stopped and pondered the idea, "her family wouldn't know anything now, if they didn't then, but the likeness is well, I could swear that she is the same woman. Same age, same colouring they are identical, as if she were a twin, so why didn't she call in when we were hunting a name for the woman?"

"Too young Sir, she would only have been fourteen in nineteen sixty two."

"True, but a fourteen year old would know if her mum was missing, wouldn't you have known? And have and contacted someone when you saw her picture in the paper or on television. I'll keep this one and perhaps speak to the Inspector up there about it," John didn't say anything as Lynda left his office; he was still starring at the photo.

It was a Sadie Jones, John read the file, and as Lynda had said she was the right height, colouring, size, shape in all aspects she was the same woman, far too close to be just a coincidence an identical twin.

A week passed, and John had rung Manchester, just a general chat, and although the likeness was so striking, he knew it couldn't be the same woman. It was unlikely that the murdered woman was even a relative, to the woman who was missing, for one thing she was an only daughter, according to the report, and as yet unmarried, and her mother the person most likely to be the dead woman, was alive and well, the only other female relative was an auntie who had died two years previous. On the Tuesday morning, an officer knocked on John's door and when told to enter came in blushing in shame.

"Sorry Sir but when I was checking the files again, I found this one, how on earth I missed it; I'll never know, I could have sworn it wasn't there last week but, there, it was this morning. It's an old unsolved case from nineteen forty two, during the war. It's a bit too old for you now, but it was the woman. The way she was laid out, throat cut, drained of blood, the position, all these things told me that you needed to see it," the constable said, now blushing with embarrassment.

John took the file without speaking and opened it; staring at him was a photograph of a dead woman, laid out exactly as the Body at the Bell had been. The cut to her throat followed the same line, severing the carotid artery and wind pipe. John studied the photo closely before reading the report even though it was war time, a murder was investigated with the same fervour as in peace time, and reports were written, photos taken, evidence collected. The resemblance was striking, the modus operandi told John that they were committed by the same person, yet twenty years apart, no serial killer waited twenty years to kill again.

John took the papers out of the folder, and a card dropped out, it was battered and faded with age, water had got on it, there was a water mark a stain, he opened it carefully and read the inscription 'to Alan from Jo,' the rest of the name was missing damaged by water. Unusually it had been written in red ink, very unusual for nineteen forty two, red ink was used for deficits at the bank. The body had been found close to the docks police station. The station had been bombed in nineteen forty two, that was probably why the card and the paper work was damaged, from the explosion, so it was not unlikely that some of the evidence was missing, as well. After reading the paper work three times, digesting all that it said, he put it to one side and called Andy into his office. John handed the file to Andy and waited for his reaction, then handed him the photo Lynda had brought in the previous day.

"Twenty years between murders, no way Sir and this photo, it is uncanny the likeness, Lynda saw it, and brought it to you, a missing person," Andy sat down confused and shocked at the turn of events, "shall I check for missing persons from that time, mind you there were so many, but I again notice that she was never named, another, Jane Doe?"

"Worth a try I suppose just in case, but I agree with you, the chances are very slim that they ever matched a missing person with this body if they had, then she wouldn't have been a Jane Doe."

"True Sir, but I meant nationwide; it won't take long with modern systems to check. What if she had come down from the north say, on a visit; it's just a thought."

"No, go ahead; let's cover all angles, but twenty years that beggars belief."

Andy did the check as he suggested, and nothing came up from that period, but Manchester sent back by mistake, the picture of a currently missing woman asking if they had a murder on their hands.

"Sir, John, look at this," Andy said as he burst into John's office and threw the photo on the desk.

John picked the photo up and studied it, then placed it on his desk and looked up at Andy; he looked as bemused, and confused as John felt.

"We have two murders twenty years apart, so unrelated, apart from the style and probable killer. We have two missing women, who look identical to the Jane Doe's that were murdered, coincidence, it can't be," John said, there was a distant look on his face, as he tried to digest the information, and assimilate it.

"Yes Sir, what the hell is happening, why," Andy said also confused by the turn of events?

"Go down to old files, and check to see if there was a murder in nineteen twenty two; let's be thorough, check, thirty two, twelve; every ten years say, to begin with," John paused whilst he thought, "from say, the turn of the century, and fifty two. No, I would have known about that, had there been a murder in nineteen fifty two I would have known. I was a new DC then, stationed at Scotland Yard, so I would have known about it, even if I wasn't directly involved."

"Yes Sir, I'll ask the officer down there to check for us, any cases similar, most of it is going onto computer now, so it should be easier for us to track any down."

It wasn't long before files started to arrive on John's desk, nineteen o two, eighteen ninety two, eighteen eighty five, now joined the nineteen forty two file and sixty two file. The officer said that they were digging farther back, but that would take a lot longer, and they would go as far back as files existed, if he wanted.

"Don't bother, there is enough here to keep me going, for now," John said, shocked at the amount of old files now standing on his desk.

"Sir, oh."

"Andy, come in."

"Sorry Sir I didn't see you, where have all those come from?"

"I asked him to go back as far as nineteen 'o' two, these files go back into the eighteen hundreds, and he was going to go back further, I told him not to. Who the hell kills every twenty years and is capable of killing well into his eighties. The oldest one here is from eighteen eighty five. When the Body at the Bell was found, the murderer would have to be eighty, and he would have had to have killed at birth, to be responsible for all these murders! There is something not right about this it's terribly wrong. So, if that is impossible we have a society, shall we say, a secret society, which demands the death of a blonde in a particular way to join? Pretty sick if you ask me, or a baby who is capable of murder; and still capable of murder, at eighty plus years of age, this is impossible."

"So that leaves us with a secret society, a ritual killing, as opposed to a sexual one, no wonder we couldn't find any evidence, we have been looking in the wrong place totally."

"I am not sure about that Andy, this has me totally confused, the way she was laid out shouted at me that it was sexual, could it be a family, a vendetta, and again I don't think so. We need to find out more about the women somehow."

"Sir couldn't we go to Manchester and look into the disappearance of the women there, see if there is any link, the files are pretty thin, and they haven't been found, just an idea Sir."

"Yes and I agree with the idea, but we have a lot of reading to do first," John said tapping the pile in front of him.

John picked up the top file and Andy sat down facing him, Andy picked up the next file, Andy was unable to see John because of the pile of files and evidence boxes between them, they began to read the files. First they scanned the file picking up pointers, and then they intended to take a closer look at the one's they agreed were identical to the Body at the Bell. It had taken them two hours before they finally looked at each other over the now empty desk, with two piles of files one by each of them on the floor.

"No question they were all the same MO," Andy said.

"So were mine, they were all killed by the same man, I say incredulously, or a sect, it has to be, but why wasn't the link seen before, even a decade apart someone usually remembers a similar case, and when checked they see that it is identical, yet here they are never checked, why? And why are nineteen twenty two, nineteen twelve, nineteen thirty two and nineteen fifty two missing if it's every ten years. Also, why eighteen eighty five, and then the second year of each decade; so we have gone from a killer who kills every twenty years to now every decade, but misses some decades why?"

"All Jane Doe's as well, the women have never been identified, ok, in the early part of the century I could understand, but latterly there were better means of identification and communication, so why were they all Jane Does?"

"Andy, I have decided to take early retirement, that," John paused trying to find a suitable name for his new Superintendent someone he considered as useless, "plonker, thank you Del Boy, sorry, they appointed as Superintendent when I declined the post, is getting up my nose with his eccentric, tight fisted attitude. Crime detection is down, and will continue to decline as long as money rules the office; you have to spend a certain amount to investigate the crime, but he doesn't seem to think so. He is always looking for the cheaper option, even when it doesn't do the job, as an option. Last night he told me that I couldn't have the funds for the lab tests on that body from the nineteen seventy file we reopened. It's vital that we get the toxicology reports, but because of the time lag between his death and the tests being done it will be more expensive."

"Sir thank you for telling me, I am thinking of applying for the Chief's job in Manchester, if I was to stay on here it would have been dead man's shoes and I don't want to retire an Inspector if I can become a Chief Inspector."

"Apply for it Andy, I would think you stood a good chance of getting the job, especially with my reference and that of the Chief Super, you're a good copper."

"Thank you Sir, I, well actually I have sent off the application form, I was going to tell you when I came earlier, but seeing that mountain made me forget," Andy said with a smile.

Chapter 7
Oddities

"John this is unusual," Andy commented as they reread the files.

It was well into the evening, and darkness had fallen early because of the thunder storm that raged outside. It wasn't uncommon for John and Andy to be in the office at eight in the evening, but tonight they were not looking into several cases bringing themselves up to date on where the cases were going, they were concentrating on the one case, sorting out the boxes of evidence and paperwork putting them into one box and viewing it as one case, the Body at the Bell had suddenly become just one in a series of cases all with the same modus operandi, there was a serial killer on the loose, an odd one, very odd, but that was where the evidence was pointing them.

"I also noticed something odd in this case, what's your oddity Andy?"

"The woman in eighteen eighty five had, had her tongue pierced with a plastic ball on gold. Did they have plastic like that in eighteen eighty five?"

"I very much doubt it, so we need to check. The woman in nineteen 'o' two had plastic bags inside her breasts filled with a gel, that was all the autopsy revealed, but we now know that they were silicone implants, or do we, some obscure ritual again perhaps, and what did the doctor mean by plastic bags, most unusual?"

"John eighteen eighty five, tongue pierced, nineteen 'o' two silicone, say implants, red ink on a card in nineteen forty two, and a missing appendix, well surgical scar in nineteen sixty two. Do you think there is something in these oddities, is the murderer telling us something and we are missing it?"

"Oh, he's telling us something, but what the hell it is I have no idea, there are no clues, yet these oddities in themselves are the clues, but why, and what is it? Shall we call it a night and begin fresh tomorrow, there is still eighteen ninety two for us to read properly, and examine the evidence," John said tired after several hours of reading statements that said they saw nothing heard nothing and didn't know who the woman was.

John came into the office first and sat down to read the eighteen ninety two file, again the statements revealed nothing, the evidence was sparse, but John extremely quickly picked up on a scrap of evidence. The woman had a mark on her arm, a burn mark, yet the doctor wasn't sure. It was as if the top layer of skin had been removed, and around the scar, there were signs that she had, had a tattoo. The doctor was so confused by the mark that he had managed to photograph it, poor though the photography of the day was by today's standards. John had to agree with the doctor that it looked very much as if a tattoo had been removed somehow surgically, leaving a nasty scar, odd, very odd.

"Morning Sir, I see you can't wait to find out about the last file," Andy said smiling.

"And interesting, to say the least, did you know that tattoos have been found on mummified Egyptians over a thousand years BC and that there are several ways to remove them, all painful. More painful than the tattooing, so much so that they use a local anaesthetic when removing them in a lot of cases, one method is wetting the area then applying salt and using a block of wood to rub the tattoo out. I mean like using sand paper to wear away the skin till the tattoo has gone, ouch."

"John, that sounds painful, very painful, really, like sand paper?"

"Yes, to wear away the skin and tattoo, or they can cut it out and sew the edges of the incision together, and it doesn't always work you can end up with a nasty scar. Now these were in operation in eighteen ninety two and prior to that, but, and it's a big but, not as effectively as this one was removed. We have our oddity, it doesn't fit the year."

Satisfied that it was another case with the same MO, John put the file on top of the others, they now had five women all killed in exactly the same way and four photos of missing women that were identical to the murdered women. Sadie Jones from nineteen sixty two, Alexandria Martins from nineteen forty two, and now a Caroline Wilson from nineteen 'o' two, and Brenda Hargreaves from eighteen ninety two, or all had identical twins, yet they couldn't be.

These murders were not the only cases the team were investigating, and John spent the rest of the day doing his other work, finishing work at seven in the evening and after a peaceful evening with Jane reading and listening to his classical music another passion of his, he went to bed, only to resume his quest for justice for the victims again the following morning.

Over the next few weeks, the Body at the Bell surfaced a few times, but it was just one of several cases they were pursuing.

It was late in the day John had told Andy that he was going home early on Friday so that they could get to the house that night, to get it ready for Andy and his wife's visit on the Saturday. They had become regular visitors to the house, now that the repairs were completed, and Andy also a keen gardener was roped into digging the newly sectioned off vegetable plot. Andy's wife Susan was an interior designer, and she helped Jane make the curtains. Jane had hunted trying to find the right curtains and hadn't been able to find the right pair, but she had seen some fabulous material. Susan looked at the fabric and agreed that it was indeed very good quality and would make lovely curtains for the lounge, a large bow window and a side window. Susan had spotted another material for the dining room patio windows, and so it went on buying the material for each set of curtains, and making them up.

John tidied his desk and picked up his coat and was making for the door when there was a knock and it opened, Lynda was stood there holding a photo from the fax machine.

"Sorry Sir but this just came in, a missing person, Manchester knew we were interested in missing women who were blonde and sent it to us,"

"I have a minute let me see it," John said holding out his hand, "I don't recognise the face not everyone who is blonde and missing will match our faces on file," he told her calmly, smiling and thanked her.

Lynda wasn't hurt and knew John wasn't upset by the minor delay, he had asked to see all photos of missing women with blonde hair, but what it did do was delay him long enough for the file clerk to arrive at his door.

"Apologies Sir, how, I still can't believe it. I am sure I checked all this area the last time, and it wasn't there, I just don't understand how it got there, I suppose I will never know. I mean."

"Why don't you just give it to me," John said calmly even though he was now slightly agitated by the delay.

The clerk handed John a file from nineteen twenty two, he opened it and pulled out the photo of the dead woman. He felt his mouth drop as he looked at the face of the missing woman, Lynda had just handed to him.

"Lynda bring that photo back will you," he called out, still not believing his eyes?

"This one Sir," she said handing the photo to him?

"Yes, I don't, here you look," he said handing her the two photos.

John walked back to his desk and sat down, he removed the paper work from the evidence box and began going through it. The woman was laid out the same, she was blonde, naked and had, all her blood drained out. There were two marks on her ankles from where she had been hung upside down. Her throat had been cut with a sharp blade and in one clean cut, the doctor who did the autopsy remarked on the cleanness of the cut. Inside her womb was a coil of some kind, similar to the coil but different, the doctor couldn't identify it, nor give a reason for it being there except as a possible contraceptive device. It looked medical, like a contraceptive device, yet there was no such item, in that type of material, in use by the medical profession at that point in time. The doctor wondered what its use was, and why it had been inserted in the uterus, he did rule out that it had anything to do with the woman's death. The gash in her neck from her left ear down severing the carotid artery and windpipe would have been enough for him in those days. Toxicology screening was in its infancy if used at all.

John picked up the phone and rang Andy's extension, asking him to come and see him.

"Andy, I was just leaving when Lynda handed me this photo," he said, handing Andy the photo of the missing woman. Andy looked at it close then away and back close-up, making sure he was satisfied that she was not one of the victims.

"No Sir she isn't one of our victims, not a very good photo but I am sure I would by now recognise every one of them no matter how bad the photo."

"Now look at this," John said handing Andy the new file.

"I, I, it can't be, she is," Andy stopped mid-sentence as he gazed dumbfounded at the two pictures.

"It can't be, but it is. Another intriguing point is that George from filing handed me that file just now after Lynda had brought the missing woman's picture in to me. George swears that the file wasn't out and that he checked the shelf himself, last month, when we asked for the old files. He swore he had checked it himself, personally, now have you ever known George to miss a file, if it had been there, then he would have seen it and brought it up, so who else is interested in this case? That is what I want to know, and how did they get the file without George knowing about it, you couldn't take a paper clip from filing without George knowing about it? We now have four women that have been murdered with identical missing women and pseudo names for the dead women, if they were the same person, which they can't be, but we have a name."

"True Sir interesting we now have six bodies all with the same MO and five photos of missing women identical to the dead women. Sir we are concentrating on Manchester, what if we widened the field a bit, say over to Leeds or Sheffield?"

"Good idea, try all that, go from Liverpool right across the country, we may be inundated with missing women, blondes, but give it a try. I am going home, before you, have to investigate my murder; I am late as it is, goodnight," John said smiling, leaving Andy to make the request, knowing, that by Monday, there would be a large pile of photos on his desk for him to view.

Chapter 8

Retirement

Andy and Susan arrived at the house at eleven 'o' clock; they parked their car in the driveway, and were greeted by Jane, John and Billy who were already hard at work in the back garden. During the week, Billy had erected a post and rail fence to segregate the vegetable plot at the bottom of the garden, cutting a section off from the main area and lining the fence with gooseberry bushes and black currant bushes. To the right hand side he had left an opening, big enough to get the wheel barrow between the border and the fence. The big plan was to plant fruit trees in front of the vegetable plot to serve as a mini orchard. Then in front of that lawns and flower beds, with apple and pear trees trained up the six foot high wall that surrounded the garden, but each year the plan had changed, and now the vegetable plot was large enough to supply them with fruit and vegetables for most of the year. There was still a lot of work to do, first in preparing the ground and laying out the redesigned lawns and flower beds.

Billy had always worked on the land, and following his divorce some ten years ago had moved to the village to work on a tied farm. Now at fifty he had become a confirmed bachelor again, so enjoyed the company of John and Jane each weekend. This weekend was special for Billy, because he had Andy and Susan to talk to, as well.

Andy took their bags upstairs to their bedroom complaining as usual that Susan had packed the kitchen sink; two full suitcases for one night, when was she intending to wear all those clothes he had asked her, Susan had just smiled, knowing that there were several yards of curtain material in one of them. Andy got changed and joined John and Billy in the garden, whilst Susan unpacked; she showed Jane the material she had bought for the two spare bedrooms, and got the sewing machine out then helped Jane prepare lunch for them. Lunch was a casual meal cheeses, ham, salad and pickles a traditional ploughman's lunch which they ate at the breakfast bar in the kitchen, Jane was not about to allow the caked up with mud men, to go into the house in their dirty clothes. Then it was back to work, Andy, John and Billy were busy planting potatoes, Billy had said that seeing as it was May, and late May at that it, was too late for the early variety and so they were planting late potatoes, carrots and putting up poles and strings for the runner beans, not that they managed all the work, but did get the potatoes and carrots in before it was time to shower and get ready to go to the pub for their dinner. Somewhat of a tradition now following, a hard day in the garden when the weather permitted, and then they always went across the road for their dinner. Billy declining as usual but was persuaded to join them, John decided that it was the offer of a couple of extra pints that made him agree.

Sunday followed a similar pattern, but in the evening, it was a shower, pack and get ready for the journey home, stopping off on the way for something to eat.

Mondays were getting to be a bore for John, he missed the country, even in the rain it was far more pleasant than the city and by the end of the first summer, Jane had decided to retire and live at the vicarage permanently, at the end of that scholastic year. John was coming up to his fifty sixth birthday in a couple of years, and decided that he would retire then, leaving just one year when Jane and he would live at the house and he would commute to the office. This was also the time when he was asked to lead the old cases squad when he told the Chief Superintendent of his plans. Andy was a good ten years younger than John and still needed to work for several years before he could consider retirement. The idea was supported by Andy and Susan who offered John a bed whenever he needed one, once their house was sold, it wasn't a good time to sell, house prices were shooting up, and getting involved in a chain could take months to realise the value of the property in a sale.

John's birthday was in May so he told the Chief Superintendent that he would like to retire in May nineteen eighty two his fifty sixth birthday, the Chief Superintendent had asked if he would work for a few years more till eighty five and lead the cold cases squad for his last three years in the force, using the Body at the Bell as a lever.

"John you never did solve that case you know three years to work on that case, very tempting isn't it," he had said whilst they were enjoying a pint after work in their local at the office?

"Not as tempting as three years in the country, but I will consider it, in one way I just want to go, you know the reason, and then I don't feel ready to retire. I am between the devil and the deep blue sea on this one. Jane is going to retire next summer so that would mean instead of one year living in the country and travelling to work I would have to do it for four years a lot longer than I wanted to, and with the purse strings getting tighter and tighter would there be enough money for me to do any investigating?"

"John, I will fund you, from another source, he will not control the budget I will, but yes I can't just dole out the money there will have to be some control."

"I will talk to Jane about it then, Andy will let me sleep there if I need to, and the way the houses are selling it may take a couple of years to sell mine."

"I knew you'd see sense, I will hold onto your retirement plans then," he had finished the conversation with a smile, knowing that John would stay and that he had not lost his touch.

Chapter 9

More and More Curious

It took two years for John to get an offer on his house, which was withdrawn, it was a blow and John decided to rent the property instead. This meant that even with the extra time he agreed to, he was only without a home in London for two years before he was due to retire.

Now with as little as eighteen months left, he was again looking at the files and in particular the new one that George; the filing officer had handed to him on Friday. John couldn't get over the striking likeness between the victim and the missing woman, they had to be closely related grandmother and granddaughter, or maybe another generation older, but they had to be from the same blood line. The date was nineteen twelve and the missing woman was named Sylvia Atherton. The initial flurry of missing women had died down somewhat, but there was at least one every month that arrived on his desk, but no matching murder victim was found.

John picked up the phone and rang the internal number for the Chief Superintendent, when he answered John said that he wanted to go up north to Manchester, just to nosey around speak to the Chief Inspector up there about his case, and show him the photos, and he wanted to take Andy with him, the Chief agreed to the trip and expenses.

They caught the train the following day, having made all the arrangements with the Chief Inspector for the visit and booked a hotel room. They intended to stay one night only catching the train back the following morning.

A car met them at the train station and took them to the police station; an officer showed them up to the Chief Inspectors office. John looked round deciding that once you had seen one policeman's office you had seen them all. Filing cabinets to his right, a desk full of files centrally with a phone that rang incessantly, a chair battered and worn with more files piled up on the floor next to the desk.

"That's what I like to see a busy office," John joked.

Raymond, the Chief Inspector, smiled back and took John's outstretched hand, "work over load, I haven't seen the top of my desk in oh, a good three years or so. The cleaners have stopped cleaning it, they couldn't get down to the top to clean it," he joked back.

"Thank you for seeing us, I have been investigating a crime since nineteen sixty two, it went onto the back burner when there was no evidence or clues for us to follow, but recently I have been given the dubious job of looking into old cases, and trying to clear some of them. We have been successful in some cases, but this one has reared its ugly head, and what makes it even more confusing is that we now have identical pictures of missing women to the murder victims, yet the murder victims were never claimed and buried as Jane Doe's. The bodies have been found every twenty years or so, which makes it only more confusing, seeing as the earliest victim we have, primarily because I didn't go any further back, was in eighteen eighty five. We have a victim for nineteen 'o' two, forty two, and sixty two and eighteen ninety two all with a photograph of a missing person from recent years, and two others for which we don't have a missing person, an identical twin. Then a couple of days ago I got another file with an identical twin one Sylvia Atherton, and her twin was killed in nineteen twelve. What I'd like to do is interview the relatives of the missing women, and ask if they know of any relatives who were murdered in the past. For one of the victims to have an identical look to a current missing woman, I would say that it was a coincidence, but for five out of seven to be identical, that stretches the imagination too much, I think there is a link."

"Hum, interesting, to say the least, of course John, we will help you in any way that we can, but, it could still be a coincidence, especially going back so far. So what do you need from us?"

"Transport, it will be quicker if we have a local copper to drive us around, apart from that there is nothing, it might be a wild goose chase, but it is the only link we have at the moment, and considering the killings have gone on for one hundred years we wondered if it is a vendetta or ritual, in the sense of joining an organisation, ridiculous but what else could it be? All the bodies were found in London, but the women who are missing are from this area, which just throws another spanner in the works."

Raymond picked up his phone and rang an internal number and asked for a car and driver to be made ready in the parking lot, John shook his hand and thanked him and left.

The first port of call was the woman from nineteen forty two; it was a terraced house in one of the outskirts of the city. A tall woman answered the door to John's knock, she was in her fifties and had dark brown hair, but there was no mistaking that she was the mother of the missing woman, same build, same facial features, and older but just the same. John introduced himself, and Andy he asked if they could enter, she invited them in. John explained that it wasn't about her missing daughter, but about another case, he was dealing with in London, and wondered if she knew of any murders in her ancestry, during the war time in London? Did she have any relatives living or who have lived in London? John drew a blank on both questions; she told him that as far as she knew her parents, grandparents and great grandparents all lived in the area she now lived in; in fact, her ancestors lived in the street next to the one she now lived in with her husband. John thanked her and left wishing her well and hoping that her daughter would be soon found, safe and sound, he shook her hand, and they left.

The driver took them to the eighteen eighty five, victims twin next, saying that it was easier to go by the address than by the date if they didn't mind, John said that he didn't, as long as he spoke to all of them the driver could take the best route to suit himself.

The next person they spoke to was the husband of the missing woman. He was a sour faced man, older than his years, balding, and curt. No, he didn't know, now unless they were going to find his wife for him, they could piss off, he had said abruptly. John wasn't very happy about this, he didn't actually think or take the time to ponder the idea just cut John off, and seeing as the man wasn't under any suspicion John was unable to pressure him. The next one was the nineteen 'o' two, case, and again it was a man, her live in boyfriend who answered the door. He at least did take the trouble to appear to be interested, and looked at the photograph of the dead woman, but it was his girlfriend's family, and he didn't know that much about them, but he gave John her parents address which coincidentally was in London, his girlfriend had come up from London to study. John noted the address, thanked him and left. Finally, they went to the family of the nineteen sixty two victim. Another terraced house all these women had come from what John considered, as the lower end of the housing market, poorer families, and as with the first person the mother answered the door and invited them in offering them a cup of tea which John took, he was dry now from all his talking. She was again a striking woman and her daughter was built in her image same eyes, nose, high cheek bones, her figure was slim and nicely proportioned, if a little over weight now around her bottom; she also didn't know of any murders in the family history and she would have, this one being that recent, her daughter would have been a child then about fourteen she reckoned, so would have known about such a disaster in the family. Apart from that they didn't have any relatives in London, she was tracing her family history and had got back as far as eighteen twenty and all her family were born and bred in Manchester since then, may be even further back than that.

As John had suspected it was a wild goose chase, but it had served a purpose in that one of the families came from London, and so there could be a link there, but it was far too tenuous a link to serve any real purpose. It was early evening when they returned to the police station, Raymond was still at his desk, and John went up to thank him, leaving Andy in the outer office whilst he went in to speak to Raymond. John told him that they would be returning to London in the morning, and he hoped that one day Raymond would be able to see his desk top again; Raymond laughed at the joke and wished John good hunting and a peaceful night. They parted, and the driver dropped them off at the hotel.

"John you are retiring in a year or so, and as you know I want to go further than an Inspector, Raymond is also going to retire soon, would you mind if I left the team and applied for his job, it will be advertised next week I was speaking to his secretary who told me," Andy said over dinner.

Andy felt that he was deserting John, but at the same time, he knew that when John retired he would be an Inspector under the man John disliked, and seeing as he had supported John, his chances of promotion were, to say the least, slim. His previous application had not been successful he believed it was down to his Super wanting to keep him. They had both been disappointed in him not getting the promotion John was just as upset knowing that Andy deserved the promotion.

"Andy if you didn't I would be very annoyed, you're a good copper and deserve better, that idiot we have for a Super is about as useful as a chocolate tea pot. I didn't think he would last long, but he seems to scrape through for some reason, and he will do a lot of damage before he does leave. Go for it, but what will Susan think about leaving London for the sticks?"

"She would have a choice, retire on an Inspectors pay or possibly a supers pay, I think money will sway her to my way of thinking," Andy said smiling; John smiled back knowing of Andy's wife's ability to spend.

They arrived back in the office just after lunchtime and were greeted by Lynda with a sullen look on her face.

"Lost a pound Lynda?" Andy asked.

"No, found two identical missing women, meet Miss Nineteen Twenty Two, and Miss Nineteen Twelve, what the hell is going on Sir? How can all six victims have identically looking women who have disappeared over the last four years? One is a coincidence, two is remarkable, but six out of six impossible, Sir we are missing something there as to be a reason," Lynda said agitated by the unjustifiable coincidence.

"My office Lynda, let's be calm about this there is a reason, we just haven't worked it out yet, come on show me the photos, but let me get my coat off first, they are dead aren't they, they're not going anywhere," John said, smiling at her impatience.

"Yes Sir, coffee Sir," she asked?

"Tea for me please, Andy what about you?"

Andy stretched and screwed his eyes up as if he had just woken up, "I hate train journey's they always make me so tired, sorry tea, no thanks, make it coffee, black no sugar let's see if that will waken me up."

John led the way to his office; it was on the second floor, at the front of the building. John kept a neat office, unlike the one Raymond was in, in Manchester, John was pedantic about his office, he would have the file he was working on out, it may cover his desk but that was the only file out. All other files were in the cabinet, and as he finished what he was doing, it would go away, and another one would be brought out. Part of his nature everything in its place and a place for everything.

Lynda followed Andy and John into his office and opened her file placing the photos on the desk; Andy pulled two chairs up to the desk and they sat down whilst John studied the photos.

"I have to agree it is remarkable." John said as he viewed the photos with the ones he had pulled from his filing cabinet.

"Remarkable!" Lynda said, as if she was aghast, "Bloody impossible," John gave her a stare, "sorry Sir, but you have to agree; these are the same women they have to be. I have done some checking," she added smiling, "Eighteen eighty five, tongue pierced, so has her look alike; nineteen 'o' two silicone implants we have to assume, because the description matches what we now know as implants, so had her look alike. It gets better, nineteen twenty two, Intrauterine device, the coil, so did her look alike. Now for one of the women, to have a look alike in the past, possible, very possible, two OK, doubtful," Lynda shook her head, "but six that is almost incalculable odds, and for three of the six to have the same er, oddity shall we say, well ten no fifteen billion to one surely Sir. I have also been on to Somerset House and of the women one was an only child, two had a brother and the third the nineteen sixty two victim, her mother had a sister, and she is alive and well, so there was no joy there either."

"Lynda has a point Sir, the odds are almost incalculable for six out of six, but for three of them to have the same oddity," Andy paused whilst he considered his words, "yes oddity, must be incalculable. Yet here is the proof, we have just that here, six out of six and three with the same oddity."

"Do we, what if they do look alike, we have to accept that the photos of the older victims are not as clear as modern photos would be, so we could be mistaken, but I have to agree they do look identical. And all of the oddities as you put it were around in those days, but perhaps not quite the same, I mean surgically improved breasts have been available."

"Sorry Sir, to cut in but, I agree that breast enhancement has been around for a lot longer than people think, but plastic? It was a crude plastic, plastic was only invented in eighteen sixty five or six, it wasn't the refined plastic of today, couldn't we exhume her body, the implants would still be there," Lynda asked?

"No point, the surgeon who removed them, kept them. I also have been doing some checking, and because no-one knew what they were when he died, and they were not in a preservative, so no-one thought that they were a medical specimen, they were thrown away. A better option would be the eighteen eighty five victim; if the piercing in her tongue were gold it would have a hallmark on it and so we could date it accurately," John added to the conversation.

"Just in case you think us Inspectors don't do any work now, except push papers around, I'll have you know that I also have been busy. The coil was again not a new invention as most people think, it was in use as far back as nineteen 'o' nine when a German amended the design, that was in use until nineteen thirty when the design was again amended, and plastic was introduced, but it wasn't until the sixties that the current one was perfected, so it would depend on the type of coil and that would give us an approximate date for its invention."

"I didn't know you cared about us women, and what we have to go through for you men," Lynda said sarcastically, smiling cheekily.

"Who said I did?"

"So what are we saying here that, these women are the missing women, come on," John said dragging out the 'on' for emphasis, "how the hell does he kill them and then leave their bodies in the past?"

"How else, we now know that they are not related, yet they are identical," Lynda said, sitting back in the chair and folding her arms.

"Sorry that is far too far-fetched we are detectives, not fantasists, you read too many novels by Jules Vern, yes the year is nineteen eighty four, and I realise that a novel has been written about this year, a science fiction book, but that doesn't mean that it is a reality; where are the cameras big brother is watching?"

"On street corners, in banks, we say that they are there to protect, but they are also, or could be the start of big brother," Andy joined in with, "I have to agree with John on this one, from the evidence, but I find it hard to agree."

"Ok, we have to go with the evidence, follow the clues and from now on I have to accept that the clues and evidence so far leads us to a serial killer, alive and working here and now. So seeing as the powers that be will suggest that I retire through ill health, mental ill health if I suggest what we are talking about. We have no option but to investigate this ourselves," John shuffled the papers around until he found the one he was looking for, "there is an oddity in the dates as well see, Miss eighteen eighty five went missing, assuming we are correct, in June nineteen eighty, yet Miss nineteen sixty two went missing in nineteen seventy eight, so there isn't a pattern there, the killer isn't burying the bodies in order, if that is what we are going to call it?"

"John there is another point here we only have seven victims spread over a five year period now, even that is too long a wait for a serial killer in my experience. I would suggest that we go back further, back to when records began if necessary."

"Good point Andy, hum, one hell of a search, and we would not be popular, think of the cost in time, the Super would not be at all pleased, wasting time and money on a wild goose chase."

"Come," John called out, in answer to the knock on his door.

A young officer entered holding a battered file and looking very sheepishly.

"Sorry Sir I could have sworn that it wasn't there the last time I looked, but there, it was now, and it was as if it jumped out off the shelf at me. I will be far more careful in the future Sir and recheck all the boxes in case I missed any others Sir."

"What did you miss, officer," John said slightly confused?

"This file Sir, the MO is the same as all the others; it is from nineteen thirty two Sir, how I missed it, I'll never know, sorry."

John took the box and opened it, he pulled out a photo of the dead woman and looked at it, yes; naked female, and blonde, throat cut, bled out, and laid out the same as the others.

"You say you just found it, you are sure it wasn't there before?"

"It must have been Sir, but I am sure it wasn't, I don't usually miss an evidence box, and the log book hasn't got a signature against the box number to say that it was out. I can only apologise, I will be more careful in the future and check again to see if there are any more that I missed."

"Ok, yes good idea and will you go further back please, as far back as possible," John said?

John didn't chastise the officer, he was too engrossed in the file, studying the papers looking for the oddity that they now knew would be there, but this far back the autopsy wouldn't have been as detailed, and it may have been missed. The officer left John's office, he hadn't been told off as expected, and somehow that made it worse, it now niggled at the back of his mind whilst he walked back to the records department, resolute in finding any more files. John hadn't given him the lecture he would have in the past for missing a file, because he was also wondering if there was something in Lynda, and Andy's suggestion. If the perpetrator was burying the bodies in the past, when would the file appear, it couldn't possibly be there before the crime, yet it had to be there after the crime, so would files now appear ad hock, whenever a murder had been committed, and a few days later a missing person be reported, so he would be reading the file after the fact as usual, but before the crime had been reported, odd, a strange situation and uncomfortable.

"Sir you didn't tell Jim, the records officer off, which is unusual for you, you were so precise and pedantic," Lynda said confused at his acceptance of the missing file.

"Yes, I wondered, and I still am wondering when the file would appear, how can a file appear in nineteen twelve say, when the woman was only murdered in nineteen eighty two say, when would the file appear," John looked at her over the rim of his glasses raising his eyebrows in a question?

"Well if the body were found in nineteen twelve, then it would be there from nineteen twelve surely," Lynda replied?

"How could it be, if the murder didn't happen till nineteen eighty two," John said still looking at her over the rim of his glasses, "the file can only appear after the murder has been committed, yet it must have been there from nineteen twelve, don't you see that?"

"Now you are confusing me, I know it isn't difficult before you say anything Andy, but how can a file just appear, it has to be written by someone?"

"It was, but only after the murder, he is changing history, he has to be. The files are not there until after the murder, but then the body is discovered, and someone has to be and is, allocated to the crime, and the file is written by them at that point in time. The crime was investigated, but it was in retrospect in so much as the crime, murder hadn't happened, yet, there was the body. The question is, how can we investigate a murder that hasn't happened; even though we have a body? Its several years old, but we have the body of a dead woman who hasn't been born yet? No wonder we couldn't get a name for our Jane Doe, she would still have been at school, up in Manchester in nineteen sixty two, aged about fourteen?"

"Another coincidence or not, but the missing woman identical to the Body at the Bell was fourteen in nineteen sixth two," Lynda said.

They continued to discuss the pros and cons of the case, wondering how to investigate it by the time the crime was investigated technically, it hadn't happened, and was it possible, if they ever found the killer, to prosecute someone for the murder of a victim that wasn't even born, and a killer who wasn't born either? They did agree on one point, that the crime of murder was when the act took place; therefore, they could prosecute, if they could prove that the actual crime had been committed in their time period; but with a body that had been buried back in the mid-eighteen hundreds say, it wasn't going to be easy.

Several months passed the nineteen thirty two, woman was as far as they were concerned identified as one Wendy Smith but couldn't do anything about it, the loved ones would never have closure because the woman would never be found alive or dead, only John and his team would ever know who she was.

John retired leaving the case unsolved, it irritated him no end he now knew how the crime was committed, and how the body was disposed of but couldn't prove anything. Country life suited John and Jane, they became extremely involved in the community, organising several things for the village such as the Morris dancers and bringing a fete to the town, there was such a carnival atmosphere when it came to their little village, several of the local villages joined in and it became a relatively large event. The local riding school started a gymkhana, which also brought all the local villages and some of the larger towns into the village, pony rides, horse and groom races, games for the young riders to show off their skills, and the abilities of the pony's they rode.

Andy and Lynda became regular visitors to the vicarage, Andy couldn't come as often as he wanted to now, being a Chief Inspector in Manchester, but he did visit as often as he could do, bringing news of the Body at the Bell whenever anything suddenly appeared. Lynda stayed at Scotland Yard in the murder squad, and moaned every time she came down about the cash and legal limitations of the present day, telling John how lucky he was to be out of it now.

"Fiscal, restraints, and do gooders, have stopped us from catching and putting away the criminals. We arrest them only to see them walk away from the court smiling. He had a poor upbringing, poor man, we felt so sorry for him; we just smacked his wrist and sent him away to try and live a good and useful life. The old lady he mugged will never lead a normal life now, she is too terrified and won't go out, she has been imprisoned by him, and the court let him off," she said one weekend when she was particularly annoyed, following the release of a second time mugger, "and he'll do it again, and we will have to arrest him again just so that we keep our arrest rate at a reasonable level, and the court will let him off again. I agree with the American three strike rule lock the bas, sorry, him up for good and throw away the key. When will they learn, when the next victim dies from the attack, and I'll bet that will be societies fault, as well. Like hell it is, he knows what he is doing, and he won't stop."

"Feel better now Lynda got that off your chest, ok, so we can now enjoy ourselves can we," John had ribbed her, joking yet not, at her sour expression and the venom of her outcry.

"Sorry Sir, yes, much better, but I'd feel better if I put a bullet in the swine."

"Oh yes you are now a firearms officer as well, how's that going?"

"I am a woman, and women don't kill; therefore, I have never been called upon, to use the skill. Perhaps they are afraid that I might just shoot the, er, sod, instead of allowing him to surrender," she said smiling.

The years passed nothing new happened, bodies were still being, well the files were still turning up from the distant past, and either Andy or Lynda kept John informed of them; also of the missing women that matched the dead women, but after the abortive attempt, he had with the Super before he retired, to get the missing women classed as murder victims, to which the Super had just said, "John I realise we don't see eye to eye, but do you honestly expect me to go to the Chief with this load of tosh, trying to make out some ridiculous idea of the missing women turning up in the past, murdered. Ridiculous I'm glad you are retiring soon it will save me having to send you for a psychological evaluation."

Chapter 10
Tragedy

Tragedy struck John in nineteen eighty nine, when Jane was diagnosed with cancer; unfortunately, it was terminal, and the doctors gave her just six months, with luck she may have twelve months to live. John and Jane gave their apologies to the village committees, John explaining why, and they began to spend as much time together as they could do. Jane had always wanted to go on a cruise, but John was sea sick, but that didn't stop John booking a cruise for them. The Mediterranean first, then the Caribbean, John was sea sick most of the time, but put a brave face on things and had to admit he enjoyed both cruises. They worked side by side in the garden with Billy, and sold a lot of their produce locally, a weekend's vegetables bought them a Sunday lunch at the pub, it was all done in fun, a pound of tomatoes and a bag of onions with three lettuces paid for their papers. On Sundays, they put a table outside, and as the tourists came passed they sold the produce to the tourists, giving the money they earned to the local cottage hospital for a new scanner, in an effort to diagnose breast cancer at an early stage.

Jane lived an active life for a good six months, then as the weight dropped off her she became tired very easily, and left John to sell some of their produce. Then it was left to John and Billy to plant the vegetables, and tend her garden, now only able to look out of the window and watch as they toiled, John looking up at the gaunt face in the window watching them, he wanted to cry at the miserable sight, but smiling instead to encourage her. A month later and the nurse told John that he could no-longer cope with Jane's illness, and she would have to go into hospital for her own good, as well as his, he was no-longer a spring chicken. John swore at her, the first time he had sworn in front of a female, let alone at her. Telling her that he was quite capable of looking after his sick wife, and she could fuck off, if she didn't like the idea. Jane would not be put out to grass until it was for her good, not his. She understood, and accepted his comments calmly realising how he felt for Jane, but she started to come daily, then twice a day, Jane was now in constant pain, and the injections the nurse and doctor were giving her, were not working as well as they had been in the earlier part of her illness.

"John, I can't prescribe a stronger dose for Jane here in her own home; she is now in constant pain and won't leave because of you. You won't let her go to hospital because you think she wants to be here. For Jane's sake, I am asking you to think of her, we have been friends since you arrived in the village and signed up with me. Please allow Jane the dignity of as much comfort as possible, and the only way of doing that is to let her go to the hospital. You are no spring chicken and the care needed will only increase as her condition deteriorates," his friend the doctor had said one day following a call out visit.

John decided that it was getting too much for him to cope with, the emotional strain, and the caring, meant that he was getting just a few hours' sleep each night. Sandra she used to come everyday dust and vacuum, and cook a meal every day for them. John had mastered several of the household chores, doing the washing and cleaning, but the cooking he never managed to get right.

It was one evening, early on in Jane's illness; they were at the pub Jane on her usual tonic water, when Sandra had joined them. Jane told her about they poached eggs John had made, hard, and in bits, laying on black toast. Which was why they had decided to dine out, it was safer. As the illness progressed Sandra called in one afternoon and cooked a stew for them, John was grateful Jane was now confined to her bed, and John going over to the pub for their evening meal and bringing it back for them to eat, so when Sandra turned up and started to cook he didn't argue, too much.

"I'll be alright," he'd said, somewhat reluctantly as he watched her.

"You can't give Jane burnt offerings every night; I'll come in each day and cook a meal for you. When was the last time you vacuumed, MEN," she snorted in disgust, then laughed with John.

Sandra was what you would describe as a typical farmers wife, rotund, rosy red cheeks, and a very jovial person, she bustled about the kitchen as if it were her own kitchen, organising things and clearing surfaces so that she could work. John's normally pedantic, organised way had gone astray, as he had tried to cope with a whole new set of rules.

"Out, go on, get out and take this tea tray up to Jane, she'll be lonely up there, I can cope," Sandra organised him.

"Yes boss," he had joked and carried the tray up to Jane; John sat by Jane's side holding her hand, as another wave of pain swept through her.

It seemed to happen so quickly, yet time just hung for John as he watched helplessly; two agonising weeks had passed since that day when Sandra had arrived and started to give him orders. Now he was too tired to argue with the doctor about where Jane should be, and agreed for her to be taken to the hospital, on the condition that he would be allowed to stay with her.

Day by day she got worse, not eating, lying there drugged up so much that she seemed like a zombie, the lucid moments became less and less as the doses of morphine increased to kill the pain. The hospital had, had a bed put in her room so that John could stay with her, he sat there a tear in his eye as he watched her deteriorate, until the monitor she was connected to screamed out it's alarm.

The doctors and nurses rushed in, and the look on their faces told John that Jane's time had come; she was now dead. John and Jane had agreed that to resuscitate would only prolong the agony, and when the alarm went then the hospital staff were not to resuscitate her, and allow her to go. John wept, he kissed her hand, for the last time, and solemnly looked at Jane, lying there, at peace, at last.

"John, John, please allow the nurses to do their job, come on," Sam the doctor had said, holding out his hand as encouragement.

Sam took John's arm and led him away, back to his office where he poured John a stiff Brandy.

Grief takes many forms, and for John, it was as if he had lost the will to live. It was after the funeral, which the entire village attended; as well as all of their friends from the force. The little chapel was full to over flowing, standing room only, even the weather cried that day, as they laid Jane to rest in the church cemetery, umbrellas went up to protect the mourners, John so much in grief didn't even notice that Andy had put his umbrella over John whilst he stood in the rain. The meal, if that is what you could call it; it was more of a feast. The meal was a selection of meats and sandwiches, pies and salads. All the food was provided free of charge by the villagers, every household made something; they took the food they had made to the pub and put it out, with the other food. John hadn't thought about that part of the proceedings. Sandra had organised it with the landlord of the pub, and the pub was where they all were now. John sat sullenly in the corner they always sat in; looking at a plate of food that had just been placed in front of him, then he got up without a word and left. Once home he locked the door to his house after him. The villagers kept an eye on the place, but nothing happened; the curtains were still drawn from the funeral, and John had never left the house; they all agreed that he was in mourning and should be allowed a period for his grief to abate, give him time they had said, Sandra was now getting worried, three days had passed and no-one had seen him not even Billy.

"You go and speak to him, ask him if he wants me to cook a meal for him Billy, go on," she had told Billy one morning at the local shop.

"He loved her so much, it will take some time for him to get over this, I have been but he won't answer the door, I will go again tomorrow," he had replied.

"Billy Hunter, he was your best friend, you will go now, or I will punch you, old as you are," she had chastised him.

"I, well I don't, I am worried about him Sandra, I was going to ask the doctor to call,"

"He has and got no reply, you need to go Billy."

"Guess so, I was giving him time, I didn't want to push it too soon."

"It's been almost a week now, go on," Sandra said encouraging him.

Billy reluctantly did as told fearful that he would upset John, who just needed more time to get over the death of his wife, but he also knew that it was time John was getting out.

Bang, bang, bang, Billy hammered on the door, just as he had done in the past; there was no response.

"John, John, come on lad open the door, are you alright," Billy had called out through the letter box? Again no reply; so he went round to the back of the house, and all the doors were locked and the curtains were drawn. He again went to the front door and hammered on it calling out to John.

"Fuck off," came the response at last, the fact that he had got a response lifted Billy's spirits, the silence made him begin to wonder if John had killed himself from the grief, but at least he was still alive.

"John open the door let me in," he called out.

"Fuck off, I want to be alone, don't you get it F-U-C-K OFF fuck off," John had yelled back at him.

"Sandra I am worried even more now. John swore at me, which is not like him at all. I'm afraid he might do something stupid," Billy told Sandra when he returned to the shop where she had been waiting.

"I told you yesterday to go, but no, leave him for another day or two. Three days he has been locked in that house, in the dark, why hasn't the doctor done something about it," she said angrily?

"Because I can't, I don't have good cause just yet, but I am also getting worried about him, and what can I do? I don't have powers of entry unless I say that he is mentally unstable, and a danger to himself, and I don't truly want to do that, just yet," the doctor said from behind Sandra.

"Sorry doctor, I am worried about John, this isn't like him, and he swore at Billy have you ever known him swear?"

"You as a friend can do more than I can officially, he is unstable, but I don't want to give him that stigma do you? I have called on him been told that he is fine. He sounded alright so I don't really have justification, very awkward, but you, well," he said leaving the sentenced unfinished and their options open.

"Well if you two wimps won't do anything then I will," she said and stormed out of the shop.

"John, John Alker I am coming in," Sandra shouted through the letter box after banging on the door.

"Piss off, I have bolted the door now go away and leave me alone," he had shouted back.

"You open this door, or I will get Jimmy with the tractor, and we will push the bloody thing in. I am coming in one way or another, now get up off your arse and open this bloody door," she yelled back, with the desired effect. John knew that she would do exactly as she had said she would do, she was not a woman to be messed with.

"Get out of my way, go and sit and sulk, all fucking day if you want; but life goes on; and, if Jane were to see you now. Look at you, unkempt, unshaven, and starving, she would turn in her grave. When was the last time you had a shower or changed your clothes, get up them stairs now, I'll open the curtains and start the cleaning, go on I don't have all day, move it," she said in her bombastic way, organising everything and everyone in sight.

She had helped John and Jane tremendously in the past, telling people what to do, following John and Jane's organisation. She did it in such a way that the people she ordered about did it willingly, with a smile, perhaps it was that, she seemed to have a smile on her lips permanently, now John saw the angry side, her face not smiling she had a fixed look on her face determined, she was in control. Standing a good two inches taller than John, and twice his width, with strong hands and arms from lifting the bails and working on the farm, she had broad shoulders and muscular legs, not the prettiest woman in the village but a lovely personality. Her angelic face beamed, when you weren't being told off by her, as John was now. Bully tactics to get him back, the soft, sympathetic route, had failed miserably, so now she was bullying him into life again.

John emerged from the shower with a towel wrapped round his waist, Sandra was leaving his bedroom having opened the curtains and stripped the bed, they looked at each other, John pale and gaunt, Sandra wanted to cry, he was so thin and feeble, he moved towards her, she grabbed hold of him and held him to her breast, whilst he got rid of all the grief he had been holding. She soothed him, and hugged him for a while, then pushed him away, tears were rolling down her cheeks, she wiped them away and looked at him.

"John get dressed, and then come down stairs I'll fix you some lunch," she said and pulled him close to her again.

John got dressed then joined her in the kitchen, his eyes still puffy and bloodshot from the crying. He ate half the bacon and eggs she had prepared, before he looked at her pushing the plate to one side. After that Sandra had visited John every day cooking a meal and cleaning, slowly she managed to get him back.

"Sandra, have I been terrible, I mean, mean and nasty, to you," he asked about a week after she had bullied him?

"Terrible it was, watching you kill yourself, but after I bullied you, you have been fine, but what about Billy, You haven't spoken to him in over two weeks, and he is also worried, and then there is Colin at the Black Bull, he has been fending all your phone calls from Andy and Lynda, they have been ringing every day since," she paused.

"Since Jane died," John said for her and paused.

"Yes, why don't you go across to the Black Bull; Billy will be there, he will again be drowning his sorrows, and he can't afford it? You owe Colin a pint, and Billy a couple, go on reunite with Billy he needs you as much as you need him right now. I need you out from under my feet so that I can clean properly, move it, or I'll box your ears for you, go on," she ordered him in a motherly way, smiling.

John got up he looked back at her and she waved him out, pushing him towards the door, it was a big step for John who hadn't left the house since he had locked himself in after the funeral. Slowly uncertain of what was waiting for him, he made his way to the pub, but he needn't have worried, they were just glad to see him up and about again. He sat in his chair, in the corner, and Colin brought over a pint of his usual, John smiled, thanked him and took a sip, it was just as he remembered, and slid down his throat like velvet.

"Sor," was all he managed to get out before he was cut off.

"John we are just glad to see you again, don't say anything, have that on me," Colin said resting his hand on John's shoulder.

"I am led to believe that I owe you a pint for fending all my phone calls, thank you."

"A pleasure, but ring Andy and Lynda, they are very worried about you."

Billy came in and stopped, looking at John then sat down in his chair and faced him, lost for words; John thought he saw a tear form in Billy's eye.

"Cold today," he said and wiped the tear away with his handkerchief.

"Yes the temperature has dropped, sorry Billy, I'll buy this one and the next one."

Chapter 11

Re-Birth

It still took a few weeks for John to begin to get over the loss of his wife, they had been inseparable, and he felt as though his right arm had been severed. He visited the pub, but it was more perfunctory than by desire; an old habit. Billy again came around every day, to help him look after the garden; he set up the stall to sell the vegetable from his garden and donated the money they raised to the hospital.

Then in the autumn of nineteen ninety, Lynda rang and spoke to Sandra; John was at the pub with Billy, she had some information for John about the Body at the Bell. Sandra suggested that she turn up at the weekend, unannounced, and force her way into the house. John was still hiding as much as he could do, she told Lynda.

As usual at the weekend John and Billy were at the vegetable stall, Billy did most of the selling, John kept the stall filled and avoided contact with the customers. Once they had cleared up they went to the pub, they seemed to sit there in silence, just the odd word, spoken, out of need, rather than conversation. Billy knew it would take some time for things to get back to normal what John needed was something to interest him.

"Morning Sir," Lynda said as she pulled up at the gate; John and Billy were at the stall serving a customer, John looked at her.

"What do you want," he asked curtly?

"I want your opinion on this; it's a photo of another missing woman, and I have the murder file as well, he has made a mistake. I went to."

"I am retired, go away."

"You miserable old sod, let her show you, go on get inside and look at the bloody thing," Sandra had butted in with her now familiar bullying way when John felt sorry for himself.

"You keep," John started, but Sandra butted in again.

"No, you need something to occupy yourself with, and that case bugged you, so solve it for them, you know you can do it, go on I'll help Billy."

John looked at her, her face set again as it had been when she burst into his house; he knew he couldn't win this one and smiled, shrugged his shoulders and led the way.

'Sir see, she has a birth mark on her buttock, and had it made into a rose, tattoos in those days were not uncommon, but for the missing girl to have a birth mark, also made into a tattoo of a rose in exactly the same place; then that is unusual, and it's on the same buttock, identical. It is the same woman, it has to be. I told the Super, and he laughed at me, saying that it was a coincidence, and almost threw me out of his office laughing at me, the bas, sorry, well from what we already know, these are the same women."

"Interesting, very interesting, but I am retired now, with a lead like that we," John paused.

"Sir, they will not investigate it as a murder, and I have cocked up my chances of the promotion by asking, please help me to prove that I am not insane, and help me investigate this one?"

"I, I don't know if I can, I have lost so much, you know of course that I gave up the will to live after Jane died and, well, I, sorry but."

"Sir, I am begging, I need you; Andy is a Super up in Manchester now, he would promote me, I know that, but I don't want to go up there, and I have been over looked three times now in London. Apart from that, he will kill again and again until we stop him. We did do a search as far back as our records went, and there are some twenty to twenty five women that he has murdered; every time we look a new file shows up. Sir we have to stop him. This file has just shown up from eighteen seventy two, the woman is an Angela Prendergast from Bury."

"You have taken the files to the Super and shown him all the evidence?"

"He won't even see me now, I have tried, but he has his head up his arse most, sorry Sir, but he has."

"Leave it with me, I will think about it."

"What is there to think about, he was a thorn in your side, he is killing innocent women, and you want to think about it, you are no better than that sod of a Super," Sandra said with disdain, and marched on passed them into the kitchen.

"How long have you been listening," John said angrily?

"Long enough, I didn't hear much except that a friend needs help, now where would you be if friends hadn't helped you," Sandra said back angrily, yet smiling in her forceful, yet friendly way.

"I'll need all the files to reacquaint myself with the case, and Lynda cleaver dick can't take them out of the office," John said to, Sandra joking yet not.

"No but I can photocopy them, and slip them into the boot of your car whilst you say hello to the other officers who you know, and apologise for being rude," Lynda joined Sandra being forceful and bossy.

"Women, always ganging up on me, ok, ok, tomorrow, sorry it's Sunday, Monday; I will come to the office at ten to thank everyone for their support during my grief, and well then it is up to you," John said a little excited but unwilling to acknowledge it.

"Thank you Sir, a cup of tea would be nice, I'll make it whilst you read the file, Sandra would you like one, you only looked at the photos," Lynda said getting up and handing him the file back then went to make tea for the four of them.

John read the file and spotted another interesting point, which he kept aside till Sandra and Lynda returned with the tea Sandra took a cup out to Billy leaving them alone.

"One, how did you get this file out, and two why didn't you tell me that she was a prostitute?"

"One it's a photo copy, things have changed, we are more technical now, and two and I missed that point."

"After all the training I have given you, and you missed an important point like that! What would you say was the easiest way to get a woman, trolling around the bars, or going to the red light district? How many of the women were prostitutes, have you checked? I'll bet all of them were, that is how come he found them so easily, and why, when they went missing it wasn't reported for a few days."

They chatted for quite some time, Lynda telling John of the new gadgets they now had, and the better means of autopsy, a more detailed report, which helped them in their work, catching the criminals, but criminals were always, or so it seemed, let off with a warning.

John took Lynda to the pub where they had lunch with Billy, before Lynda had to go back to London. In the afternoon, John read and reread the file absorbing all the information about this recent victim.

That evening when Sandra was leaving she saw a spark in John's eye she hadn't seen in a long time, "See you tomorrow John," she called out as usual, but got no reply, his head buried once again in the file, seconds later he had shouted bye, but too late, she was out of ear shot by then.

John was up and dressed, he had got back into his old routine mainly because if he didn't Sandra was wandering into his bedroom opening the curtains before he was up. The first time she did he looked up at her in shock, "Well it's almost nine 'o' clock, half the day is gone, I've seen it all before come on, I want to make your bed," she had said unashamedly.

"Yes ma'am, sorry ma'am," he answered her, and got out of bed as she left the room, he wasn't going to get caught again.

John answered the door, stood there expectantly was Jenny, another bombastic woman, a sour look on her face.

"Well move to one side, I can't clean out here," she had said forcefully.

"Where's Sandra?"

"On holiday, I know she told you that I was going to be doing for you whilst she went away for a week. Now come on; move it."

"Oh, I must have forgotten, but there is no need, I mean, I can manage for a week."

"Look John, Sandra organised this; now if you want me to tell her that you wouldn't let me in, fine, but you can face her anger. Please, give me plenty of warning, so that I can leave the county before she gets to you," Jenny said and cocked her head to one side daring him.

"I didn't mean to offend you, but you have your own family to look after, and well, I appreciate the offer but, I mean, well, you'd better come in then."

"John, don't worry, I am doing it because I owe you and Jane, a lot see these," she put her hands under her well-formed breasts and lifted them, John nodded but didn't look, "they are mine, all real. From the money, you and Jane raised, they put in a breast screening unit. Had it not been for that, and Jane pushing me into going to have them checked, they would not have found the cancer, and it could have killed me, or at the least left me flat chested. I am proud of my double 'D' breasts, even though now they are well not as firm as when I was in my teens, but they are mine and I still have them because of the work you and Jane did. So out of my way, go and get me the veg for lunch," she said and pushed past him.

John smiled to himself, Jane had done a lot of charitable work for the village and local hospital, helping organise events to raise money.

John went outside just as Billy was walking up the drive way, "You look happy with yourself John," he said, as they met by the back door.

"Yes I have seen the good work Jane has done for the village, I now know it wasn't in vain, not that I ever thought it was, but, well, let's just say that it was all worthwhile," John smiled to himself as he remembered the two monsters she had pushed under his nose.

John dug up a cauliflower and took it inside for Jenny to cook for lunch; along with some carrots, gave them to Jenny then joined Billy helping him dig up some more vegetables for them to sell and laid out the stall in readiness.

Monday again John was up early, he had given the keys to his house to Jenny, because he wanted to leave early, and he didn't like the idea of driving through London, so had decided to leave the car on the outskirts and catch the underground. What a mess, he hadn't realised the volume of traffic from the outskirts, and missed the first train, because it was full of commuters; even the next one was nearly full, but there was standing room for him. He got off at the nearest station to New Scotland Yard and walked the few yards to the entrance. He looked up at the building and shrugged his shoulders, this wasn't easy it had been a long time since he retired, and he had to make a deliberate effort to enter the building, afraid of speaking to his ex-colleagues, not knowing what to say, he had ignored them for so long now.

"John great to see you, sorry, you look great," he knew they would lie, he looked terrible, he still hadn't put on all the weight he had lost during Jane's illness.

"Yes Sir how may I help you," the officer behind the desk said?

He was tall, very tall six foot six John reckoned, and he had broad shoulders a square jaw and deep blue eyes, a thick shock of hair covered his head even though it had been shaved right down to a sever length, giving the officer a hard look, "no wonder people are not as friendly to the cops of today as they were when I joined," John thought, "he looks like a thug."

"Ex-Chief Inspector Alker to see Sergeant Summers," John said in an official tone.

"Yes Sir, just one moment, please," the officer replied.

The words were spoken nicely, but the intonation was one of, if I decide to, were you really a policeman, hah well?

"Sir, glad you could come, the lads are all waiting to see you, what's left of the team, that is, where's your car?"

"Lynda, sorry Sergeant, I left it at Sevenoaks, I decided to get the tube in, and I am glad I did the traffic is terrible."

"Not a good idea, but I will think of something, come on," she said, and opened the electronic lock, showing him through to her office, "David you remember Inspector Alker don't you?"

"Yes nice to see you again, I worked with you on several murders, I was just a DC then, when you took on the old crimes section, just before you retired, I stayed in the murder squad, I'm an Inspector now for my sins; Lynda, John must be dying of thirst, a coffee please?"

"Yes please, that would be great, who else is here?"

"John I have an errand to do, sorry, but you chat to the guys for a little while, and then I'll run you back to your car, can't have you using the tube can we," Lynda said, with meaning?

"Oh, I don't mind, it's so long since I drove in London and the traffic, to be honest I was nervous."

"I won't hear of it, you remember the Super, no he was Chief Super when you retired, wasn't he, he had just been promoted; well he's dying to see you again. Have a coffee; I'll get someone to show John up to the Chief's office?"

"No problem, Simon, after the Inspector has finished his coffee, please take him up to see the Chief Super," David said eagerly?

"Yes Sir," the young DC said, John looked at him and decided that the saying was right; as you got older the police officers got younger he didn't look old enough to join let alone be a DC.

Lynda left the office and the officer called Simon spoke to John about policing and the changes since John had left, to some degree at a loss as to what to say, he had, had an ex-senior officer dumped on his lap without warning, and although John tried to help him by asking questions about the new set up, it never actually got anywhere, and John was as relieved as he was sure Simon was when the Chief Super entered.

"John, how are you, we were all worried about you when you became a re-cluse, but it was understandable Jane was a beautiful woman in many respects, so what brings you to London," the Chief Super said leading the way to his office?

"Visiting old haunts as it were, seeing who is left, Andy has gone north, and Lynda for some unknown reason is still a sergeant. She would make an excellent Inspector, got the sense, the feeling, she uses the gut reaction, a lot of the officers who were with me didn't have that, but they are Inspectors now, sexism is it?"

"John now come on, you know we can't be like that, no she just ruffled a few feathers that she shouldn't have."

"You mean told face ache the truth, and he didn't like it, come on he should never have been made a Super."

"No John he shouldn't, but the man who should be, refused the job, remember?"

The conversation continued for a good half hour before Lynda knocked at the Chief Super's door and entered, telling John that she would need to go now because she had an interview to conduct, and time was short. John took the hint, shook hands with the Chief Super and said his goodbyes, following Lynda out to the car park.

Once clear of the building Lynda turned to John. "You forgot didn't you, how can I put the files in your boot if the car is in Sevenoaks," she said with a smile?

"Sorry Lynda, your right I was so afraid of driving in London that it never entered my mind, and that was the reason for coming, are you sure I can be of help, I am getting forgetful?"

"Sir you remembered to come, that is the important part, all the files are there, a copy at least, I came in yesterday, to copy them. Read them and get that brain working, half of your brain is better than half of the forces full brains today, idiots."

John felt stupid for forgetting, but as Lynda drove through the traffic he was glad he had. It used to be bad, but now it was just a solid block of traffic, going in every direction and half the streets were blocked off, he began to wonder if he could have found New Scotland Yard, with all the one way streets that had suddenly appeared.

"John I have put the files in your boot, please read them and then ring me, I think your idea about them all being prostitutes is a good one. I have contacted Andy and told him, he wants to help. So I asked him to check if any of the missing women were on the game, he hasn't got back to me yet, I will let you know when he does."

John took Lynda's hand as she offered it and pulled her to him, "Thank you," he said hugging her, and gave her a peck on the cheek, she smiled at him, and they parted.

John drove home feeling more alive than he had done in a long time, it was now some eight months since Jane started with her illness; all the pain and suffering he had gone through watching her, unable to help, a feeling of loss, of being useless, had hurt him deeply.

When he arrived home, he reversed the car up the drive and went in by the back door, to the most gorgeous smell.

"Jenny what is that, it smells gorgeous?"

"Ragout de Beouf," she said with a smile, "I got it from one of my recipe books; the one I bought, written by the chef on the tele."

"Well if it tastes half as good as it smells, it will be great," John said sniffing the air near the oven.

"My, you're in a good mood, met a woman," Jenny said laughing.

"Yes, a very demanding female, a criminal file. Far more demanding than any woman I have ever met," he said, his eyes gleaming from excitement.

"Can I stay for dinner Jenny, is there enough, it smells lovely," Billy shouted from outside the back door.

John and Billy carried the files in and put them in the morning room, which was at the back of the house and out of sight from prying eyes. The files although they were old were still not allowed out of the office because they were sensitive, even the ones from over a hundred years ago, but mixed in with them were the recent disappearances, and they were highly confidential. John looked around the room and decided that he would need to rearrange the room to accommodate his office. Billy piled the files up on the floor then helped John rearrange the furniture, and bring in a desk from John's study, which was too small for him to use as an incident room. Next he rang the GPO to get a phone installed in the room, an extension, then went out and bought some materials he would need, a blackboard, white board, and a cork board, pins, a map of England and a street map of Manchester, a map of that area including Sheffield and Leeds. Some pens, coloured pens, highlighters and pencils. The woman in the shop had asked if he was setting up an office; John had told her that he was. She suggested a photocopying machine and fax machine. John decided that he wasn't ready for that much technology yet, and left. Billy helped him load the boot of the car and then unload it into the morning room. It took the rest of that day, and till lunch time the next day, for them to get the room as John wanted.

"Billy much as I trust you, I cannot involve you in this, these files are for police officers eyes only, even I shouldn't have them as an ex-copper, and I will have to lock the door to stop Jenny or Sandra from coming in, I am so sorry."

"John, I understand, I do, but as you full well know, if it is gossip I will tell you all about it, but you say mum's the word, and a team of wild horse wouldn't drag it out of me, we are a team, and I want to help you."

"True," John said, and the phone rang, Billy was nearest and took the call.

"John it's Andy, he says that so far all the women he has checked up on, were on the game, four of them, two he thinks were, but their friends shall we say, wouldn't admit it. What women," he asked curiously pushing John?

"See, that is why I can't allow you in."

"No, I don't see, you need someone you can trust, to listen to you; even if I am not a policeman I am a good listener, and voicing ideas aloud helps sometimes. Someone to mull ideas over with, well it always worked for me."

John walked away from Billy thinking, lost in the concept; trying to work out if he had a point, then turned to face Billy and walked back slowly, still considering the idea. His hand rubbing his jaw, his eyes screwed up as he pondered, "hum," head bowed slightly looking at Billy through the tops of his eyes as he considered the proposal.

"I agree you have a point, but I must warn you the pictures take some getting used to; it isn't just writing and things like that, and you will need to know as much about this as I do. You will have a lot of reading to do to bring you up to date, and you will have to read the files here, they mustn't leave this house OK?"

"A done deal, where do I begin," Billy said eagerly?

"See those boxes; well, all of them," John said trying to put Billy off, or test his commitment to the task.

Billy looked at the stack of boxes in the corner and began to wonder if he had made the right choice, there were a dozen large boxes piled up in the corner, it would take him years to read all those.

"Yes," he said uncertainly.

"Start by opening them up and reading them, they are not in an order, and they don't need to be. The bodies didn't er, arrive, or appear in any order. What you need to see is the similarity, what the statements say, little or nothing, but that is where you would begin. I'll finish doing the work room then, oh hell I don't know, is it all worthwhile, I mean I am retired, I don't have the energy, and seeing your face when I told you what you needed to do, well?"

"John, I will read them, and I will view the photos, but you need a reason to live. I was close to committing suicide when I met you, alone, no job, yeah, I lied, I was on the dole, but I was a land worker, so I did know what I was doing. Working for or with you, gave me that something, I was needed, and I did a good job. You need that something, something to live for and you need to close this case, for your own peace of mind."

"There is no disputing that Billy; I don't know how we would have managed without you, so I owe you one; the boxes are not full, there is a box for each murder, it won't take you so long, honestly, I was trying to put you off, seeing if you, well, sorry."

Billy opened the first box there was a file with a few pieces of paper inside, which he read, and several photos of a young woman from various angles. John put up the white board and placed the pens on the ledge, then screwed the blackboard to the wall. Billy held it for him, and then returned to his reading. By the evening, Billy and John were stood not in a morning room, but an incident room, with phone, and all the boards with photos and notes on them in readiness.

The week passed slowly for both of them; by Thursday, Billy was in a restless mood, he asked John if this was what police work was like; all this sitting around, reading and waiting for something to happen? John had laughed at him, telling him that he wished it was. He would have about a dozen files on the go at any one time, sometimes more. Some murders were easily solved within a day say, when it was the husband, or the murderer had slipped up and was seen, some took years to solve, and everyday reports interviews and evidence gathering meant that he worked never less than a ten hour day. Now was different they had only one murder, or one case, a serial killer. The same man had committed all the murders, and the crime scene was not known, the victims until recently, and John still was unsure, but they were not known either. When the murder was committed was not known, how the victims were abducted, trapped, was not known, they had so little to go on, just the fact that all the dead women had a twin, a missing person from the present day. John waved his hand across the board, where the photographs of the victims and missing women were now pinned in pairs.

On Saturday, there was some relief, from the tedium of reading and looking at the boards. Each morning they had met in the incident room and read the files again, then out into the garden, when the weather permitted, but on Saturday Lynda was coming to see them and staying the weekend.

She arrived late Saturday morning, and her smile was a welcome greeting which lit any room, she had news and John recognised it in her face.

"Well, come on don't keep us waiting," he said anxiously, almost as soon as Lynda had entered the house?

"Let me get my coat off," her smile lit the room as she beamed, "Andy is going to help us, he was always the sceptic, but he has agreed to help; there has been another missing woman reported. Normally they would have told the woman who reported it to wait for twenty four hours, but Andy had told the lads that any missing woman with blonde hair had to be taken seriously, no matter how short the time. She was supposed to be at her sister's house at ten yesterday morning, by twelve, her sister was in the police station reporting her missing. Unusual, but it was the woman's birthday and the missing woman was always so punctual, she was pedantic about punctuality, and she worked as a prostitute, a private one, so knew when she was booked and when she was free, she never went on the streets, she took no chances like that. She began with an agency, but now had a client list and didn't need the agency, although from time to time she did do them a favour if you like."

"So has she been found, I mean on our murdered women's list," John asked?

"No but, how far back has he buried them, maybe she will never be found her body turning up before records began."

"Doubtful but possible I suppose, even the Romans kept records and good ones, but you have a point, hum, is Andy starting a murder enquiry?"

"Sir, please, he is taking a risk just accepting the report so soon after her disappearance; to open a murder enquiry would be suicide, work wise I mean, he is hoping for the Super's job."

"Interesting, but there is nothing to stop us; Billy needs some field training, and I need to be more involved, get out and do some digging. Monday we will go to Manchester, Billy, two days will be enough, leave first thing Monday morning, and we'll be back Tuesday for dinner in the Bull."

"Sounds good to me boss," Billy said, now smiling at the idea of not only going to a place he had never been before, but at his involvement; John hadn't hesitated in assuming that he would be going along as well, without asking him, he was now a part of the team.

They all went into the incident room, Lynda looked round and was surprised at the array of boards, and all the equipment John had bought, she had said that it was almost fully equipped, just like her office at the station, but only one case, as opposed to the ten she was investigating. The weekend passed extremely quickly, John and Billy both got on exceedingly well with Lynda, and as they weeded and dug up unwanted plants, Billy was surprised at the energy she put into the job, commenting on it to her, Lynda had just smiled and thrown some grass cuttings at him, starting a grass cutting fight.

John and Billy left the house early, the dawn was just breaking at seven in the morning which was unusually early for them these days; John drove, it was a long drive taking till two in the afternoon for them to get to Manchester. John stuck to fifty miles per hour, mumbling about the lunatics that raced down the outside lane, in excess of the speed limit; he was sure. Time was taken by the stops as well, stopping for breakfast around nine, coffee at eleven, lunch at one, but it made it a pleasant drive. By three, they had booked into the hotel Andy had booked for them, and they were sat in his office, with yet another cup of coffee in front of them. Andy handed John a copy of the woman's file, John studied the file then after a brief chat whilst Billy also looked at the file, they left for the woman's house with a copy of the file. Andy had asked the sister if it would be alright for a friend, a private investigator, to look at the woman's home, she had agreed.

Four thirty and John was knocking on the woman's door, Billy a step behind him, having been told to listen, and watch the woman, mainly her body language, leave all the talking to John.

The woman placed the tea tray in front of them and poured three cups of tea, and then sat down.

"Allow me to explain, we are looking into the case of a missing person near London, and Chief Inspector Green, an old friend and ex-colleague sent your missing person report to me, because it was very similar to the one I was investigating. The police investigate crimes and look into reports were a crime may have been committed. Your case doesn't fit either of those criteria, but if you don't mind, I would like to take it on, as an extension to the one I am looking into. My fee, I can see the question in your face," John said and smiled at her, "there will be no fee. I am hoping, that one case will help to solve the other one; so don't worry about a fee from you; I will not be."

"I, well, we are not well off, but I do have some savings so I can er, well contribute something say," the woman said nervously.

"No, as I said my fee, as it were, is covered. I understand that your sister worked in the entertainment business as an escort. Can you tell me where she got her clients from?"

"She," the woman hesitated, as if ashamed, yet accepting the fact that John needed to know about her work, "she had a list of her clients; all private and well-heeled as we say. She didn't work the streets, she wasn't like that. She even had a couple of men who came up from London, they came from all over the country, and very select she was."

"Can I see her house please, I need to get an understanding of how she lived, and where she worked, was it from home?"

"I don't know, she kept that part of her life very private. I know what she did, but that was about it, except that her clients weren't all local, very few were, in fact. If it will help, I can show you where she lived?"

"It will, a great deal, I will need to look around, and if that upsets you, to see the other side of your sister shall we say, there is no need for you to be there. I can assure you that I do need to look; I do not judge a person that is not my job. I just want to find her for you."

It took another half hour for John to convince her of the need for him to go into her sister's house, and open drawers, to get the feel of the person. He thought back to when he had been called in to find a missing person, or investigate a robbery, or murder, and the shock when the people left behind saw what their loved ones had in their possession, secrets, secret lives, unbeknown to them. It always surprised the relatives what secrets they were keeping, even shocked them in some cases, it was easier when the relatives were not there. The number of times he heard, 'oh, my god,' or, 'who the hell left that there,' as if it didn't belong in their loved one's lives.

At last John had the key, and the authority to enter her sister's house without escort. Billy had done as he had been told, and sat there listening watching the woman. On the way to the house, John spoke to Billy about the woman and her body language. Billy was observant and had picked up on all the points John raised, like her folding her arms when she wasn't interested or leaning forward when she was interested, it had been a venture into the science of body language, for Billy. He was to watch, as John looked around the house and learn.

It was a Victorian, end terrace house; it was larger than the rest of the houses in the row. Originally it had been built for the rent collector, or a junior manager would have lived in this house, that was in the days when it was owned by the mill, or colliery. It had an entrance hall with a coat rack on one wall, a single light bulb illuminated the hall, there were three doors of the hall one to the front room, a small but neatly furnished and well decorated room, a settee with two seats, and two arm chairs were set round the fire place. Along the back wall was a small cabinet, John didn't open it yet. The next door opened into a dining room with a central table and four chairs around it, a large display cabinet stood against the wall by the door, next to that was the stairs to the bedrooms, with a fireplace in the opposite wall, which had been bricked up, a gas fire had been set in the opening. Off this room was the kitchen, again well set out, neat, tidy and clean, everything had been put away there was nothing on the sides. They went back into the entrance hall and opened the third door; this went down into a cellar. John closed the door and went upstairs, first, there were two bedrooms and a bathroom, all decorated to the same standard as the ground floor rooms. From this general view, he determined that she was pedantic about cleanliness, tidiness, and didn't like anything on show, except what was designed to be on show. She had excellent taste, and knew what worked in decor, and what didn't.

"Billy first we look round, well I do, and see if I can assess the person, this person is clean, tidy, and has an excellent eye for decor, and she has an organised mind, she knew what she wanted and what worked, see her colour schemes, and the way she blended things into it. Now we dig deeper, we open the drawers, and the cupboards, she would have had a diary, a book of her clients, she was too well organised not to have. She would have kept records of what they paid, probably in code, and even their likes and dislikes."

"Likes and dislikes I thought she was a prostitute?"

"Not everybody does it the missionary style, Billy."

"No, I suppose not, I hadn't thought of that."

"First of all, let's take a quick look round the cellar, that shouldn't take too long," John said leading the way.

At the bottom of the stairs, John stopped, and looked at the two doors in front of them, both closed. John tried the first one, it was locked, he then tried the second one, and that was also locked.

Billy felt along the top of the door surround and handed John a key, he put it in the lock and the door opened. Beyond it was a steel barred gate, also locked, they peered into the darkness trying to see what was so unusual that it was behind two locked doors. Billy left the area and checked the corridor, finding the switch he switched on the light. Behind the gate was a mattress on the floor with a blanket on it, a bucket stood in the corner and chains hung from the ceiling, with manacles attached.

"A prison cell," Billy said shocked.

"Yes Billy that is what it is, but she wasn't the police, so this now begs a question what was it used for? Was she a kidnapper, and has someone taken revenge to get even with her by kidnapping her?"

"John, do you think she was a kidnapper, why, where, when, how, I mean, why wasn't it in police records?"

John smiled to himself, "because Billy, she did it for money, her clients paid her to kidnap them and lock them up."

"You're having me on, you mean, like I would pay her to kidnap you say?"

"No Billy, you would pay her to kidnap you, a dominatrix, I'll bet the next room was her dungeon where she would cane them."

"Fuck off John! Sorry, you're having me on again!"

"This time I am not, men would pay her to cane them, to lock them up, chain them up, and do other things as well," John smiled to himself at the naivety of Billy.

"So she'd beat them, and then had sex with them, how?"

"No, well yes, it would depend, some of the dominatrix did offer some sort of sex, a hand job or oral but very, very few would offer full sex; usually the men got off on being controlled mentally and physically, to ejaculate was a no, no, unless the dominatrix said that they could come, they were not allowed to."

"How do you know about this then, hey, did Jane know about it?"

"My job, I investigated a murder several years ago, and I interviewed a dominatrix, she was a nice lady actually, very nice; and the interview, well went on and I learned a lot about what she did, oh, and yes we did get the murderer, her evidence led to his arrest, but she would have been no use at the trial."

"Here we are the other key, not a safe hiding place," Billy said.

Billy handed the key to John who opened the door to the other room, as he had imagined it was her dungeon, her room of punishment for the errant, albeit, anticipated with pleasure rather than foreboding, slave. John hadn't seen the dominatrix's dungeon when he had interviewed her, and was as amazed at the vista, as was Billy. Along the far wall hung an array of canes, floggers, and whips, next to that was a cabinet. John opened the door to find various small implements, he didn't have any idea what they could be used for, in many cases, but assumed that they were all designed to cause pain, or inflict some sort of discomfort or binding. In the centre stood a box, angled and padded with straps on the four corners, and a belt on the side. John thought it odd that she would worry about the comfort of her victims; he patted the foam filled pseudo leather covered box. Fixed to the wall on one side was a cross with anchor points at the end of each leg of the cross, facing it on the other side of the box was a hoist bolted to the ceiling, with a bar and anchor points on the ends of the bar. John picked up some of the items and studied them; Billy also picked some up, more from curiosity than to glean any information about the item and the woman's trade.

From there, they went up to the ground floor, and John now happy with his feeling for the house began opening drawers and cupboards, seeing what was inside, and opening books, just to make sure that there wasn't anything inside that would help them in their search. Next they went upstairs and again John opened drawers and felt underneath for a cello taped note pad or diary. Into her wardrobe and John took out some of her dresses slinky silk, sexy gowns, low cut and revealing, yet not crude. Her underwear was very similar enough to tantalise, to get her companion worked up randy, but there was always that element of concealment. A see through silk gown, very revealing yet all was seen behind a veil, an invitation, but not total availability. She was good, she offered herself, without being too crude, too in your face. In a drawer, he found some underwear, the usual, what might be described as normal underwear; in the next one the underwear was totally different. This one contains 'G' strings, crotch less panties, bra's, with the front missing, peek-a-boo, one was labelled, and at the bottom, he found what he really wanted a note book. He opened it and read the code, 'SL Code 3 Wed, 27a, b, p, ws, 24, c, L3. On the next line, it read S, DL, code 1, Fri 1wk b, p, sh, wby 52, c, f, n, b, L5, as.

"Billy I've got what I wanted, I'll make a few notes if we take it, we would be stealing, so see if there is anything else of interest whilst I make my notes."

"You mean there is something here that isn't interesting, what does she do with these," Billy said holding up a pair of very uncomfortable looking shoes, the heels were extremely thin and high and extremely close to the sole, the woman wearing those would have almost walked on tip toe they were at such an acute angle?

"Wear them, I suppose, but I bet she complained all night about her shoes, they look like a form of torture."

"Yeah they sure do, why don't you use the photocopier that way you can copy the whole book?"

"Guess I'm not as modern as you, where is it, and how do I use it? Then again it is your suggestion; so I suppose, you do know how to use it?'

"Brian at the Bull showed me one evening when I was waiting for you; they have one. Here, switch it on like so, and then just put the book on here and press the button, simple see," Billy said, happy that he knew about something John didn't for once.

John photocopied the book and then put it back, and switched the machine off, they left; returning the key, and then went to their hotel. John showed Billy the papers he had copied and together they tried to decipher the code.

"What would you start the list with Billy," John asked to ensure he felt involved?

"No idea all gobbled gook to me, just a series of letters and numbers."

"That is what it is meant to look like; personally, I would start with the person's name. The first two or three letters are usually different, but the others are the same; so I would say that the first two letters are the client's name, their initials. With an extra letter when the initials were the same. Then the date and time, I would say; so 'A' would be afternoon perhaps?" John said as a question, "making 'E' evening, but 'WK', week? No too long; I doubt, anyone wanting to spend a week in her hands; mind you, it is possible, but more probably a weekend, perhaps, hum? What these all mean I don't have a clue, 'C', 'B', 'P', could be anything, the type of punishment, but what? Here, is something intriguing, apparently DL hopes to be Chief, I found another set of notes at the back, these are to remind her about her client, something to talk about, or ridicule him about perhaps, so that she would remember to ask him, making it personal, hum."

They spent the evening going over the papers trying to understand the meaning of the codes but, to little avail. John also rang Andy and thanked him, telling him that they would be leaving early the next morning. It had been a long day, especially for John who was now feeling the effects of retirement, no-longer used to working such long hours, they went to bed, the next morning they drove back to the vicarage.

John's first job the following day after a long nights rest was to ring Lynda and ask her to go into the old files. A case he worked on in nineteen seventy five, a murder of one James Williams, he wanted her to find the phone number for one of the witness's a Sylvia George, it was a long shot but worth the effort. Lynda rang that night with a phone number for him.

"Sir it isn't the one in the file, she has now retired and moved, but I managed to find her number for you," she told him cheerfully.

John thanked her and rang the number, "Hello, Miss George, I'm, well I was Inspector Alker when we last met."

"Inspector, how are you?' she replied cheerfully.

"I am very well and you?"

After a few more pleasantries, he went to the point of the call, "I am investigating an old murder that has me baffled, and, well I know what you worked as, and hoped you could help me decode a note book?"

"Still in the force, I would have said that you retired a few years ago but if I can help I will, of course."

"Yes I did retire, but this murder bugged me, and I am now working the case for my own, er, pleasure, is the wrong word, satisfaction perhaps, so I can't force anyone to help me, but I thought you would help me."

"With pleasure, what is the problem?"

"I have come across a note book from a lady, shall we say in your trade?"

"A dominatrix, that is what I was, and I did a good job, ask my ex clients, well perhaps not," she joked, "they rely on discretion."

"I would imagine so, I will need to meet you so that you can see the book and hopefully explain the coding, when would it be possible and where can we meet?"

"I don't suppose your wife would be too pleased, if I turned up at your home; so please, come to me, I am single; no man would or could, live with me, I'm too powerful."

"A pussy cat, with claws, I'm shocked you think no man would have you, I thought you were very charming," he flattered her.

"Flattery will get you nowhere with me, but that was sweet of you, thank you tomorrow at say ten?"

"I live in the country now, a good two hour drive from London, what is your address?"

She gave John her address and to his surprise it was only a half hour drive away, north of the village where he lived.

John went to visit Sylvia alone this time, Billy would have been in the way, and his presence would have made the conversation awkward. He arrived a few minutes late getting lost on the way.

"You're late," she admonished him on arrival.

"S, sorry," he replied rather taken aback.

"See what I mean, no man, could put up with my power, my forcefulness. You are not a potential client, after I had spoken to them like that, I would expect them to grovel, on their hands and knees. Is that what you are after, what we actually do, how we intimidate our slaves," she was smiling, now and her voice was normal not the commanding bark of a dominatrix at work.

"No, not really, I must say you look very smart, and time has done you no harm at all I would have recognised you, you haven't aged at all."

"You sweetie, for being so nice, normally I would cane you, presuming that was what you wanted me to do; and normally I would cane you again, for not doing it on your knees. Now what is it then, seriously now?"

"These are copies from her book, I guessed that the first initials were her client's initials, then a date and perhaps a time, but what do these letters mean?"

"Not a good code or perhaps too good, 'B' I would have said was bondage, and 'C' the cane, but these are guesses, can I hold onto this for a day or so, so that I can, shall we say, make enquiries on your behalf?"

"Sorry I can't, it is too confidential, I shouldn't really be showing it to you, in the old days I would have handed it to one of the lads to decipher, but I can't now."

"Hum, ok, please stay here I will ring someone to help, I could tell you the names of certain politicians, high ranking judges, high ranking policemen even, but they trusted me, I can be trusted. My work relied on trust, on confidentiality," she said smiling, but accepted what John had said and left the room.

"Ok, you got this off or from Joan Davies, she works Manchester, she used to work London then left to set up, up there. London now is so overcrowded with doms. The code is as straightforward as I thought; each letter stands for a punishment, and the code with a number is the degree, so, 'C' is the cane, 'Bg' is bondage, 'N' is for nipples, whoever he is liked to have his nipples tortured, 'B' is balls, we can make your eyes water when we get going on them, squeezing, crushing them."

"Don't the thought of it, is making my eyes water."

"Ok, take the first one then, SL, the client's initials, code three, that's the price we all had our friends say that we charged less for, so there are several prices. Wed 27 a, that is the date and appointment he was booked for the afternoon, not an hour if it were an hour then it would have read capital 'A' and a time, like 'A two' for two o'clock. 'Bg' is bondage, 'P' is prison, oh she managed to build one then, good for her. This client like to be dressed as a woman, that's the 'W' and the 'S' means slutty, he has taken twenty four strokes of the cane, that's the twenty four 'C' at level three, medium to low pain threshold, does that help you?"

"That is wonderful, it's all explained I am sure we can work out the other items," John said perusing the papers, "no sorry, what can an 'As' be?"

"Show me ah yes, it's at the end; the position of the letter is also important. The punishment is over, as it were, she'd have bound him and imprisoned him; then she would cane him and dressed him, now was the final act, she would fuck him. She would be using a dildo, we call them strap-ons and buggered, I think you will understand the meaning of that word, hum."

"What, you mean used it on him up his er, excuse me, anus?"

"To put it in the proverbial fucked him up his ass, Inspector you are so naive on certain points, it's so sweet," she said and gave him a peck on the cheek.

"So it is in order as well then, thank you," he added blushing.

"Well of course dear, but we can change the order to suit ourselves, or confuse the client; so that he doesn't know what will happen to him next. I remember once I did that to a particular client, and he came. I'd spent quite a bit of time dressing him up in a ball gown, the wig was perfect, the make-up took ages, but we had all evening, he was staying overnight, well the idea. Sorry, his dream scenario was that he was taken prisoner, dressed as a woman, locked in my cell for the night. The next morning, I would take him out, and I would punish him with a dozen strokes of the cane, before we ate breakfast. All went well until I decided to change things around. I punished him with six strokes of the cane first of all; then, I dressed him, and locked him in the cell. I handcuffed his hands, on this side of the bars. Now I teased him, I pulled his dress up and put my hand inside his knickers, that was all; he was so worked up he came in my hand so I left him as he was, handcuffed to the bars that was my mistake. I had gone too far, he didn't come back, ah well those were the good old days when you lost one and two came to your door."

"Thank you, Miss George, you have been a great help to me, I must go now, Billy will be waiting for the answer to the code."

"Don't be shy now, come and visit me anytime, personally, not professionally, I don't do much these days, just enough to keep me satisfied, so always ring first, please," she said smiling now, a pleasant smile, very inviting.

"I will, and thank you again for all your help, oh just one more thing, this at the back what is that any idea."

"That would be unprofessional of me."

"It is a murder enquiry; so far some twenty four women have been murdered, all from your profession, help me stop it happening twenty four more times, please?"

"I can't, but what if I were to say that you know, or knew the guy, professionally I mean, but you didn't hear it from me."

"I understand and thank you again, here is my address, and you are welcome to visit me unprofessionally of course," John said smiling and with meaning.

They shook hands then she kissed him on the cheek, smiled at him again and closed the door, John returned home.

What puzzled John was her words, that he knew DL professionally, he pondered all the criminals he had, had contact with, going slowly through the list that he could remember, who else, what else had she said about her profession, control, the sub relinquished control, yet they were in control, an odd relationship, a controlling person, powerful person. Billy knew not to interrupt John, when he was thinking like this, deep, thoughts, trawling the depths of his memory, for a person who wanted to control and have power. That, he thought matched almost all the villains he had encountered. Billy got up from the arm chair he lounged in and made a pot of tea, always better from a pot John had said once when Billy made a brew in the cup. Billy had now got into the habit of always brewing his own tea, even at home in a pot. He returned and placed the tea tray on the coffee table, he found it odd, because they always drank tea; so why call it a coffee table?

A full hour passed as John dredged for the person he knew, then slowly the light dawned on him, why look just at criminals, who else did he know professionally, who was power hungry and a control freak, the Super, his old Super, a fast track officer destined for high position, a Super still wet behind the ears, qualifications coming out of his ears but no experience, a politician, proficient with figures, an egotistical, moron when it came to actual policing, but very good at making the accounts balance, even if it meant allowing criminals to go on doing their deeds, well that was John's opinion of him.

"Damian Lockwood, yes he fits the profile perfectly, a control freak, power hungry, and useless as a policeman," John said smiling.

Billy looked at him, shrugged his shoulders not knowing what was going on, or what the hell John was talking about, but just accepted the fact that John had now found whatever he was pondering. Billy stood up and handed the tea cup to John who took it still smiling, his eyes bright with the pleasure of realising who she had been talking about.

"Billy I have the swine, just let him talk down to me ever again, and I will ram this piece of news right up his nostril," John said.

"Who, what," Billy said confused

"Sorry Billy, I was miles away, deep in thought, and I really, well what the hell, my ex-Super he has visited a dominatrix, I don't think that would look too good on his CV do you?"

"Well, no; if I knew what you were talking about," Billy said still confused.

"He visited a woman, who used to cane his behind for him, it's not sex like a prostitute, but it is very sexual, in a kinky way."

"Oh, I see, and that will help us find the murderer how?"

"It won't, but it will give me a lever, for er, well blackmail if I need it."

"But isn't that illegal, and you a copper as well, tut, tut, tut," Billy said now smiling at his joke.

Three weeks passed it was going to be a long, hard slog, John knew this; he didn't have the men on the street now, and where would he send them if he had. The murders were officially in London, but the victims were from the future and up in the Manchester area. John was sure that the murderer would make a mistake, but the question was when and would they recognise it?

The garden never looked better John and Billy worked hard on keeping up to the standard Jane had set, out of respect and his undying love for her, but the investigation had ground to a halt.

The phone rang, and John answered it, he was pleased when he heard Lynda's voice, this meant that she had some news, especially when she informed him that she would be visiting them at the weekend. John hung up and told Billy the news. Billy smiled the sale of the vegetables, which they still did, even though almost all their own grown vegetables were now exhausted, a scant array of tired vegetables were to be put on display, for sale would now be secondary to Lynda's visit. The new crop was by now full grown and ripening and would soon be ready for sale, then it would begin again in earnest.

Lynda pulled up, putting her car in the drive and carrying her bag into the house, where she dumped it on the floor. John looked at her, her face was set, her eyes mere slits, as she controlled her anger, "Bastard," she said, angrily, "F, fucking, bastard, sorry but I am so, so annoyed. Do you remember that oink, a miserable, useless, kid still wet behind the ears?"

"Not really I probably had retired by then," John said calmly.

"That, that useless ingrate the Super, he promoted him, the oink, over my head again, yet another person that I trained promoted over me, I have been a sergeant now for ten years, I have trained three other constables, who are Inspectors, who the fuck trained them so well, me, yes me, a woman, well I've had it, on Monday I will resign," she said and flopped into a chair.

"Lynda you are a good copper, a very good one."

"Yeah well why then don't I get my rewards like the men do hey, answer me that," she was now yelling?

"Please, let me finish as I was saying before you rudely interrupted me. You are a good copper, but, there is still an element of sexism in the force; also you are not a politician, you ruffle feathers, to get the job done, and the powers that be don't like that. To be honest your success is why you don't get a promotion, they are afraid of you, but leave this one to me, now after you have put your bag in your room, you can give me the information you have for me whilst you do that I will put the kettle on, to help you calm down and be more civilised," John said calmly smiling at her.

It was the way he controlled his officers, he was so calm, so in control, and that was what punished you, when you let rip. As Lynda, had just done; she knew that she had been told off by him, but he hadn't raised his voice, he didn't need to, the intonation was enough. He managed it without shouting at her. It was a calm, controlled, telling off, for losing control, she knew exactly, what she had done wrong. Lynda looked at John her eyes glazed with anger, near to tears, yet she was in control now, she attempted a smile which turned into a deep grin, picked her bag up and went upstairs.

It only took a few moments for her to unpack her clothes and then she returned to the sitting room where John sat in his arm chair, Billy in his and the tea tray on the table in front of them. Lynda looked at both of them in turn, sighed and sat down on the settee with a flump.

"Now Lynda, what do you have for us," John asked calmly.

"First off Sir, sorry for the outburst, but it was this afternoon when the oink came in and told me to get him a coffee. That was something you never did, we all made for each other, but he was making sure that I knew he was now my boss. Perhaps that was what hurt the most, he wasn't just made Inspector in another section, or station, like the others were; he was made Inspector over me personally. I am still second in command in the section you ran before the old case section was brought into force. When you left, then we all went back into the murder squad. Anyway what I have for you is another missing person, again Manchester area, again she was a prostitute, and again it came in just yesterday. The difference is that we don't have a body to match this one either, so it might be a wild goose chase."

John had listened carefully whilst he poured the tea and handed them round, finished Lynda took a sip of her tea.

"Lovely, just what I needed John, thank you," she said, relaxing.

"Yes, pot brewed tea does taste, much nicer, doesn't it? Now we have a missing person in Manchester, with no matching body, ok, what if the body is buried before records began; I think it is worth another trip up to Manchester to view the woman's house. But first, I need to speak to Damian, I need some help, will you run us into London with you on Monday, then we will go by train to Manchester. I'll get Andy to book us in the same hotel for one night. The last trip was too tiring for me, all that driving."

"Sure boss, but we will need to leave at five in the morning for me to get to work on time."

"Leave that to me, seven will be early enough."

John left the room and made a phone call then came back and told them that he had spoken to the Super, who had confirmed that Lynda could be late in that morning.

The weekend passed as every weekend when Lynda came, reviewing the files and selling the produce, dinner at the pub and then a quiet night watching some television until Billy and John went to the pub for their usual pint or two, then bed.

Monday came and they were all loaded into the car with John and Billy's overnight bag in the boot, arriving at New Scotland Yard for ten thirty, Lynda went to her office, Billy followed her and sat by her desk with a cup of coffee watching her, whilst John went to see the Super.

"Good morning Damian, I am so pleased that you were able to see me at such short notice, and allowing Lynda to drive me here making her late, thank you. Now I have a copy of a book, as I told you, it was copied at a woman's place of business, a dominatrix, I think they are called. She went missing over a month ago, just another missing person except that she fits the criteria for the serial killer I am hunting. You do know about that don't you," the Super said that he did then folded his arms and sat back uninterested was the message John got from his body language, John smiled to himself?

"Well it was from the home of one Joan Davies in Manchester, and I have reason by way of the coded book, to believe that you knew her, see the initials DL, and then more letters and numbers I am not interested in these people, except that one of them may be the killer; a distinct possibility don't you think? So I am anxious to trace them, all of them. Oh and there is one other point, this DL, apparently I know the person in a professional capacity, so I was reliably informed, and I can only think of one person that I know with those initials. Now the other point I wish to raise, Lynda an excellent policewoman don't you think, one that is under rated terribly much, she needs a promotion, urgently, it would be a shame if that book got into the wrong hands don't you think. Well Damian thank you for your time I know that this DL didn't commit the crimes, but any information they have, may be useful so if you can think of anyone like that I would be most grateful, oh and don't forget Lynda, when Williams retires next month."

"John that is blackmail and you know it, the best person for the job will be chosen as usual and as for the initials DL well you know several people with those initials, sorry I can't be of help to you."

"Not in a senior position, and who I knew personally, and professionally, some chances just are not worth taking, and with your recommendation behind Lynda, I am sure she will get the job, thank you again Damian; it's always, a pleasure to see you. I will give your regards to Andy later today when we meet up. Oh the book, well, that is now in Andy's hands, he is hoping that I can help him decipher it. I was always adept at that wasn't I, good day,' John said and held out his hand, Damian took it, a sour look on his face, he knew that John knew who the DL was and that he would use it, if he had to.

In Manchester Billy and John with the help of Andy who provided a car and driver from the pool, went to the house, this time there wasn't a key for them from the woman who had reported her missing, so John went to the house next door to the missing woman's address.

"Hello sorry to trouble you but I am a private investigator, and I wondered if you had the key for next door, she has been reported missing, and her family have asked me to investigate her disappearance?" John said.

The woman who answered his knock was taller than he was and much wider her tubby stomach hung like a fold over the waist band of the track suit bottoms she wore, and a white mass bulging out from under the ill-fitting top. Her hair was unkempt and straggly, her nails were dirty, and eye shadow as black as night and so old it was cracked. John thought the only thing missing from the ragged ensemble was a roll-up fag in the corner of her mouth.

"No, try number twenty five, they was friends," she said bluntly and closed the door in his face.

"Nice woman that Billy, very helpful, I don't think."

"Well she did give us a house to call at, so rude and ugly yes, but helpful I would say that she was, you're getting too fussy in your old age John," Billy said with a laugh in his voice

John repeated the process at the next house, number twenty five without any success. The house was in darkness, and appeared empty, so they left and went to get something to eat. The driver and car were only available till the end of the drivers shift so he went after dropping them at a local cafe where they ate before calling a taxi back to the house.

John and Billy took a taxi back to the house, and this time they saw lights on as the taxi pulled up, John paid the driver and they walked up the short drive of the modern semi-detached house. John rang the doorbell, and they waited a few moments for it to be answered.

"Forgot your, oh sorry, yes," the woman who answered the door said.

She was much younger than the other woman, somewhere in her late twenties, slim, jet black hair that hung straight from her crown down to the nape of her neck. She smiled when she realised that it wasn't the person she expected.

"I am sorry to trouble you, but, may we have a few moments of your time please? We are investigating the missing woman from number twenty four, a relative has asked us to look for her and we understand that you knew her."

"Yes come in out of the cold it's about to rain as well, how can I help you?"

John and Billy followed the woman into the house; she led them up the short hallway and turned left into the front room where the television was on loudly, with her two young children sat on the floor in front of it.

"We understand that she went missing on Friday, her sister reported her missing," John began?

"Yes, the three of us were going shopping and, she was always so punctual, and when she said that she would be there, she was. I had asked her and her sister to join me for a female day out for my birthday, shopping and the like, and she had said that she would, but never turned up. I saw on the news that the police wanted us to report any woman missing, as soon as we knew that they were missing, especially if they were blonde, so I rang her sister, and she reported it that afternoon when she didn't meet us as planned."

"Do you have a key to her house, it would help me if I could look around, and do you know where she worked?"

"Yes to both questions, but I can't just hand out her front door key. Do you have any form of proof that you are who you say you are? As for her job, well that was at a new club in town, The Topaz club, it does very well so I believe, but when I went to see Joan it seemed empty, and she looked nervous and ushered me out quickly."

"I don't have a warrant card any more being retired, but I do have."

"Who are you, we don't want double glazing, or any more insurance," a man's stern voice said, from behind John, he looked round and stood up holding out his hand.

"I have explained to your wife that I am investigating Joan's disappearance, we are not selling anything, my name is John Alker," John said waiting for the man to take his hand, but he didn't, and John dropped his hand.

"You stupid woman, do you know these men, no, and with all the robberies round here you invite them into our home, call the police," he said angrily.

"There is no need Sir I am ex-Chief Inspector Alker of New Scotland Yard retired, and I am as I said investigating Joan's disappearance, if you wish we will leave?"

"I said call the police, they could be assessing the place you know setting us up, finding out about our security then telling their friends, and we get robbed next week when we have forgotten about them, you aren't leaving till the police have been."

John assessed the man, in his late twenties, fit, broad shoulders, a man who worked with his hands, firm and strong, "There really is no need, but if you wish we have done nothing wrong, it is a waste of police time, but so be it," John said and sat down again.

"John what will happen," Billy said anxiously.

"Nothing, we were invited in, and we asked our questions, and if asked to leave we would have, but we were told to stay, and we have."

It was an uncomfortable wait till the police car arrived outside, and the policemen were invited into the lounge. The officers who came didn't recognise John; he didn't expect them to and explained who he was, and what he was doing. To verify his name he showed his driving licence to the lead officer, who suggested that he leave police work, to the police and that he was too old to be a private eye. John took exception to this, and suggested that he spoke to Chief Inspector Andrew Green in the morning; the officer looked at him knowing that he obviously knew the Chief.

"So if I may I would still like to see around Joan's house, if possible, I need to understand the woman, to see if there are any clues, I very much doubt that the local force has looked round?"

"I'll show you round in the morning, Mr Alker I feel so ashamed calling the police when you haven't done anything wrong, and were an officer," she said giving her husband a nasty look.

"Don't let that bother you, my advice to your husband would be to do exactly what he did do if in doubt; he did the right thing calling the police, especially if there are a lot of burglaries around here. Officer where can I find a public phone to ring for a taxi," John added turning to the officer.

"I'll ring one for you," the lady of the house said calmly, pushing past her husband in annoyance.

John arranged to meet the woman at ten outside the house, he was as usual on time this time in the unmarked police car, he told the driver to go and return in about an hour after he had, had time to look round.

"Just to put your mind at rest this is Constable Graham, he is my driver for the day." John said, introducing the woman to the uniformed officer.

She smiled, and said, "Hello," then, led them into the house, as he set off down the road back on duty.

"How will you get back, isn't he going staying with you," she asked, concerned?

"He is going out on patrol, but will pick us up in an hour or so, give me time to look around fully," John informed her

"Oh, I didn't realise it would take so long, I have to be at school in half an hour."

"Don't worry we will be alright alone, and I will post the key through your letter box, or if you prefer, I can leave it at the main police station for you to collect?"

John was pleased that she couldn't stay and hoped that she would go and leave him to look around alone. She smiled at him, still feeling a little embarrassed from last night, and felt obliged to allow him to stay, and said that he could drop the key in her letter box, if he wouldn't mind, and left them.

The house was the same as hers, except the opposite way round, with the front room to the right off the hall, as with the last time, Billy watched John, who entered each room and stood there registering the room before going on to the next room. The other door in the hall was at the far end and led directly into the kitchen with a small dining room off that. Upstairs there were three bedrooms, all small with a bathroom at the top of the stairs. John looked up as he stood on the landing and saw the hook for a loft door; he opened that and went up. The attic was full of empty suitcases and some boxes with odds and ends in, nothing of real importance, so he came back down to the bedrooms. He looked in the small one first. In here there was a computer, he was totally lost about them and left the room, and there was no paper work in there. The next room was a bedroom used as a guest room, the wardrobe and drawers were all empty. The final room was her bedroom; in here, he found what he was looking for, the type of clothes she wore, they were expensive, as were the few jewels she had in a jewel box. He had expected to find some sexy clothes to match the job she had, but there were none.

John felt under the drawers for a book or note pad taped to the bottom with her code in it hopefully, but he found nothing, he had hoped that she was also a prostitute, that would have been another piece of the puzzle solved, but there was nothing to suggest that she was a prostitute to be found in the house so far. This threw John slightly, was she just another missing person who happened to be blonde, or was she another victim? If he could find out whether or not she was a prostitute, then that would help. His fingers ran along the base of the wardrobe seeing if it had a false bottom, but that was another dead end.

"Billy it looks as though she is just another missing person, and probably not one of his victims, there is no note book of her engagements, I'm afraid it's been a wild goose chase, but interesting, what with being almost arrested last night, that was fun, I've never been in that position before."

"For you, may be, but I found it distressing, I have never been in trouble with the police. John if I wanted to hide something I wouldn't hide it in my bedroom, would you; that would be too obvious, what if she hid it in the next room, or her office?'

John decided that Billy had a point and began his search of the other rooms, but again to no avail. They went down stairs and checked down there, looking and feeling in all her drawers and cupboards; as they searched each room, not disturbing anything, they could avoid, disturbing. Finally in the kitchen they found a set of keys. John looked at them and tried them in the doors, but they didn't fit.

"Billy what would you say these keys were to?"

"House keys to me; that is a mortise key, I have only ever seen them on houses or garages, why?"

"Good question, why have a set of keys that doesn't fit any of the locks in the house?"

"Because they are to another house, like these were, at Mrs French's house."

"Logical, they could belong to Mrs French's house, but I don't think so, didn't she have a Yale on her front door?"

The knock at the front door startled them not expecting anyone to call, John answered the door it was Mrs French, she had returned early. John stood to one side to allow her to enter then asked if Joan had her front door keys, in case of emergency. Mrs French said that she didn't, being out most of the day, but she did have the keys to another house, one she rented out, or so Mrs French thought.

John studied the idea for a few moments wondering why she had a house to rent, yet lived in this poorer class area, and where did she find the money for a second house when she worked in a club, unusual. He said nothing more about the keys having, slipped them in his pocket.

"Do you know where the house is," he asked Mrs French?

"Yes twenty seven Windmill Street in Bury," she replied.

"Thank you for your time and help, we do appreciate it, ah my car has returned, like I said, about an hour, thank you once again Mrs French," John said with a courteous nod of his head, and they left.

"Take us to the hotel, please, we need some lunch, then, I need a bit of time to think, before we catch the train home. Can you pick us up at say six forty five, I realise it is late, so better still drop us at the hotel and go back to work, we can get a taxi to the station thank you," John said thinking as he spoke, when he was a policeman this came easily to him, but now he wasn't as quick to think and talk at the same time.

John thanked the officer for his help and then rang Andy to do the same, telling him that he would get a taxi to the station, and then rang a taxi firm to book a taxi for two in the afternoon, to go to Windmill Street.

They had lunch and waited for the taxi to arrive, he did more or less on time, just ten minutes late. John told him that he needed to be at the train station for six thirty, allowing quarter of an hour for him to be late, plus the quarter of an hour he had already allowed with, another fifteen minutes, to get from the taxi to the train catching the seven fifteen train to Euston, the driver booked it for him.

What a difference this house was from the other one, far more upper class, a large four bedroom house set in its own garden, a large corner plot. John estimated that this house would fetch twice, if not three times, the price of the one they had visited before. This observation only raised more questions. Why live in a poor district, when you owned one in an upper class district? Where did the money come from to afford this house, let alone the two of them, questions, questions?

John followed by Billy walked up the drive to the newish house, John estimated that it was about five years old, the garden was still in its infancy, the plants not fully established yet. They went to the front door and rang the bell, no reply, John told Billy to stay at the front whilst he went around the back, John peered in through the windows, there was no-one in, and it was very clean and tidy, expensive furniture from what he could see. He then went around the front and repeated the exercise, then took out the keys and tried them in the front door. One worked and he opened it, stepping inside.

"John can we do this?" Billy's nervous voice echoed in his ears as he wondered the same.

He didn't have cause as such, but then again he had the keys, so it wasn't breaking and entering, but it was trespass, because he didn't have permission to enter. Oh if only he had kept up with the changes in the law, not that he now remembered all the laws from when he was in the force, and not being in the robbery division, he wasn't as familiar with these laws.

"Of course Billy, we have the key," he bluffed.

They both felt odd, not like the last two houses where they had been officially invited in, now they were on dangerous ground. John quickly walked round the house. Its position was such that people could come and go without being seen, unless someone was purposely watching the house. John considered this, it would have been ideal for a house of ill repute, secluded, yet easy to get to, a bus route ran past the end of the road about fifty yards away, it was a nice area for expensive clients.

If she were also a dominatrix, then, it was a quiet and secluded site for her client's anguished yells, which would not be heard too loud, a basement would be ideal, they wouldn't be heard at all from there. John felt along the top of the door to under the stairs, the door was locked. He then took the bunch of keys and tried them, but none fitted the lock. Billy looked around the kitchen for anything, and shouted to John that he had found another set of keys. John took them eagerly and tried them in the door, one worked there were three more keys on the ring. John opened the door and went down the stairs into a cellar, this one had a lower ceiling than the first one they had seen, but again there was a short corridor with three doors leading off it.

John tried all three keys in the first lock, the last one opened it. He switched the light behind the door on, and they stood there in amazement. The room was a torture chamber, literally, with all kinds of implements to create pain, some from medieval times. A full sized rack stood in the centre, a cross on the far wall, shackles hung from the ceiling; no hoist just the shackles, a cupboard with a full array of whips, canes, paddles, floggers, even a hair brush, and a slipper, she went from the playful to the extreme. In the next cupboard, there were all sort of clamps, and funny looking things like upside down parachutes or umbrellas, lead weights, from a gram up to a kilo, creams they had never heard of, including a jar of deep heat rub, and what looked like a branding iron. John took pictures with the camera he had brought along. He still had two more keys and two doors, the next one opened with the first key. This was her cell an outer door and a barred gate the second key opened this cell door, a mattress lay on the floor, and bucket stood in the corner. The cell was narrow just three feet wide and about seven feet long. That left a final door, Billy felt along the top of the door and found the final key, the next door opened with it, this room was L shaped, going behind the cell, where there was a video camera linked to a screen so that she could view her victim. John wished that he had the technical team with him to see what she used the video for, apart from the obvious. In here there was a place to make tea and a sink a bed and a settee and a wardrobe fully fitted with a variety of sizes in dresses and underwear. Several wigs were lined up on a shelf, and a dressing table full of make-up, was next to the shelf, again as with the rest of the house all the items on the table were lined up in neat rows, and there wasn't a spot of dust anywhere.

"What is this room for," Billy asked intrigued and hoping John would know?

"Well some men like to be dressed as women; like my ex-Super, I think it is called a TV room, short for transvestite."

"Yeah like you're having me on, she deals with poofs then?"

"No, Billy they aren't like that, just like to dress as women for their kicks, let's not judge them, I don't like the idea and from what you say you don't, but it doesn't hurt anyone, so I ignore it."

"Humph, poofs," Billy said, disgusted.

John left Billy still starring at the room and made his way upstairs, Billy closed and locked the door then followed John, locking all the doors as he went, and putting the keys back. John was now feeling under the drawers, and all around inside the wardrobe then he went to the next room where he finally found her book and slipped it in his pocket. They went down stairs just as the policeman entered the house.

"Do you own this house Sir," he asked officiously.

"No officer I don't, but I do have the key and permission to be here," he lied.

"Oh, so why then didn't you turn the silent alarm off, I think we need to go to the police station, and you need to answer a few questions, don't you Sir," he said in an aloof tone.

"If you so wish, I have no problem with that, please contact Chief Inspector Andrew Green for me will you," Billy knew John was annoyed with the tone of voice he used, it was just as aloof as the officers, he even walked out of the door with his head held up, cocky in attitude.

They sat in the back of the police car and were taken to Bury police station, where they were escorted into an interview room each, John had managed to tell Billy not to say anything except his name and address and to demand a solicitor, and to say nothing else.

A sergeant entered the room John was in and looked at him, then sat down facing him, the officer from the house sat next to the sergeant and the other officer from the house stayed by the door.

"I have to inform you that we will be taping this interview and that anything you say will be taken down and used in evidence against you, do you understand?"

"Fully, thank you," John said still aloof.

"Name," the officer asked John?

"Are you asking a question, very shoddy, do you require my name?"

"We have a right one here, yes Sir, please tell us your name," the sergeant said smarmily.

"Chief Inspector John Alker of New Scotland Yard, retired."

"Address?"

"Yes I do have one, have you managed to call Chief Inspector Green yet?"

"What is your address, Sir please, and not yet?"

"Oh, right my address is The Vicarage, Vicarage Road, Hampton that is in Essex, now unless you are going to charge me, I wish to leave, or have my phone call?"

"We haven't decided yet what the charge will be."

"Don't worry, just let me phone Andrew, sorry, the Chief Inspector."

"Oh Andrew is it, know him do you?"

"I should do, he was my sergeant, then he became my Inspector, until his move to Manchester as Chief Inspector, now what is it to be, the phone, or a lift back to my hotel?"

"A phone, I don't like your attitude, who do you think you are, demanding things when we have arrested you and may bring charges against you," the Sergeant was shouting now and stood up; sending his chair skidding across the floor in temper. John just sat there apparently unmoved yet inside he was trembling, he knew he had stolen that book and his bluff was being called Andrew was his only hope.

The phone arrived, and he rang Andrew, he suggested that the officer listen in to save time.

"Andy, sorry it's John I have been arrested, I am unsure as to the crime, I entered a house with the keys which were given to me. In the old days, I would have broken in as you know, when following a lead, but I am no-longer in the position to do that, can you help me please?"

All Andy wanted was the station, and then they hung up, it wasn't long before the sergeant came back in and told John he could go, but to be very careful, he still didn't like John's attitude. John said that the feeling was mutual.

Back at the hotel Andy was waiting for them, and gave John a telling off for making such a stupid mistake, he had made an enemy at Bury police station, John smiled at Andy and accepted the telling off with grace. John handed back the keys to Andy, telling him that the woman was as they suspected and that he was now sure that she was another victim and would, therefore, not be returning to press any charges. John bought Andy a drink, and they chatted for a while until the taxi arrived to take them to the station. John said goodbye and a thank you to Andy, Billy also thanked Andy but not as John had like a friend, he was shy and reticent feeling a debt of gratitude to Andy for getting them out of a tight situation. Andy smiled knowing that John had done what needed to be done, just as he would have done in the past, but for Billy, a brush with the law was a bad thing, and the experience had unnerved him.

The train was a modern one without private compartments, even so John pulled out the book he had technically stolen, and Billy's face was a picture when he recognised the book, shock and horror both were visible. John ignored the look Billy gave him and carried on reading the book, again it was a code book, the code more complex than the previous one, and John decided that another visit to Sylvia George was needed. John decided not to waste time by waiting till tomorrow and instead to ring Sylvia as soon as they arrived home. Lynda had agreed to collect them from the station and run them home. As they exited the station Lynda was waiting in a no parking zone, but then she was a policewoman and a flash of her card sent traffic wardens scurrying away, or so Billy believed.

On the way home they talked about the trip, Billy telling Lynda that John had got them both arrested, and the reason, and then he told her about the book. John sat in the front seat and listened, as Lynda mockingly told John off for getting Billy into trouble, and then asked if the book would be of any use. John looked at her and smiled a knowing smile.

"Once I have broken the code I am sure it will reveal quite a bit, but whether it will help us in finding the killer or not I honestly don't know, I will be looking for two sets of similar initials from both books, which will hopefully lead me to the name of the killer, but with only two, and the chances that a person may have visited both women, well it's definitely a long shot."

Billy was intent on telling Lynda all about the trip; John closed his eyes and allowed Billy the chance of retelling their adventure, which is what it was to Billy. He explained about the types of equipment they found, expressing doubts as to their use except to cause pain. Lynda had a broad grin on her face at the amount of shock Billy enthused, describing the equipment, and that men dressed as women. Lynda told him that she had worked in vice and would probably be able to explain the use of the equipment to him. He apologised for telling her, it wasn't fit for ladies ears, but by then it was too late, he had already described most of the items, John chuckled as he imagined Billy's red face when he realised what he had just done, in describing the items to someone he considered a lady.

"Billy, the upside down parachute as you described, it is a ball stretcher, the strap goes around the scrotum, and then the dominatrix puts weights in the parachute part. Those clamp things are for your nipples they crush them painfully. The deep heat rub is for your balls it burns. What else did you want to know?"

"Nothing that's fine er oops they actually want that done to them?"

"Yes Billy, they do, and pay for it, being honest, it doesn't hurt anyone, except the person who wants it, and so I say let them get on with it."

"Suppose so, but dressing up, well," Lynda laughed at his apparent shock.

As soon as they arrived home John rang Sylvia George and made an appointment with her, suggesting that she visit him, if she so wished, Sylvia accepted the invitation, and told him that she would be there for ten thirty tomorrow.

The three of them went across to the pub for their usual, and then retired for the night, Lynda wasn't due on duty till the afternoon so John crept around the following morning, allowing her to sleep in till eleven, or that was the plan; except she woke up when the doorbell rang to announce on time Sylvia George.

John showed her the book, and sat back whilst she digested the contents.

"Interesting, yes she uses her own code and it's not as straightforward as Sadie's. I am going to need a bit more time with this one. I have an idea what her code is, from the recurrence of similar letters, and the number of times they reoccur. This suggests the implement or implements she used on her clients. You see John this symbol here is repeated in most of the cases, and the most used symbol would indicate the cane, being probably the most used implement, mind you bondage isn't that far behind. As for the others with less use, well then I would be guessing. I accept that I am not allowed to take the book; but may I copy the symbols so that I can ask around. You say she was from Czechoslovakia, I know of a couple of girls from there, and these symbols may be from their language, as opposed to English, would you mind?"

John looked at the woman before him and decided that she was a very striking woman, at both previous meetings he had been more interested in the book and breaking the code, or as in the first time solving the case, now he was more relaxed in his own home and able to take in more about her. Her hair was pulled back in a tight bun, quite severe make-up, making her look more of a school ma'am, a Victorian teacher, especially since she was wearing a knee length, tweed skirt and a white blouse with a cardigan over it, flat black shoes lace up style and deep red finger nails.

"May I say how striking you look today, very, um, very?"

"School ma'am, I am off to work, he wants a teacher, a very severe teacher, strict and well able to use the cane, sorry if I have offended you, but you asked. I am not ashamed of what I do, retired or not, I still command two hundred pounds for this two hour session. When did you last earn one hundred pounds an hour John?"

John was lost for words, very unusual for him, she had floored him with a few words, "well never, it pays that well does it, I'm sorry I shouldn't have asked that, it's private."

"Yes, it does, but I may only have one or two clients a week, so really that is four hundred pounds a week, if I get two clients; still not to be sniffed at is it? Now may I copy these symbols?"

"Yes, please do, would you like a pen and paper," John said making to get up?

"John a teacher without pen and paper, I am surprised at you," she mocked him.

Sylvia made a note of the symbols, and then they parted. Lynda came into the room and said that she was ready to leave and thanked John for the accommodation. John thanked her for the lift to and from the station; he kissed her on the cheek and said goodbye. All visitors' gone, John went into his incident room, he put the book in with the other evidence, after making a few notes in a separate book, about the conversation with Sylvia George, this book he kept in a drawer, in the lounge.

Billy arrived as he had said he would do about twelve, and they went into the garden, John ribbed Billy about their adventure and Billy's embarrassment at his story telling in the car.

"Lynda has seen it all, and read about it all, vice isn't just about catching hookers, street girls, cleaning up the streets you know. She was involved in a kid pornography case; they did catch and prosecute the paedophile. She was also involved in catching a gang; they were kidnapping young women, bring them to London and using them as prostitutes. Drugged up to the eye balls with cocaine, beaten till they couldn't stand or sit, raped repeatedly until they just didn't give a damn, well used and abused, a blow-up doll had more life in them," John spat the last few words out in disgust, at the treatment these women had endured, "and what did the kidnappers' get, twelve months, because one of the officers failed to dot an 'I' or cross a 'T', they were found guilty on a lesser charge. A few days after their release, one of them was found floating in the river, two others were never heard of again, the forth one, well prison would be a safer place for him," John turned away and dug with more energy as he tried to vent his contempt for these animals on the soil.

Chapter 12
Promotion

Outside John heard the screech of brakes and left the rear garden in a hurry to see what had happened. Lynda's car was parked across his drive, and she was almost running up the drive.

"What the hell's going on Lynda, is something terribly wrong," John quizzed her in a worried tone?

"No the opposite, and I wanted you to be the first to know," she said, her face a picture of happiness.

"You got the promotion," John said as if excited, knowing that his talk with the Super had worked.

"Yes and I have you to thank for it, I don't know why but I know I do," she said and kissed him.

"Me, Why me," he said in mock surprise.

"I said, I don't know what you did, but it was a done job when I went for the interview yesterday, even as I walked out I felt that I had got the promotion, but I had to wait until today, to get the confirmation. What did you do or say to the Super, hey?"

"Me," John said as if he was shocked at the suggestion.

"Yes you, come on what was it; I want to know, you crafty old fox?"

"Let's say that I suggested that sexual discrimination was not allowed these days."

"Let's not, let's say that you had something on him that made him give me the job," she said cocking her head to one side as if questioning him?

"Do you deserve the promotion?"

"Yes I do, I have worked hard for it."

"Then accept it with grace, in the knowledge that someone has your back, just like in the old days, ok. Say no more; congratulations," John said, and kissed Lynda on the cheek.

"Bullshit, ok, thank you," she knew he wouldn't tell her and accepted it.

Once they were inside, Lynda removed her jacket and sat in the arm chair to John's left. Lynda looked across at John, he was beginning to look his age, he was showing signs of his age now, she leaned forward and took his hand in her's.

"John, I owe you one; I never knew my father, he died before I was born. I would have been proud to be his daughter, if he were anything like you, just as proud as if I were your daughter."

"Don't, you're going to have tears in my eyes in a bit," he smiled at her, "but thank you anyway," he added, with a wink.

"I have something else to tell you, how can I explain it, it was like a deja vu moment, as if I had been there at that time, yet I wasn't, odd really, do you remember the case of the woman found in nineteen seventy two?"

"One of our women?"

"Yes, I remember it, yet don't, why do I remember it? I wasn't on the case, nor were you, Inspector Howard was the lead on it, well I felt kind of odd last night, and then this morning for some unknown reason, I just had to go down into records and pull the file. I copied it, yet you must have a copy, one so recent, so why did I copy it?"

"Ok, don't worry about it, show me the file and I will tell you whether or not I have a copy of it.'

Lynda opened her brief case and pulled out the file, John looked at it and knew straight away that he didn't have this file, not only was it not in with the files in his office, but he hadn't seen it before, yet, there in the picture was the woman he had just been to Manchester to look into her disappearance. A cold shiver went down his spine as he read the reports, now far more detailed than ever before, with a lot more information, new, small elements, that helped in the investigation.

"Lynda, we are dealing with someone who buries the bodies in the past, we know that, even though the powers that be will not accept that fact. Now when did the murder take place in nineteen seventy two, no, it didn't, it only happened last weekend, so the file would not have been in records till then. It couldn't have been, but like with my case I investigated it when the body appeared, but she was only a child then and still at school, so only when the murder took place would the file appear in the Archives, even though I investigated it."

"Sir you are confusing me, how could you investigate a murder in nineteen sixty two when she was only murdered in nineteen eighty say?"

"Because he has changed the time line, he has changed history. There wasn't a murder in nineteen sixty two, only a body. The murder, the crime took place, in nineteen seventy eight, but, because he sent the body back in time to nineteen sixty two, that, is when the murder was investigated. Because that, is when the murdered woman was found. So how could I have caught the murderer, hey? He may not have been born, in nineteen sixty two? We don't know, whether he was alive or not, or how old he was? He may also have been at school at that point in time? We were looking for a murderer who didn't exist; we could never have found him, and as we now know she died in nineteen seventy eight."

"So how can we prosecute him now for a murder he committed in nineteen sixty two then?"

"That is a good question, perhaps we can't, unless we can prove that he killed them at the present time, and then we can, but how?"

"Find his time machine?"

"Excellent idea how do we do that? We will not get a search warrant; that is for sure; a pass to a lunatic asylum yes, but not a search warrant. And if we did, where do we search, we, that is the three of us Billy as well, we know that the missing women are dead, so he is active now, but where? Does he have to be in England even? Just because, he is killing English prostitutes, doesn't mean that he has to reside in England, does it? Consider this why does he have to be in England, or alive today, if he can bury the bodies in time, why not come back from the future kill, and then bury the bodies in time. We know that he is active now, but is he alive now?"

Lynda thought for a while she got up and paced up and down considering John's comments, her head bowed deep in thought; she lifted her head and looked at him a searching look and pursed her lips.

"John he is in England, I am sure, a gut reaction, he lives in the north, Manchester area I believe, and dumps the bodies in London via this time machine thing whatever, but I am convinced he lives up north."

"I agree, that is my gut feeling as well, but, I also have a feeling that he is alive now, he is a genius. A very talented a scientist, as a profession working in nuclear, quantum, or, some physics that, requires tremendous knowledge and skill, an Einstein of today. That said we still have to catch the bugger that is the hard part, where to look. The last woman she worked in a night club in Manchester, I don't know what as, but I wonder if it might be a good place to look. Andy retires in a few weeks, and I assume you also have been invited to the do?"

"Yes, but I can't go, I'm too busy, and just getting the appointment, I don't want to be caught lacking, so I have had to decline his invitation," Lynda said dejectedly.

"Ok, I will go, I can't take Billy although he was a good help, believe it or not, he found the keys at both houses, and spotted other things, but I will have to go alone on this one. Do you know any of the policewomen up there, it would be interesting to wander among the street girls, to get the news on the hoof as it were, they must be aware of what is going on, all these disappearances?"

"No, not really but I could ring Andy I'm sure he would send a couple of WPC's out for you."

John picked up the file and started to read it again, as he read through the notes his face changed; it was getting more and more thoughtful, as if he were looking for something that wasn't there. Then his face lightened, "Of course, why, I must be getting senile."

"What on earth are you on about John?"

"He has these moments, lost he is for ages, then all of a sudden the light appears, and he is ok," Billy said joking.

"Cheeky sod Billy, good morning."

Lynda said hello to Billy, who had just entered, then they looked at John whose face was beaming, as the idea had settled, into a fact he could understand.

"Lynda, have you read the file?"

"Yes Sir before I left why?"

"Didn't you notice anything odd?"

"No, a usual autopsy report and the attending officers report all as usual."

"Correct, all as usual, nothing odd about the body, that was what confused me, all the rest had something out of place, this one hasn't, and it confused me, why nothing odd? There is a comment about a scar from keyhole surgery, that was fairly new then but not odd, like in sixty two when keyhole surgery didn't exist, or earlier when silicone implants didn't exist, now they are common place, you can even get them on the National Health Service. There is nothing odd, nothing out of place. That in itself is odd; the oddity with this body is that there is nothing odd. He is telling us that he is around now. All the oddities were telling us that he was burying the bodies in time, but we had to wait until we had caught up in time for him to tell us that, don't you see? I think we are dealing with a schizoid personality, he wants to be caught, rather than the normal personality does," John said beaming.

"It's too early for me," Billy said

"I get it, yes, he wants us to know that the time is now, this is when he is killing the women, but how does that help us," Lynda said nodding her head in agreement.

"Well as a Chief Inspector, I could start a full investigation, but as a retired one, I can't, and seeing as Andy is about to retire, we are still on our own. Except that, Andy will have good contacts, unlike me, all I have is you Lynda, and a bloody good help you are, but even you can't get a full blown enquiry going without support from above."

"No but you have a lever Sir, you used it once, perhaps this is a good time to er, use it again say?"

"I can't, not in Manchester, which is where the investigation needs to take place, unfortunately."

Over the weekend, more notes, tags, photos and coloured pins adorned the now overflowing cork board and white board, the blackboard still had some space for more notes, but even that was beginning to get full. As Lynda loaded her car with her bags, she turned to John and smiled.

"Why do I get the funny feeling that you are about to make an unwelcome suggestion," he said, also smiling knowing that she was uneasy about the suggestion she was about to make.

"John I know Sandra and Billy have nagged you about getting a lodger, and I have no wish to interfere but," she paused giving John the opening.

"Well don't then, I am taking it under consideration, it is a large house, and I do have space, which means that the lodger and I wouldn't need to meet, very much as it were, but it is still my home, and I am not sure I want a stranger living with me. Or as Billy crudely put it, even if it were a single woman and we, well Jane wouldn't object, she would be happy that I had found love again, she was that type of woman. Then I posed the point that it may be a man, then, what would they think hey, alright to have a woman in the house alone with me at night, but a man?"

"Not as easy as it seems, is it? Think about it, either way I am sure the village would not think badly of you; they know you too well for that John," she said kissed him goodbye and left.

Chapter 13

A New Line

John arranged to go to Andy's retirement do leaving on the Tuesday morning staying once again at the hotel Andy had first booked him and Billy into, then going to the party at the same hotel, and staying overnight. What Andy didn't know, was that John also booked an extra two nights, intending to do some snooping, although he hated the word, but it best suited his intentions.

He arrived at the hotel and settled into his room, then washed and got dressed ready for the party. The evening was an enormous success, John felt a little like a fish out of water because all the other guests were from Andy's Manchester area, and had known him now for some ten years; John was the only person who had retired earlier and was not part of the team. Andy and Susan both made him very welcome, and Susan made sure that he was never alone. John was not a party person, especially now that he was alone. When Jane was alive they didn't party as such except with their close friends, at home, small, select parties. This was when Jane and John enjoyed parties, when they did the entertaining, as a guest he felt awkward. Even so the officials and officers attending welcomed him and he made a few new friends, but he was reticent to broach the subject of the case he was working on, and asking for help.

The following morning, John woke early and took a taxi ride around the town, in particular, the red light district. He wanted to see the area in daylight, before his planned night time tour. He wanted to get the layout in his mind, so that when he returned, at night, when the place was vibrant, even if it was in a seedy way; he'd know his way around. From there the driver took him to the Topaz club, each time John had asked for the destination the driver had given him a funny look, knowing the sort of places they were. This told John as much about the Topaz club's reputation as he expected to find when he visited it, it was a pick up place for prostitutes, protected by the club, safe for them to have a drink and assess the client prior to going away with the client alone, he spotted an opening to some stairs leading off the entrance corridor, which he assumed led to bedrooms which the club allowed the women to use for a price.

He had lunch in a cafe and spent the afternoon looking around the exhibition at the G-Mex centre. He returned to the hotel around four in the afternoon then went to bed for a couple of hours, knowing that he wasn't used to being up late and that it was going to be a late night for him.

John showered and got dressed then went down to diner, and waited in reception till nine o'clock when the taxi he had booked earlier came for him.

"Hi boss, are you sure you want the Topaz club, I wouldn't have said it was your scene, there's a good film on at the multiplex," the driver said, concerned for him.

"Thank you but I am sure, I have to do this," John replied smiling at the driver's well-meaning offer, "pick me up at say ten o'clock please."

"Ok boss, but I, well it's none of my business," he said and moved off, dropping John outside the Topaz.

John felt uncomfortable, he was not a policeman now, just an old man looking for sex, or so it appeared, and was viewed as that as he passed the doorman, a stout overweight man about five ten and well-rounded shoulders. He obviously did some weight training by the bulging muscles of his biceps. John held his head up as he walked past the doorman; he was not going to be intimidated by him, for no other reason than he knew he wasn't there to pick up a woman.

The Topaz club was a dingy place, very poor lighting, all small, dark alcoves and round seating, where several men and women sat laughing and drinking. Along the far wall, facing the door was the bar, a busty, red head, stood behind the bar, ample cleavage on display to get the men into the mood. John walked up to the bar and leaned on it.

"Take a seat in that alcove and I'll send someone over to you with the bottle of champagne," she said indicating an alcove to the left of the entrance door.

John went to the alcove indicated and sat down, a young woman came over to him carrying a tray with two glasses and a bottle of cheap champagne; she smiled at him and put the tray on the table. She opened the bottle and poured the two glasses then sat down next to him and put her arm round his shoulder.

"Hi sweetie, I'm Sandy, what shall I call you," she hummed, oozing with the come on?

"John, ahem," John coughed he was getting hot under the collar from the uneasiness he felt.

"Well John it's a hundred for the champagne, and fifty for me, I will show you a good time for that. I sense that it is your first time, sweaty palms and the unease, relax I won't hurt you, unless you want me to, we have a dungeon as well for the men who like that sort of thing, but I don't think that is your scene somehow?"

"Actually no, I don't want anything except a chat; I was hoping to meet Joan here," John said as a question?

"Know Joan do you, then why the discomfort? I don't think you do; so why ask for her, and as I said, I need fifty plus the champagne that's another hundred, one fifty, please," she said, holding out her hand.

John took out his wallet and handed her the one hundred and fifty pounds, "now, tell me about Joan, she isn't answering her phone and hasn't been seen for a few weeks now?"

"So you do know her then?"

"Yes, and I want to know why she hasn't been seen," John coughed again and rubbed his hand round his collar.

"Gone on holiday, back to France, that's where she comes from; you did know that didn't you."

"Back to, her home country, but she comes from Czechoslovakia, so why go back to France?"

"Just testing, so back there then, am I not good enough for you," she said as if hurt?

"Like I said, I am not here for sex; I am looking for her and wanted some back ground information. She worked here so I was told, and you just confirmed it, now, did she have some personal clients, what did she offer to her clients, and where did she get them, here?"

"I think you ought to leave now, before I call the security," she said switching off the friendly attitude.

"I paid for an hour, so why can't we chat, if that is what I want, there is no rule that says I have to have sex, is there?"

"No, there isn't, but that depends on what we talk about."

"Look she has disappeared and if you're a friend of hers then why don't you want to find her? Why push me away, when I am looking for her?"

"Ok, you want to chat we will, for another half hour, and then piss off ok, Joan hasn't been in here for over a month, after she had a row with the boss, he doesn't like the girls getting above their station, we presumed that he told her not to come back, now that ends that conversation."

"Thank you, so you don't see her other than here then, do any of the other girls here know her better than you, I need to get to know about her?"

"Look John, if that is your name; we each get fifty, plus a hundred for the champagne, so if you want another girl then it's another one fifty, how important is it that you find her?"

"I don't have that much, but it is very important that I find out what happened to her, I believe she is dead, don't ask me to explain you wouldn't understand, but that is what I believe," John said taking a chance that she might ease up a little and help him, knowing that fact.

"I, I didn't, don't think, they would go so far, no, I mean, you don't think, that they killed her, do you," she said shocked, the reaction John had hoped he'd get.

"No, I don't, in fact, I very much doubt it, but I need to get into her mind, to know where she went, and with whom she met, about a month ago; do you know of any appointments she had, or where I can begin to look?"

The woman looked at John studying him for a moment, her head pushed back as if assessing him, trying to work out what the hell he was doing. He was too old to be a policeman, and too eager to be just a friend, but there was something about John that just didn't sit right with her, and John sensed it.

"I am an ex-policeman I am retired, and I need help. The police force will not believe what I know is fact, and neither will you, but please, you are a blonde, so be very, very careful about whom you entertain alone."

"Oi you, times up, come on there are others waiting for her company," the door man said forcefully but not aggressively, except for the fact that he leaned on the table in a commanding and threatening manner.

"Hum, yes ok, remember what I said, be very careful."

"What for old man; threatening her are you?"

"No just being polite, and hoping to see her again," John said smiling, she smiled back.

"Tony, its ok, I'll show him to the door thank you," she said, now grinning and nodding her head.

"Look tomorrow at Wendy's cafe on Walter street, meet me at ten, no make it eleven," she said as she showed him out.

John looked at his watch it was just five to ten, he waited uneasily till the taxi arrived virtually on time and took him to the red light district.

"Well you're a glutton for punishment twice in one night," he said as John got in the taxi; John just smiled if only he knew.

"Ok, the red light district then please, where the street girls are."

The taxi driver shook his head, put the car into gear and drove off.

"Look mate, I don't mean to be, interfering, it's none of my business, but, why a street girl, I can take you to a discreet lady, she will look after you, you're a nice guy, and I don't want you to get mugged."

"Thank you for your concerns, I'm not as fit as I used to be you're right, but that is where I need to be, and I'm not feeble yet either," John said touching his driver on the shoulder to show that he appreciated the concern.

"Ok, I will be back at the same point I drop you off at midnight, that is when I finish, if you're not there then, I will call the police, unless you call me before then to pick you up, ok."

John smiled to himself at the concern expressed by the driver, and wondered if there was as much danger, as the driver seemed to think, "Fine I'll be there, probably before twelve, I'm not used to such late nights these days."

"Just be careful, I have two pickups to do; otherwise I would have stayed with you."

"Again I thank you, for your concerns, but I will be fine."

"Famous last words, those."

He dropped John off at the corner and told him that the women were usually a few yards down on the left, with their minders, pimps and the like, John thanked him again and got out.

The night was extremely balmy, a clear sky and bright stars shone when visible through the glare of the street lights. The street was dimly lit for the most part, several shops had their windows illuminated that cast light onto the pavement; as he passed by the doorways he saw a few women hanging back in the doorway. He walked down the street assessing the women and the street; he felt that as long as he was on the street then he was safe enough and seeing as he had no intention of going with any of the women he relaxed. Now clear of the area occupied by the women, he started back; this seemed to be a signal for them to take an interest, as several of them came to the front of the doorways in which they were standing.

John stopped at the first door way, and a woman came over to him, "Can you manage it dear, it's fifty for the lot, extra if you want extras," she said in a northern accent.

"I'd like you to look at some photos for me; I wondered if you knew any of these ladies?"

"Look love I sell sex, are you interested or not, if not piss off," she said putting her hands on her hips and looking down on him from the raised step in the doorway, in a disinterested manner.

"Fifty you said, for how long, half an hour?"

'Yeah about that, if you can manage so long," she said with a mocking laugh.

"Ok, here's twenty pounds, for ten minutes, I want you to look at these photos, is that fair enough?"

"Suppose so, just to look?"

"Yes, just to look and tell me if you recognise any of them, and there's twenty for anyone else who is willing to look, you don't seem very busy considering the time, I would have expected you all to be, well, you know."

"Girls come here and look at these photo's holiday snaps I think of the women he has bedded," she mocked him and laughed then looked at the first photo, "Christ! You sick fuck, piss off, she's dead!"

"They all are dead, and they were working in Manchester as prostitutes, now I want to find the killer, to do that I need to know who they were, and where they worked. Otherwise, you are all in danger, especially you," John said pointing to a blonde woman.

"Fuck off, you silly old git, we don't know any of them," she said and threw the photos on the floor in disgust.

"You didn't look very closely, and I did pay you, so if you would please?"

"Come with me," the woman he had pointed out said, John followed her into a door way.

"Do you know any of them," John asked?

"I think I do, this one, she worked at thirty two Windsor Street, we all have from time to time, but it costs an extra twenty five for a room there. So our punters prefer to go around the back, cheaper that way, and her Alexandria yeah Alexandria, that was what she said her name was when she was here, but that was a good, oh, twelve months ago, she got in with a bad crowd, plenty of money but drugs and the like, I'd rather take my chances here than be involved with them."

John pulled the other one out, she had identified, and asked if she knew her name; again it was just her street name, Sadie, she didn't know if that was her real name or not. He pushed her for a surname, but she didn't know what that was. John thanked her and moved off at each door way he met with the same answers, telling him to go away, too old and if they took the bait of twenty pounds then they usually shunned away when they saw the photo, calling him a pervert. John decided to call for his taxi when one woman called in her minder who directly threatened John, he decided that enough was enough and to call Andy next morning to see if he could help. John didn't feel that it had been a waste of time, he now knew that Joan used a street name of Alison, and one of the girls used an address her real name was Alison Thomas. Satisfied he went to the corner and waited for his taxi, even though he was nervous, he had underestimated the reaction to his enquiries by a long way. Was he now too old, was he getting senile as Billy had once said jokingly. It was a stupid idea, yet there seemed no other option, and his technique had gone, he had rushed in, pushed the point when it was a gentle approach that may have got the results he needed.

Finally, the taxi arrived; he got in flushed and in disarray, he hadn't realised how flushed he was and how ruffled he looked, but the taxi driver noticed.

"You ok mate," he asked very concerned about John's state.

"Yes, yes just a slight misunderstanding, I am fine, just take me back to the hotel please, I am too old for this sort of work now."

"Work, what do you mean if I may ask? I'd have thought you were retired by now?"

"I am; how long have you been a taxi driver?"

"Some twenty years now, great job, I get to drive a nice car and have the private use of it, and get paid to drive it. Most of my customers are like you, nice people, and I enjoy the natter and their company."

"When we stop I'd like you to look at some photos please, see if you remember picking any of them up, where you picked them up, and where you took them, I am asking a lot of your memory, but if they were regular customers, hopefully you'll remember them?"

"Yeah sure, if I can help I will, here we are," he said as they pulled up at the front of John's hotel.

John handed him the photos and waited, the driver studied each one pulling a face as he looked at them and shaking his head, realising that they were all dead.

"An odd bunch of photos, where did you get them, if I can ask?"

"I'd rather not say, but I was a policeman, a Chief Inspector, and can we say that these are old unsolved files?"

"Yes we can, you're the boss, and this woman I recognise her, but the photo is so old; she was in my taxi, oh, say one, two years ago, I remember her because she always gave me a good tip, very good, she was a prostitute, and I kept my mouth shut, so she rewarded my silence. But I haven't seen her in a couple of years or there about, does that help you, I mean, it isn't her obviously, this photo is so old, but whoever she is, she's the spitting image of her."

"You have helped me a lot, that is just what I wanted to hear, please believe me, you wouldn't understand why, but you have helped me, thank you. Do you remember where you took her, or where she worked, her home perhaps?"

"You want me to pick you up tomorrow afternoon to go to the station, give me till then, I'll try and remember, but it was a long time ago now. On condition, you tell me what it is you are doing, deal?"

"You won't believe me, but it's a deal as you say, till tomorrow then, oh where is Wendy's cafe on Walter street do you know it?"

"Sure do, you go to some of the seediest places around if you don't mind me saying so. What time shall I pick you up; it's a long walk from here near the Topaz?"

"Oh, I need to be there for eleven, so what ten thirty?"

"It's not that far, quarter to eleven that will be early enough."

"I can't afford to be late, I'd rather wait a quarter of an hour than be late, it's important, very important."

"Ok ten thirty then, I'll be on time don't you worry."

"I know you will, thank you and good night, and thanks again for your concern appreciated," John said and gave him a hefty tip.

Back in his room he turned the photos over and wrote on the back of the photos the names; he now had for them, their street names and their real names if he knew them. He put them on the side table and got ready for bed climbed in and went straight to sleep, exhausted from the day's work. It had been a long, time since he had worked that hard and for that long.

He woke up with a startle, and looked at the clock, it said nine, he jumped out of bed and showered then went down stairs just in time to have breakfast before it finished, he drank a second cup of tea and began to relax, allowing the sleep to evaporate from his head. He looked round to see all the tables cleared ready to be set for lunch and asked if he could have a third cup in the lobby so as not to delay them, the waiter told him to go through, and he would bring him a fresh pot, John thanked him and got up.

Ten thirty on the dot, the taxi pulled up outside, the driver, went in to the hotel for John, having seen him sat with his back to the window.

"Ready Sir," he asked gently so as not to make John Jump?

"Yes and I saw you pull up, but I wanted to finish my tea, a lovely cup, shall we go?"

The driver took John to the cafe and told him to ring him when John was ready, he wasn't on duty till four that afternoon, but he would look after John, John paid and thanked him, telling him that he didn't know how long he would be, but would ring him when he was ready.

John entered the cafe, more of a greasy spoon than cafe, he thought back to when he was a beat copper and the sort of cafes he frequented in those days, this one was not that much better if as good. A dilapidated; dirty looking cafe, a large window looking out on to the street, a dirty net curtain half covered it. Gingham table clothes stained with tea, grease and other various types of food and sauces, wooden seats, hard yet comfortable for a short time. He began to wonder if this had been the start of fast food in Britain, along with fish and chips, before all the foreign food places arrived. All the food was fried in deep oil, quick sustaining, but very unhealthy, or so they now told us. He ordered tea, wishing that he hadn't had so many at the hotel; he now needed a toilet and asked where it was. The waitress, was a buxom woman in her late fifties, she was dressed in a floral dress, with a scruffy apron over it. She told him that it was down the street, that is, if it were open, a public one. John sighed and went down the street, he was lucky it was open and used it, holding his breath as he did, again it was a long time since he had, had to use these facilities, and had forgotten how much they smelled. Back in the cafe he took a seat in the far corner, so that he could watch the door for the woman entering. His tea came in a thick almost white, and crazed mug, the spoon standing up in the cup, no saucer for him to put the spoon in, and now that smoking had been banned in public places, there wasn't even the ashtray for him to put it in, so he did as the other clients had done before him, the evidence was in the table cloth, and put it on the table, wet.

He didn't have to wait for long before the woman entered; she saw him, came over and sat down next to him, there were two other tables taken, one with a man on his own and the other with two women. They exchanged greetings, and she ordered a cup of coffee then looked at John.

"You asked me to meet you here, I presumed you had some information for me," John said calmly and quietly.

"Yes, I, no first of all I want something. How did you get hold of those photos, they are all of dead women, aren't they," she began; giving him a stern look?

"Ok, yes they are, and I am trying to find their killer, so if you can help me, please do, otherwise don't waste my time," John was firm and blunt, he had, had enough of the run around he was getting from these women.

"You didn't answer my question how did you get hold of them," she said forcing the point?

"That my dear is none of your business, I have them legally, as an ex-police officer I am privy to this type of information, now what information do you have for me?"

"An ex-police officer, where, which station did you used to work from?"

"Look, do you, or don't you have any information for me?"

"As a serving police officer," she said showing him her warrant card, "I have the right to ask you these questions, and retired or not, those photographs should never have left the station. You could be in serious trouble and whoever gave them to you. Now answer my questions or would you rather go down to the police station and answer my questions there?"

"If only I had, had that power last night, I am ex-Chief Inspector John Alker of New Scotland Yard, retired, the photos were given to me by an ex-officer who worked with me, they are of women, who as you can see are all dead, and they all died over the last six years. Yet their bodies were found over the last hundred years or so. Now, if I go to your boss and tell him that, he will have me thrown out as a senile old man, correct? And I can tell from your face that you don't believe me either, so I am on my own, now either you can or cannot help me. What is it to be, can you help me to stop this serial killer?"

"Hum," she said and sat back, looking John up and down, pondering what to make of this old man sat before her.

The point was as ludicrous as he said it was, so he was no fool, he knew what he had told her would be viewed with far more than just scepticism, yet he was so factual, he knew they were killed recently, but the photos were ranging from sepia to full colour of recent years, schizoid, no yet, what the hell she decided to help him.

"I don't believe what you told me, but I can't honestly say that your lying, can you prove anything you told me, no matter how tenuous, just something that I can say perhaps to?"

"Not here, but in my hotel room, I have more photos, ones of these women alive, I didn't bring them because I wanted the shock factor and because by you identifying them proves in an odd way that I am right. I have definite identifications on two of the women, apart from the. Well my hotel room shall we say in half an hour, I need to ring my very concerned taxi driver, if I don't, he will be down to the police station before we reach the hotel," John said laughing.

"I don't have a car for this job, so a lift would be appreciated, but don't tell him who I am, please?"

"Undercover, things have changed; we would never allow a woman to do what you do."

"Don't make assumptions; I don't do what you are thinking, and there is no way that a male officer could do the job I am doing, is there?"

"Sorry I am getting as bad as everyone else, like last night when they all assumed I wanted sex," John said and got up to pull her chair out for her.

"In a place where men pick up women for sex, what did you expect, thank you?"

They went outside as the taxi pulled up, he looked at them and said nothing, just drove them to John's hotel, but he did smile all the way John watched him in the mirror and smiled to himself, assumptions!

They went up to John's room, and he pulled out a set of photos from his brief case and handed them to her.

"Ok, all dead women, from eighteen seventy two, but we believe there may be some going back even further," he then handed her a new set of photos, "all missing women from Manchester, now do you see any likenesses?"

"Oh, oh," she said as she matched the photos, "all from Manchester and all dead, and I have seen her, and her, I have been in vice now for three years. Sergeant Collins Sir, Detective Sergeant Jenny Collins, proof yes, I agree, that one maybe two have a look alike, but six never, and as I said, I have dealt with these two, for soliciting. I had presumed they had got out of the business, because I haven't seen them for so long," she paused and looked at them again and shook her head, "so now what?"

"Well," John paused, shocked that she hadn't laughed at him, "I am shocked, I expected you to laugh at me at least."

"What, when I knew her, I can't quite remember her name, it was, let me see now nineteen seventy eight, yes, that was it. I had gone to Wigan from college then transferred to Manchester, and it was my first collar here, you always remember them don't you, your first collar in a new station?" John thought back to his first arrests, and he remembered them better than all the others.

"Drunk and disorderly, that was it yes, when I took her in it was as if she were returning home, they all knew her by her first name, but I can't recall that just now, but it will come to me, a regular apparently. Usually for soliciting, that was it J, her name began with Jan, no Jones, I forget her Christian name, but I can look it up, it was several weeks later, when one of her companions, female, was brought in for soliciting; I was on the desk and they commented that Jones hadn't been seen for a bit. Now you have a photo of someone that looks exactly like her, exactly, and it isn't very old, well it's in colour, so you may have a point."

"Great, that's the best news I have had in years, and I mean years, I have someone who actually believes me apart from the two officers that have worked with me. Her name is Sadie Jones, I was an Inspector at the time, and your Sadie turned up in a pub called the Bell, I had a new sergeant with me a cocky little sod he was, a nice guy, did you ever meet Chief Superintendent Green?"

"Yes once, I, I'm a bit embarrassed about it, I was awarded a merit for some work I did, and he gave it to me, why?"

"My old sergeant, and don't ever be embarrassed about an award, you earned it, be proud of it. We were the investigating officers on the case, there was no way that the body could have been put where it was found, yet there, it was. I have been hunting this guy since then on and off. Now I am in the time zone he is operating in, so if we are going to stop him now is the time, but I am too old, I made a mess of things last night, I did some stupid and dangerous things, but I have to stop him, no-one else will believe me."

The bedroom phone rang, John picked up the receiver, "Hello,———, Andy, great to hear from you, how are you getting used to retirement,———, yes I have a young lady with me,———, yes in my bedroom, don't get any funny ideas. She was about to arrest me, and with you not being there to help me, I decided to tell her the truth, and she arrested, the Body at the Bell how's that for a coincidence,———, yes for drunken disorderly. Now we know that he is burying the bodies in time, and the women all disappeared from Manchester, and they all disappeared within the last ten years. We also know that the last body, which you haven't seen yet, well the photo, didn't have anything odd commented about it.———, I wondered that, but what he has told us is that he is operating now, by that fact alone. What a pity you can't help now being retired and call for a full murder investigation,———, true they would have laughed at you and suggested you see a psychiatrist, but then again maybe we are mad, thinking what we are,———, Ok see you at the weekend at my place, we can go over things there,———, Sergeant Collins sends her regards, bye."

"Sir there isn't a lot I can do, but whatever you ask if I can, I will help you, oh, and I get one man a night, just to get things clear, about the case, he is DC Allen, a regular of mine. We sit and chat for an hour, just enough for it to appear that I am working, I don't have sex with anyone, unless I choose to and in private not for money, ok."

"Ok, what are you doing at the Topaz anyway I told you my story," John said with a smile, a questioning and gently encouraging smile?

"Drugs Sir, we think they are one of the main suppliers, but I am new to the place and needed a cover, a client to give me more time to ingratiate myself."

"Or a key, go to Bury station and get the set of keys to number two, Sycamore Drive, it belonged to a Joan Davies, and there may be something there to help you, I can't give you more, except that she is dead," John said and handed her the photo.

"I will make enquiries about that Sir, thank you; well I had better be on my way, good luck, and if I can do anything, please let me know," she said holding out her hand and shaking John's, then left. John finished packing and went down to meet the taxi.

John told the driver a story, close to the truth, but not the truth about the photos, something about women who looked like a dead person, was it reincarnation? Upon his retirement, he had decided to investigate it as a hobby. Unfortunately, the women had all worked as prostitutes, so that, was where he had to go; if he were to be able to find out if there were anything in the suggestion, or theory. John wasn't sure if the driver accepted it or not, but he seemed to accept it.

Back home, John pencilled in a date, for him to return to Manchester, to go back to two Sycamore drive, and hoped that Sergeant Collins would be able to assist him then.

He told Billy of his exploits, and that made Billy wish he had been able to go, he wondered why he was so upset at being arrested, yet now wished he'd been with John, when yet again he found himself at odds with the law, even if it turned out for the best. He also wished he had been there when John was talking to the prostitutes; he had never met one, or been in a place like that.

Andy and Susan came down to the house, and Lynda also arrived for the weekend, it was like old times they mused as they sat in the incident room looking over the old files, and reading the new one. Whilst listening to John's exploits and the information he had acquired from his visit in Manchester. Andy told John off for a second time, this time for being so stupid as to go into that type of district alone, and as for going to the Topaz club; he said that even he wouldn't go there, alone, just to ask questions. Did he know what went on there, and that it was under investigation? John informed him that he did, now, Detective Sergeant Collins had told him. This brought Billy up to date along with the rest of them.

Billy and John set up the stall as usual with Andy also helping whilst Lynda decided that she was going to cook lunch for them with Susan. After dinner at the pub on the Sunday Lynda went home, she still had to go to work the following day, whilst John, Andy and Susan planned another few days together. Sandra was pleased to see Susan on the Monday morning when she arrived as usual, they chatted about John taking in a lodger, and Sandra found another helper to get John to take in a lodger.

"I think it's a great idea John, company, I know you have Billy, but with three of you, there will be even more to talk about, especially if they work, I think it's the best idea I've heard in a long time, why don't you do it," Susan enthused?

"Because, for one, I like being my own boss, doing what I want when I want, two, I like the peace, not having to listen to the noise they call music these days, three, there isn't a three but give me time I'll think of one and I'll think of a four, that one as well," he said joking, yet meaning it.

"Pardon, being your own boss with Sandra around, I don't think so," Susan said teasing him.

John did like his own company and Billy's; he wasn't short of money although recent trips had eaten into his savings quite a bit. John still had the income from the house he rented out in London and with his police pension he could afford these excursions. Within a few weeks, his savings would be back to where they were, that is until he went to Manchester again, and that was beginning to worry him slightly, the cost of speaking to the women was far more than he had expected. He was no-longer able to use his powers as a policeman and now was regarded as just another man, who paid.

John's early vegetables were now ready for sale, Andy and Billy had helped him set up the stall again inside the gate of his drive, ready for the new season. John had to agree that it was getting harder and harder for him with age to set up the stall, but he also knew that the locals would lend a hand should he need it. By Friday, Andy and Susan needed to go home, Susan had a hospital appointment on Monday, and she wanted to prepare for it. John had been upset by the news that she had cancer of the breast, the same one that had taken Jane from him. Susan had been more fortunate in that her cancer had been diagnosed early enough for them to be able to do something about it. Even though, it would mean the removal of a breast and then reconstruction, which was bad enough, but the prognosis was excellent and she expected to recover fully.

Chapter 14

A New Convert

During the next few weeks, John organised a trip to Manchester, he met up with Jenny, and they looked around the house, they found several packages in the loft. This effectively closed the case for Jenny, the packages were all labelled, and Jenny was able to follow that up. Lynda rang whenever she found a new victim, now they were older and older, but the missing women were still from the Manchester area. Although he had moved out into the outlying towns more, like Bury, Oldham, Rochdale, these and other areas were now fast becoming the killer's hunting ground. John decided to try and count the number of victims from the obvious ones with photos of the dead women, and then from the number of missing women, some of the missing women he decided would be as per normal; people disappeared every day and so it would not be correct to assume that they were all victims. John decided to deduct ten per cent from the list of missing women, which still left him with a hundred or so women who fit the killer's requirements, missing, and presumed dead.

He shook his head, as he realised, that, in the short space of ten years, he had killed at least, one woman every month. And John had to admit to himself that this was only an estimate, derived from the number of missing women who had been reported, how many went missing that were not reported, he had no idea. His conclusion was that the killer was active every month, if not more often. He then checked the dates on the files, to see if that calculation were correct, and realised that if it had been to a pattern, then he now stood a chance, of catching the killer, because he would know when to expect the next murder to take place.

He worked on the theory all that day, trying to find a common date, week or time of the month, but nothing was predictable. One woman went missing on the first of the month, or that was when she was reported missing, then there was a gap of six weeks before the next one was reported. Then there were two in one month, then a gap of a month before the next one was reported, and so it went on, no system or regularity to the reports at all.

John decided that he must assume that all the women were victims of the killer, even allowing for the ten per cent, and in particular which of the women that were missing, were that element; he didn't know, there was no regular pattern to be discerned.

Why, oh why was that, most serial killers followed a pattern, the area, his safe zone, a commonality, apart from being prostitutes and blonde, that was it, but he got the women from all over the area now. All were prostitutes, but some were street women and some private, he must meet them somewhere they feel safe, and then somehow get them to go with him but how?

John decided to try again, walking the streets, talking to the women, but this time he would try and take back up with him. Sergeant Collins, yes he was sure she would help him, if she was in a position to do so, just as, he made up his mind to ring her, the phone rang it was Lynda; there had been another case appeared, nineteen fifty two. As soon as she told him that he felt a shiver run down his spine. He had been a sergeant then and in the murder squad so why hadn't he known about it, like the nineteen sixty two murder. Slowly as, Lynda read the file to him he became more and more aware of the events. He had not been on the case because he had been given special duties with the coronation coming up he had been seconded to crowd control and security duties, and was on training courses for much of that period. He was to mingle in the crowd as a spectator, move around to keep an eye on the crowds; he had been selected because he didn't look like a copper, so his Inspector had told him with a smirk, which had amused him at the time, not knowing what a copper looked like.

As the information came over the telephone to him, he remembered that there was a case being investigated by an Inspector who had now retired well before he did, and when he was in the office there were photos and notes being circulated. That crime was just like his was; they never even identified the woman. Deja vu Lynda had called it, a feeling that you knew about the crime but didn't, and that is exactly what he felt now. It was as if he had known about it all along, and yet he now knew that the crime had just been committed, it was an odd, uncomfortable, and somehow sickening feeling, all at the same time.

John asked Lynda what was the oddity, she hadn't found one, which she found odd it was early enough for there to be an oddity yet, there didn't seem to be one.

"Lynda I must be getting too old for this, of course he has already told us that he is operating now, so why bother telling us that he is burying the bodies in time, wait a day or two, and then if you haven't received a missing person report, ring Sergeant Collins at Manchester and ask her to see if anyone has been reported missing in the last say three days."

"John they, well the new Super has decided that it was a waste of time and cancelled the urgency, I won't get a report now until it goes nationwide," she said apologetically.

"Well then ring her, no I'll do it, at a personal level, I have something else I want to speak to her about anyway, ok can you bring the file down on Saturday?"

"See you Saturday, but I am on duty for the two following Saturdays so I'll post anything else I get for you ok?"

John said that it was fine and then hung up, he turned to get his diary with Collins phone number in and the phone rang again, this time he was surprised to hear Sergeant Collins voice.

"Sir, I have been told that we no-longer send out missing persons as urgent, so I thought you ought to know that a blonde has been reported missing."

"Thank you Jenny, for ringing me, she is five six, average height and weight, blonde hair, a small tattoo on her left buttock, her belly button has been pierced, and her nipples, she is about twenty nine and slim, she works as a prostitute, now I am guessing, but I think she worked in the Bury area, how was that?"

"Brilliant, why do we bother, you know it all without a report," she said surprised, "and her name?"

"Sorry I don't have that; Lynda has just rung me, to tell me that the woman I have just described to you, was found dead in nineteen fifty two. Now how is that for proof that our boy is somehow burying the bodies in time?"

"I am in, I can't risk my career by suggesting that is what is happening, but I do agree that, that is the only possible solution, I'll keep you informed."

"Thank you for calling I appreciate it, and can I ask a big favour of you if you can't do it then I will understand, but I want to visit the red light district again and an address used by the women, can you help me, be my back up say tomorrow night?"

"Sorry Sir I can't I've pulled an all-nighter, what about the following night is it that important that it is tomorrow night I mean?"

"No, Thursday, will be fine, I'll come up tomorrow in the afternoon, Billy will be with me as well and you can meet him, he's a nice guy, friendly and chatty you'll like him."

Arrangements made, John hung up and went back into the garden to help Billy, who had arrived and was digging up some carrots.

Chapter 15

Street Walk

The receptionist recognised John when he booked into the hotel, taking two rooms, John always able to remember faces, acknowledged her greeting, and introduced Billy as a friend; she gave Billy a warm, welcoming smile.

They went to their rooms and unpacked, they had decided to stay for two nights, just in case they needed to follow up on any leads. John was a half full glass man, always the optimist, 'something will turn up and then, we will have him, or her,' he would tell his subordinates, and also telling them never ignore their gut feeling, that had caught as many villains as evidence. Unfortunately to proceed to court they needed evidence, but once they knew who the perpetrator was, then they could concentrate on getting the proof.

They met up at seven for dinner, then had a leisurely pint in the bar before the taxi arrived to take them to the agreed meeting point with Sergeant Collins, she was already there waiting as they pulled up.

"Keen aren't you, and thank you for being punctual," John said jokingly.

"I spoke to an ex-Chief Super earlier, and he told me not to be late, if I wanted to get off on the right foot with you, he also welcomed me to the case, and told me to watch you; professionally that is, and to stop you from getting into too much trouble. He wishes he could be with us, but Susan isn't feeling too well today, and he needs to be with her, she has been for her chemo."

"Ten years ago I would have been flattered by that comment and probably agreed with him, but now, I am, forgetting things," John said with a sigh.

They made their way down the street again, as before the women were sheltering in the door ways waiting for their punters. John as before was about to walk along the street assessing the women before talking to any of them, Collins stopped at the first door way, John carried on, Collins gave him an odd look wondering what he was doing, weren't they there to talk to the women she wondered, gave a shrug and followed him.

It was a cold night the women were dressed to protect them from the wind that had an icy edge to it, not unusual for the month, October was the start of the cold weather not that it had been a hot summer. John seemed to Collins to be just going for a walk, a few of the women approached him, gave a shrug of disinterest,

126

then stepped back onto the shelter of the doorway when he didn't look at them. At the far end of the street, he stopped and turned round to face Collins.

"Well, what did you see," he asked as if there was anything to see apart from closed shops and ten or so women.

"I, well, just a group of women in shop doorways Sir, why?"

"There were two blondes, of about the right age group; the two men over the road were, or are, the pimps for some of the women. The ones that approached me, I would guess are controlled by the men, none of the ones to approach me, were the right age, or colouring, they did it because they had to, because of the men. The women I want to speak to are the two blondes. Firstly to warn them, but I also need to speak to the others in the hopes that they knew the missing women. So have your warrant card ready, just in case we need it, soliciting is still against the law isn't it," he said, looking at her over the rim of his glasses like a school teacher?

"Yes Sir it is, but so is curb crawling, and it could be said that, that is what we just did, viewing the merchandise before making our choice."

"True, I suppose, but we do have the law on our side, don't we," the question was rhetorical Jenny smiled her broad smile that illuminated her face, and raised her eyebrows as a question?

John started back along the street and stopped at the first doorway; he pulled out the photos of the missing women and asked if any of the women, stood in the doorway, knew any of the women in the photos? They all said that they didn't, but were polite enough to look, which encouraged him. He had told them that he was a private detective and looking for the women for their relatives, whether or not they believed him didn't seem to bother him, in fact, it didn't.

John assumed it was a quiet night because they took the trouble to look, he caught sight of one of the men crossing the street and going to the women stood in the next doorway.

John led the way to the next doorway and stepped into it, two women were in this one, there had been three in the previous one; both of the women were not of English extraction, being he guessed from Eastern Europe, bordering on Russia, if not Russian, which was confirmed by their accent when they spoke.

"Look mister our time is valuable, it's twenty for a fondle, or ten minutes," one of them said, not looking at John, but past him at the man who had spoken to them.

"Very polite to call it a fondle but I don't want one. I just want to show you these pictures of missing prostitutes, women like you who are now dead, and ask if you knew them. Now you can look at them here, or this young lady will escort you to the police station for questioning. I presume you do have the paper work to allow you to be here in Britain, it can be a very long and very unprofitable night if she has to do that, don't you think?"

Collins pulled out her warrant card proving that she was an officer of the law.

"Oh, well let me see them again," one said showing the photos to her companion after she had looked at them, "seriously Sir, I don't know any of them, they don't or haven't worked this street in the last two months, since we started working here."

"Thank you, now are you here because you want to be, or is he forcing you to be here, because she can arrest him just as easily, if he is forcing you to do this to pay off a debt, that is illegal."

"We don't want any trouble; best you just go, we honestly have never seen them women."

John watched her as she spoke and decided that she was telling the truth, in that they hadn't seen the women before, but wondered about the circumstances in which they were working.

The group moved on to the next doorway, and another group of two women were in this doorway, who had also been warned, and they also were reticent about acknowledging knowing the women in the photos.

John looked at them for a while testing them, wondering if they were, in fact, telling the truth. Collins warrant card had only the effect of frightening them, making them defend their position. John again decided that they were telling the truth and moved on. They moved on, two blondes were sheltering in the next doorway; the women in the previous doorway had approached John, hoping for a fee, for their services. These two seemed to move further back into the doorway, not really wanting to sell their wares to such an old man, or again they had been warned off, but John hadn't seen anyone, approach their doorway.

"Ladies, I would like you to look at these photos please, I am a private eye, and I am looking for the women in these photos, will you please look at them?"

"Granddad, go away, we are working, unless you are willing to pay for our time, piss off," one said vehemently.

"No, I am not willing to pay you, so let's begin again, these women are all dead, they had one or two things in common with both of you, they were all blondes, natural or bleached, they all worked in your profession, and they all came from Manchester. Two I know of came from this area, so count one you have been warned of the danger to your lives. Secondly either you look at the photos with some interest, or this young police officer will escort you down to the station and then we will find enough photos for you to look at, that it will be dawn before you get out. So which is it to be?"

The women looked at Collins, who nodded, knowing that it was a bluff, she didn't have enough on them, to drag in more officers to take them to the station, but she went along with the bluff. They looked at John to see any sign of nerves, but he just stood there unmoved, and waiting, now getting impatient, and turned to Collins.

"Ok, ok, we'll look," one of them said, afraid of calling his bluff in case it wasn't a bluff.

They went through the first few, then the one who had done all the talking stopped and handed the photo to her friend, who showed signs of recognition, it was obvious to John that she knew the woman.

"Her we knew her, she hasn't been her for oh, two months or so Caroline, nice she was, very nice, I was wondering why we hadn't seen her, she's dead," she said looking John in the eye and now concern showed, in her eyes.

"Yes, do you know her surname," they said that they didn't, "thank you, and I ask you to be very careful, very careful indeed, because he befriends the woman first, a nice person to all intents and purposes, she must feel relaxed; then he kills her. I can't do anything except warn you, and hope that you don't turn up on a mortuary slab, and thank you for helping me. Can you tell me anything about her, who her clients were and where she found them? I am looking for a name that comes up in several client lists, and then I will have my man, until then please be careful."

"Ok, thank you for the warning, but we can look after ourselves," she said and showed him a knife, John frowned, "as for her clients as you put it, no I can't help you, but try thirty two Windsor Street," she smiled and stepped back into the shadows, end of the conversation.

John thanked her and continued to the next doorway.

The next doorway had three women stood in it, and again the way they reacted at first showed that they had also been warned off, but Collins warrant card made them more amenable to the idea of helping John. Once again they drew a blank; the women obviously didn't know any of the women in the photos.

Collins offered John and Billy a lift back to their hotel which they accepted; it also gave them a chance to talk about the evening and what they had found out. John expressed a great deal of interest in the address they had been given because that was the second time that particular address had been mentioned in connection with a missing woman. Collins said that she couldn't do anything officially because it wasn't a current crime under investigation, and she wouldn't be able to get a search warrant to gain entry, but she would again be willing to use her warrant card if necessary to gain entry. John thanked Jenny remembering the number of times in the past he had used his card in an unofficial capacity when an official means of entry, by applying for a search warrant was doubtful because the grounds were too weak. Most people would stand aside and allow him in when he showed his card, whereas, as an ordinary man they wouldn't have; and if, after showing the card, they still objected, then that raised its own conclusions, perhaps not about the case he was interested in, but he wondered what they had to hide. Collins was off the next day, and she agreed to pick them up at ten to take them to the address, John told Billy that he would be better on his own in there, he didn't want to be seen to bully or show strength and suggested that he wait at the hotel for them to return, Billy reluctantly agreed.

Chapter 16
Sexual Encounters

The sun was out, and it promised to be a nice day, the air had warmed up quite a bit from the previous night, but there was still a cool chill to the breeze as John stepped out of the hotel into the morning sun. Collins waited in her car, having seen him wave to her from the reception area window, when she pulled up outside.

There was the usual exchange of greetings, and they left for the address on Windsor Street. During the journey, they talked about the case, and how to progress it, the main problem was still the fact that they couldn't prove that the bodies were from a current murder. They now had over thirty confirmed missing women, none of whom would ever be found; unless they could prove beyond any shadow of doubt that the women had been murdered.

John asked Collins to stay in the car, he didn't want a police presence at this meeting, hoping that a friendly chat with an older man who posed no threat would get the results he wanted, but just in case he had her park opposite the bay window of the Victorian detached house.

The house was set in its own grounds with a short walk from the pavement to the door, a low hedge provided some seclusion and a barrier to the pavement; the original wall having been demolished some time before. John stood in the entrance porch and rang the doorbell. There was no reply, he had heard the ringing so knew that it worked, but they didn't seem to want to answer. He rang it again, this time in his police method, long and persistent, a voice from behind the door said that he should go away; getting an answer he spoke to the voice.

"I wish to speak to you in connection with Joan, she asked me to meet her here, this is 32 Windsor Street isn't it," he said appealing to her.

"We're not open yet, go away," the voice said bluntly.

"I wish to see her, is she here, she said that if she wasn't then ask for Alison and she would help me," John knew that neither of the women would be there, but hoped that it would trigger a positive response.

"She's not here either," the voice said calmly.

"What a pity, I had promised her a hundred, obviously that was for her and well never mind, I'll just find someone else, but she was so nice and helpful."

"How much," the voice asked as if shocked?

"I don't want to make a scene by shouting, perhaps if you open the door then we could discuss this inside quietly, I mean I am stood out here, and people are passing."

"Ok, I'll ask, Madam."

John waited patiently for the door to finally open, and for him to be allowed in, facing him was a bevy of women, about eight of them, all in various stages of undress, some were in underwear with dressing gowns over but not fastened, or in night dresses, some made up and some obviously still not fully awake. John appraised the view before him and decided that although not all were pretty, he would have given them all a second look in his youth, allowing for the sleep in several eyes.

"How may we help you Joan and Alison, are not here and haven't been for some time, so unless one of these lovely ladies can help you, you are wasting our time," a large lady said from the rear, as the women opened up a gap for her to come closer to John.

John noticed the woman he had spoken to the previous night, who had shown him the knife, and he wondered if she now had it hidden somewhere in her underwear, not that there was much room to hide the offensive weapon in the flimsy garments.

"I am looking for some women, and two or three of them used this address for their," John paused and looked round at the unashamed semi-nakedness of the women, "business, I believe that they were murdered, and the police are unable to investigate this aspect, so as an ex-policeman I have taken it upon myself to investigate the crime. I need your help, if I don't stop him, you are all in danger, especially the blondes amongst you, natural or bleached, he doesn't seem to mind that," John said, still stood in the entrance hall, the door closed behind him.

"Why should we help you, they work for money, time is money, and you said a hundred plus, for what, some will go further than others, extras like spanking naughty little boys, is that what you want," the Madam said with a marked reference.

"No, I just want to ask you a few questions, about the girls I mentioned, ahem," John coughed forgetting that age does not reduce the urge when faced with so much on offer.

"Ok, how many women do you want to talk to then, and is it a hundred each," she asked coldly adding, "plus my expenses as it were?"

"Ouch, I can give you a hundred, to be divided, I am on the pension, but I accept that you get paid for your time, then again how much is it worth to have this lunatic arrested, and be free to earn your money without the fear of being killed. How many of you must die before you realise that by helping me, you are helping catch this madman?"

"Show him into the lounge and make him comfortable, Andria put the kettle on. You have half an hour, then a client is due so make the most of it, but no sex, just ask your questions and we will answer the ones we choose to, that is my deal for one hundred, accept it or get out," now she was being forceful and decisive, her eyes closed to slits, and her face set to make the point that it was not negotiable.

"I accept," John said and followed the three women the Madam had indicated into the lounge.

The Madam and two others walked off, including Andria who had already left the group, John presumed to make the tea for them, after a few moments the other two also came into the lounge sitting on stools one on each side again surrounding John in an intimidating way.

"Sure you don't want a quickie ducky," a woman with a Nottinghamshire accent said, making eyes at him.

"No, thank you all the same, but I, well I am no-longer interested," he lied.

John wondered if he could manage to keep his arousal as private as he wanted to, as the women, who were sat either side of him, on the settee for three people, sat closer to him than the arms; he was sure it was deliberate to fence him in, guard him as it were.

The two on either side of him were in their mid-twenties, and in just a bra and knickers, he guessed to arouse him, making his task harder. As an officer, he would not have allowed himself to be intimidated like this, but he was on a sticky wicket, and needed their help. Without the power he had as an officer, he felt that he would have to allow his predicament to continue.

The woman to his left was shorter than he was, and as he turned to acknowledge her with a smile, he couldn't help but notice her ample cleavage, a large expanse of white flesh supported by a black bra, emphasising the expanse she allowed to be visible, she smiled back and suck her chest out invitingly.

John had always thought that a semi-clad woman was more exciting than a naked one, there was that element of mystery, which when naked was removed. He felt his loins react, so turned to smile at the one on his right. She was not as well developed, but still had a rather large expanse of breast on display, captured in the bra to her Basque. The suspenders of the Basque were attached to black stockings, and her crotch hidden by a black 'G' string that seemed to emphasise her groin. She also smiled at him invitingly, whether it was done intentionally to make him feel uncomfortable, or a genuine invitation he didn't know, but it was having a detrimental effect on his ability to concentrate.

The other young lady, he now turned his attention to, was wearing a dressing gown over her underwear, which she had, allowed to fall open, exposing the Basque and her naked crotch, she opened her legs and leaned backward to ensure John had a good view. John realised that he had never felt so intimidated in all his life, yet here they were not threatening, but inviting him to the treasures they held, he coughed again and swallowed hard.

The two women who entered later and were sat on the stools and wore a nightdress even so the nightdress left little to the imagination, one being so short that it was little more than a 'T' shirt, and the other so shear that it a veil would have hidden more.

Sweat was beginning to form on his brow as he looked from one to the other, and so he decided to start asking some questions to occupy his mind.

"You all knew Joan, did she always bring a new client here first," he asked, clearing his throat before he spoke.

"Yes, but we would rather wait till the Madam has come back, that is what she said we should do, so, please talk if you wish but no questions," the one opposite said calmly, opening her legs even more, John looked around the room to avoid the views offered.

The room had been decorated in a nice red flowery paper, slightly faded now from years of use, as was the white paintwork. A good quality Wilton carpet, well-worn now covered the floor, leaving just a two foot border in wood around the side. The furniture again well-worn but had originally been expensive, and good quality, a sideboard and chest of drawers with a few coffee tables scattered round the room ready to be set when needed were the final bits of furniture. John looked up and was pleased to see that the original central moulding very often found in houses of this character and age was still in place as were the edge mouldings round the ceiling. By now he had surveyed the room, and its furnishings, he was still waiting, for the Madam to return. The silence was much more than a pregnant pause, it was imposing, drowning him whilst the women sat there comfortable and oozing sex appeal; he was uncomfortable. He knew that it was deliberate, a ploy used by the Madam, to make him feel uneasy, to take control of the situation away from him, but he wasn't going to allow that to happen, he must keep control of his desires, but he also realised that the longer she left him the harder it would be, so he again started to talk.

"Will she be long I mean she said that, this is terrible calling the lady she, what's her name?"

"She is the Madam, that is what she is called," the one sat next to him said, resting her hand on his knee.

"Right, yes, the Madam will she be long, she did say that I only had half an hour when does that begin, I mean a hundred for a full half hour was what?"

"Cynthia," the Madam called out from behind John; he didn't jump at her voice because his old training was still in effect, not as efficient, but still there and he heard the squeak of the door as she entered.

The woman opposite John closed her knees; John was sure he saw half a wink as she pulled the dressing gown over her knees and sat back.

The Madam sat in the chair that was vacant, and the two women with her sat on the arms of the settee, she poured the tea and handed him a cup all in silence, John took the cup offered and thanked her, she looked at him. It wasn't a sour face but forceful, decisive and controlled.

"To answer your question, it begins now, but we will not answer a question until my tribute has been paid," she said holding out her hand. John took out his wallet and gave her the hundred, "because of what you said about the murders I am allowing the girls to speak to you, for what to us is a mere pittance, so be precise in your questions, time is short."

The Madam sat back and waited for John to ask his questions, sipping her tea.

"I need to find out if a name on a client list appears on several lists, so that I can find the killer, I also need to know where the clients as you call them, come from, where the ladies," John cleared his throat, "meet them?"

"We will not tell you any names that would destroy our reputation, apart from the fact that they usually use false names, so only regulars will tell us their real names. Secondly, the ladies, as you said, get their clients from several sources, some from the street as you found out, and then we do advertise the service in newspapers, and phone boxes, so they would be called telephone bookings. When a lady picks up on the street, they always bring them here for the first meeting, when you arrived four of the girls saw you and appraised you. That is our security if we don't like the look of a client then we do not open the door," she replied.

"So only because of my persistence did you open the door, what if the er, client was just as persistent?"

"No, we opened the door because Cindy said that she knew you, or rather had met you and you were all right, if the client were too persistent, then we can ring a number and the person would be removed, forcibly if necessary."

"The two women I mentioned, do you know of a client they both er, helped, had, er what do you call it?"

"No we don't, that was their business."

"So if as I am assuming with reason, they did both have the same client, who killed them both, your women are at risk, because he knows of this address and what he can find here, and because he has already been here he will be allowed access again, to murder again, someone like Cynthia that is what you called her wasn't it, a pretty blonde just his type?"

"We are very careful, sorry I didn't get your name?"

"John; I have no problem in you having my name, or telephone number, in fact, I will give them to you. I will also give you the telephone number of the lady you saw in the car opposite, in case you remember anything after I have left. I am Ex-Chief Inspector John Alker retired, and the lady outside, is Detective Sergeant Collins, this enquiry is a private one because of the circumstances surrounding it. The police force does not believe that the women are dead, just missing, and they are actively looking for them, but as you will see from the photographs I am about to show you, they are very dead," John said and pulled the photos out from the brief case he had with him, handing them around.

"What the hell are they doing using sepia on mug shots hey, and it feels and looks old that's odd, but this one is Caroline, alright see the mole in the shape of a heart she was proud of that, a warm heart she had said just above her tit, below it and you wouldn't have seen it, but there she said it was just right. I haven't seen her in oh, two years or so," Cynthia said as she looked at the photo once she had got over the shock of the gash in the woman's throat.

"Her real name is Angela Prendergast, and she was found dead in nineteen seventy two and reported missing in nineteen eighty nine," John said confirming her identification.

John looked at the women each in turn, there was a look of recognition on some faces and a blank, if shocked look, on others. He waited for a few moments, to allow them to pass the photos round, and as they did he watched, seeing recognition with each new face they looked at. He now knew that there were some faces that were not known here, but out of the six he showed them, four were recognised by at least one woman.

"I need names and addresses so that I can build a picture, of their activities; I need to find out if one name keeps cropping up, he may use a false name, but at least I would have a name. It would also help me if I knew what his requirements were. With these things, I can give you a good warning. I can tell you not to go with a John Thomas say, or avoid going with a man that asked for a certain type of sexual gratification. I do not want to see anymore dead women, women who have been killed by this man."

"Ok, you have made your point this is Joan, that's her street name she was Russian, and she lived at twenty seven Windmill Street, this one was Caroline as you already know, I never knew her address, she used here all the time, or so I thought. The girls use this place when they don't have a secure or private place of their own, but I do rent out rooms to girls who want a secure location for the first meeting, if everything is ok: then they take them to their own place after that. As I told you earlier, when a client arrives usually two or three women see them, and express an opinion, like watch him, or he's ok, just wants a good fuck," the Madam said accepting that John really did need their help.

"Thank you, that isn't a help, unfortunately, I already know about Joan, and I have seen her home, and where she met her clients, what about the other two, do you know where they lived and worked?"

"Georgia that was the time of the 'G's for names. You will have realised that all the girls names begin with a 'C' here today, well we change the initial every month, just so as to keep some anonymity for them, confuses the clients no end, today with Annabel, next week because it's a new month she is Georgette, or Cristobel, see what I mean," the Madam said, John smiled and nodded, "So even I don't or should I say that I am not sure of their real names, but I think she was," the Madam paused, "Wendy yes, Wendy Westcott, now she lived out of the city I think it was Bury, or Radcliffe."

John had a name and from that Collins should be able to get an address for Miss Nineteen Twenty Two with luck.

"The other one, we called her Juliana, her real name escapes me, but one of the girls, she's not here now, knew her, I will contact her for you, I can't give you her name or address etcetera obviously, but I will make contact later today and ring you."

"I would appreciate that, and ask her if she would allow me to talk to her, please," John didn't want to push his luck too far, now that he had their co-operation.

"There is another one that I recognise, but I don't remember her name, this one," the Madam showed John the photo of miss eighteen eighty five, "We are very particular about hygiene, every girl has to provide a certificate from the doctor to say that she is, shall we say clean, before we allow them to use our facilities, we have a reputation to protect. She brought one and then several days later, a week or so, her client rang to tell me that he had caught something from her. She never used our facilities again I sent her away the next time she showed up."

"You can't remember the date can you, it may just link in with one of the murders, then a description of the man," John realised that he was clutching at straws, but that was all he had at the moment.

"The simple answer is no, it was a few years ago now, but I found it odd that she looked disappointed, yet he was not smiling as such, but seemed pleased, as if he didn't want to come here."

"Thank you, try and remember anything you can about him, and call me on this number, please, it could be very important," John said, writing down his phone number and handing it to her.

"Thank you; I will contact you if I remember anything."

"That's all I can ask, and thank you for the tea, good day ladies," John said and stood up, he wanted to ask more but thought that by applying as little pressure as possible at this time, he would be made welcome if he needed to return.

They all stood up and shook his hand, some allowing their robes to fall open giving him a view of sexy underwear and bare breasts as the case may be, he smiled to himself still in control of his emotions for the moment although he had to admit the view was as stimulating as he was sure they had intended.

The rain had just started as John left the house, he made a run for the car and got in; he looked back at the old house and smiled again, as Collins started the car. It reminded him of his own house, the deep red brick and mullioned windows, a porch open at the front with low walls, providing shelter from the rain, whilst the visitor waited, for the door to open. Inside had also been somewhat of a surprise, the quality of the decoration, although faded with time and use, yet still in good order. Considering the use of the house now, he felt that it was odd, such a quality building, being used for such a basic requirement.

He told Billy about the meeting, and what he had found out, he realised that Billy would tease him about the women and their mode of dress, but decided to tell him anyway, just for the hell of it, and laughed with Billy about the situation he had found himself in, Billy was as cryptic as John had expected.

During that week, John and Billy worked in the garden and rearranged the photos and details they now had, a picture was slowly forming, but it was still too vague to come to any conclusions, apart from the ones they already had. Lynda came down that weekend and studied the boards, she was impressed by what she saw, but as with John and Billy couldn't draw any conclusions, except that they would now be able to build a better profile of the person they were looking for helping them to catch the killer.

"We now know that he started to murder the women in nineteen seventy eight, he was then in his late twenties early thirties, male of course, wealthy," Lynda said.

"Why wealthy," Billy asked?

"We know that he has a time machine and those things will not be cheap, they use a lot of power, and you would need a massive area, he must own a warehouse or some such building."

"Very presumptuous of you Lynda, how do you know this," John asked?

"Well perhaps not, I don't know, but I presume, have you any ideas on this?"

"No I don't, but all we do know, and that is what this session is about, is that it is a male and because he has a time machine of some sorts he is very intelligent, because he must have built it, I haven't seen any for sale, so I think that is substantiated, working in some or other field of science."

"Quantum Physics will be the field," Lynda joined in with.

"Like that TV programme Quantum Leap," Billy asked?

"Yes, like that, now that is a government programme, military, that is why I think he has a lot of money, very rich."

"But Lynda we don't know how much it would cost, it might be cheap, an accident during an experiment, and he turned the result to his use, quite a lot of things we now accept, were found by accident. There is no justification to believe that it is large, expensive, or costly to run, I agree that it is a natural assumption, but we are police officers and do not assume. We work on known facts, and gut reactions, mine tells me that it is the opposite. Cheap to run, and cheap to build, otherwise he would not have been able to build one, a logical assumption?"

"Yes, I have to admit that point, so male, thirtyish, intelligent, possibly scientist, strong, he subdues the victims without injury, he needs to be a bodybuilder type," Lynda continued.

"Another assumption, sorry Lynda but he could drug them, remember the nineteen sixty two case we found a drug in her system not known then, perhaps it is now?"

"John, why didn't I think of that, we can prove that they are buried in the past? The air gets into the body and carries any pollutants that are airborne with it; these enter the body and get into the bone and hair, so they will now be in the bones of the women buried in the nineteenth century. There will be sulphur, from the heavy air pollution of that period, smog, and acid rain, from the volume of coal they were burning. By the mid to late sixties, this had become a major problem, and the clean air act came into power, and in as little as three years, the air purity was much better, almost clean as it were, so these chemicals would not be in the bones of the victims. I know a pathologist, he is a friend of mine, and, I well, I will try and get him to do some tests on the victims bones, and if there isn't any of these chemicals in their bones, then we will have proven that he is indeed burying the bodies in time," Lynda said with much aplomb.

"And how do we get the bodies exhumed, your honour we want to prove that this woman lived in the mid-twentieth century, can we dig her up?"

"John, ok, I agree, getting, permission to exhume the bodies won't be easy, but if we don't try then we may never have the proof we need. I will ask another friend, she works in the Old Baily and hopefully she will help us with a judge, ok?"

"Excellent, I will leave that in your capable hands. Just to shut you all up, I have put the room in the hands of an estate agent, to let one room with semiprivate bathroom and use of the house."

"Great, I am sure that it will provide company and a small income for you," Lynda said, pleased he was listening to them.

The rest of the weekend went as usual; working in the garden in the rain for some of the time, but John needed to get the garden prepared for his vegetables as usual, so he and Billy worked in the rain whilst Lynda cooked for them, and did some cleaning.

"Hey you two, get those muddy boots off before you enter, I have just mopped the kitchen floor," she shouted at them as they came in finished.

"I thought I was married then, nagging women," John said joking.

"Nag, I will nag if you muddy my floor with, oh my god, did you leave any soil in the garden?"

Lynda looked at the two of them as they stood before her, black from head to toe, both of them had slipped and fallen face down in the muddy ground, John began to sing 'Mammy' waving his arms like the Black and White Minstrels used to do, Billy joined in as they sidestepped across the entrance porch.

"I will go into the office whilst you two strip, and go upstairs and have a shower, leave those clothes where they are and when you have passed the office, better still, when you are on the stairs call me, and I will come out, now move, before I get cross."

"That's telling us Billy, no sense of humour women these days," John said with irony.

"Never did have, as far as I can remember," Billy said, just as ironical.

They waited till Lynda was out of sight and then they stripped and went upstairs John shouted to her when he was half way up, and then went to shower and change. Dressed in clean clothes they came back down to a Lynda stood her hands on her hips and a sour expression on her face.

"Look at my floor you two, foot prints from your dirty socks, I warned you not to dirty my floor."

"She did Billy, she warned us, and I suppose we had better wipe the floor clean, or, we may not be having any supper as punishment."

"Lynda wouldn't do that, would she," Billy said, as if shocked?

"Too bloody right I would; Billy, now there's the mop," she said as if angry.

John picked up the mop and mopped the area, whilst Billy stood to one side and pointed out bits John had missed, whilst Lynda stood still, her hands never leaving her hips and with a fixed, stern look on her face, yet she was just as eager to laugh as they were. Seeing these two aged men mopping the floor whilst she stood over them like an ogre, with Billy giving John instructions.

By the March of nineteen ninety two, a week after John had put the room in the estate agents hands, the first phone call from the agent to tell John that he had somebody interested in the room. A good person with a job locally in the new industrial site; it had been built a few miles away from there; the potential client was a lady. John indicated that he wasn't too sure, the client being a female and him a single male alone in the house, what would the neighbours think? The estate agent said that it was a separate room, and she would be able to lock it, so there was no cause for alarm. John told him that he would ring the estate agent back and rang Lynda and told her.

"John, what happens, happens, just because she is a woman doesn't mean that you have to bed her, you may not even want to, and as we told you, even if you did, the villagers would be pleased for you. Don't be so Victorian, it's the early nineties we are almost in the twenty first century, you lived through the sixties free love and all that. I missed out on that period," Lynda said ruefully.

"Ok, ok, I'll ring the estate agent tomorrow, then and tell him to send her over."

John rang the estate agent the following morning and told him to send her over to view the place, it was arranged for six that evening, John said that it would be dark then, but the estate agent told him to relax.

Six on the dot he heard a car pull up outside, and looked out of the window, to see a woman struggling up the drive, not that it was up hill, but she was so obese that she didn't walk but rolled, waddling from side to side, panting she rang the doorbell.

"Miss Evans I presume," John said as he opened the door.

"Yes Mr Alker, wow what a walk from the drive to the front door wow, I need to sit down," she said, John showed her into the lounge.

"The room is it far; I have a bad chest and can't walk too far."

"Well it is at the rear of the house, and the stairs are longer than usual, because of the high ceiling, perhaps you should reconsider the accommodation, if it were a struggle to get from the car to the front door," John said hoping that she would agree.

"I've come, so I might as well see the room," she replied, still panting.

"Ok, get your breath back first, what made you decide to move out here?"

"Fresh air, to help my lungs, the fresh country air, but the smells, they are nasty especially just now, I don't know why, but there was a horrible smell as I entered the village."

"That, oh that's Andrew, he's been muck spreading, normal for this time of the year, he will leave that field fallow and make hay from it, then put crops in next year, where do you come from then if I may ask?"

"Just outside London, the company I work for built a new plant on the industrial site near here and I asked to be transferred for my health, and they agreed, I'm a shop floor supervisor, next step is management," she said proudly.

John looked at her and wondered how she managed to do her job, especially if she had to walk round the shop floor, to ensure that the work was being done properly. He asked some more questions about her job, and found out that it was a firm that made clothing and her job was to lead a section of women. Helping and training them in the machinery they were using, and then to watch them, and correct as needed, so she would need to walk, and again it struck John that she was not the most agile of women.

Billy arrived as John was showing her upstairs, he said that he would put the kettle on John gave him a look of disdain to which Billy smiled, she said that she wouldn't be able to cope with the stairs, so would not be taking the room. John was relieved, he could see himself having to help her up to her room, and if she fell, then there was no way that he would be able to lift her, he would need a crane to do that. Once she had left, John and Billy talked about her and her size.

"Bad chest, I didn't think it was that bad," Billy joked.

"All fat Billy, like the rest of her, bad chest, try being almost twenty stone overweight; lose a lot of that and she would be able to breath a lot better. The stairs groaned, when she stepped on them, they actually creaked. Anyway she said that she wouldn't be taking the room, thank goodness."

For the next week, a stream of potential lodgers arrived at the vicarage, one was a young lad barely twenty who wanted the room but couldn't afford it. John didn't fancy becoming a pseudo parent, luckily the lad decided to rent a cheaper place. A Business man or so he said, but John had his doubts from the manner of his transport and dress, he guessed that the man was more of a con merchant, if reputable then more of a representative or salesman. There was a young lady a bright person, cheerful and intelligent who called, and John for all his forebodings previously was interested in allowing her to stay. A rather pretty young woman, slim, tall, elegantly dressed of about twenty five, dark hair in loose curls, and her face was made-up with taste, emphasising her attributes. Her other attributes were well defined as well, which Billy was quick to point out, once she had left, but it was not to be. She misunderstood what was up for let, and wanted the whole property, but that didn't stop her from staying for a cup of tea and biscuits when John offered them. John was becoming disillusioned by the end of the week, he had shown several people the room, and either they did not suit him, or they didn't think the country smelled as much as it did. City dwellers that wanted the country life without all that made it what it was.

Saturday dawned and the telephone rang it was the estate agent again, with yet another potential lodger, a man in his thirties, who had just started work at the laboratory on the technology and science estate, next to the industrial estate. Would it be possible for him to view in half an hour? John, always an early riser was dressed and said that the place needed a clean, but if the man would accept it as it was, then he had no objection to him coming to view the room.

Just over the half hour later, a car pulled up and a young man got out, he strode up the drive with confidence, and his ring was a firm ring, unlike some of the pathetic people, John had been forced to deal with during the week.

John opened the door and invited him in, "Hello John Alker," he said holding out his hand in greeting.

"Hello Alan Winston, pleased to meet you," the man said.

John liked him, a firm handshake, confidence and manners oozed from him, John showed him the room and then they settled in the lounge with a pot of tea and three cups, Billy was due. John had told Alan that a friend would be joining them soon.

"So Alan what is it that you do then," John asked as he poured the tea?

"I am the new head of the science facility, my discipline is Quantum Physics."

"What do they do there, if you are allowed to tell us," John asked?

"It is secret, but basically, I am dealing with atoms and their power, we know that when the atom splits there is tremendous energy released, and we are studying how we can harness that energy, we already use the energy in atomic power stations, but we are left with radioactive waste. Here, we are trying to find a way of harnessing that energy, without the waste product being left. It's very interesting, a way of creating perpetual energy, which was never thought possible until now, we have our sceptics that say it's not possible, but I believe it is, that is why I got the job, apart from the fact that I devised the theorem."

"How do you do that, do you split the atom?"

"No, that requires energy, it's difficult to explain, we collide atoms, this splits the atom, which in itself then creates a chain reaction splitting more atoms, and this is where we derive our energy. Once split they are channelled into another chamber, as it were, that is where we reattach them. Then we can split them again, over and over. To join them surprisingly enough, we have to get them to collide again, but that is a very simplified description of the system."

"I do understand, even though I don't, no that's wrong I follow, but don't fully understand. If it takes energy to split the atom, then where does the energy come from that you derive from the system?"

"From the second and subsequent collision, and it takes an equal amount of energy to re-join the atoms but again they now generate their own energy after the first joining, with our system."

"Fascinating, I am still lost, but I hope it works for you, how much will the cost of electricity go up, by with this method?"

"It won't, it will come down by about fifty per cent, unless the moguls get greedy," there was an irony to Alan's voice.

"Well to change the subject; I am happy for you to move in, if you are happy, then when would be convenient?"

"I am very happy, it's a lovely room and big enough for me to do some work at home, you won't see much of me, say this Saturday, if that's alright with you?"

John agreed, and they chatted for a while then Alan left just as Billy arrived.

"Another dead duck is it, I think you frighten them off deliberately," Billy said as if dejected at the loss of another potential lodger

144

"That's where you would be wrong Billy, he moves in on Saturday," John said smiling.

That week went quickly with all the phone calls John got and, the work in the garden preparing the ground for the year's vegetables.

Lynda rang to tell him that her friend Glynn was very interested in testing the bones to prove that the bodies were from another period in history. Especially seeing as the bodies were actually, from the future, well at the time of burial they were. He felt that it would be interesting and a challenge for him. Andrew rang he was pleased to hear from Lynda that John had a lodger, and showed interest in the scientific approach they were now looking into, he commented that if they could prove that the bodies were buried in time, then the authorities would have to open at least an investigation, if not a full murder enquiry. Sandra also expressed her delight at the new lodger, even if she didn't understand what he did for a living, but liked the idea of cheaper electricity.

Saturday arrived as did Alan with a small van, loaded with his belongings, John was surprised at the size of the van just for clothing, which was what he thought Alan would be bringing with him, and the room was fully furnished.

"Mr Alker I'm sorry, perhaps I didn't fully explain myself, when I said that I would be working at home, or bringing work home with me, I meant just that. In my work, there is a lot of number crunching, complicated numbers and equations, and, for that I need a computer, there are only two suit cases and a couple of bags in there, of personal items, the rest is my computer. Large but it doesn't use a lot of electricity once I have booted it up, and obviously the company will compensate you for the energy I use. I presume being as well organised as you are you pay by direct debit monthly, so it will be very simple to calculate any extra power I use, and I will pay you, and claim it back from the company."

"That isn't the problem, but I appreciate the offer, if the use is excessive, I wondered where you would fit it in the room, there isn't much room left in there for extra furniture."

"It will fit next to the bed, I will need to rearrange the furniture a bit, but that isn't problem for me, as long as it isn't for you?"

"No, the room is yours; please arrange it as you wish would you like a hand carrying it in?"

"I can manage thank you, I will set it up as I bring it in, to save having to try and work in a mess, so I am better on my own. I have the van for the weekend and if you don't mind, can I leave it parked in the drive where it will be safe, my computer is very expensive and some items are very hard to get?"

"Please do, I am not going out in the car this week end; come on Billy, let Alan get himself organised, and we will plant the cabbages, unless you have other ideas?"

"What's a computer," Billy asked?

"An electronic abacus and data, information, storage piece of equipment," John said smiling, he hadn't used one, but they were being talked about when he retired, and Andy had got one in his office, which he had, shown John.

"Hey? Electronic abacus, what the hell is an abacus?"

"The Chinese invented it for counting, ten rows of ten beads so, I'll tell you whilst we work come on; or we'll never get finished."

John and Billy set to work in the garden; John explained what an abacus was and how it worked to Billy whilst they worked. Sandra had made a stew for them, which John heated up and then called out to Alan that lunch was ready, he joined them, and they chatted generally.

John always inquisitive asked him where he used to live. He told John that he was born in the Manchester area, in a place called Wigan, just north of Manchester and that he went to Manchester University, then on to Cambridge for a second degree, he was forty five, and never been married, and as far as he was aware no children; they all laughed at his joke. Girls got in the way of his studying and career dreams, which were now fulfilled, but that was just the start, his work now was what drove him, and gave him the most satisfaction. He aspired to be an Einstein; he admired several physicists, and hoped that, in time, his work would be recognised, and brought into fruition.

"I have rearranged the room slightly, and started to bring in my computer, and as I bring in the parts I am assembling it. I am building my computer a lot quicker than I expected, with a bit of luck I will empty the van tonight, and be able to boot the computer up tomorrow, and then I can get it set up and remove any gremlins that have crept in so that by tomorrow night, I will be settled in."

"Good, I'm glad you are getting on so well, sure we can't help you?"

"Sure how many vegetables do you plant; it seems a large area of the garden?"

"We sell them to raise funds for the local hospital, it is only a cottage hospital so needs all the help we can give it to stop them from closing it down," John explained.

"I wish you well then, is it just you and Billy who work on the garden, it seems to me a mammoth task?"

"Yes, to an outsider that is one not used to such a large garden, I can imagine it would appear so, but we are used to it now, even though we are not as young as we were, and we are slowing down quite a bit, so need to work longer, less time for the pub," John said joking.

"Don't you believe him, we still get our refreshment when we have finished, and can he down the pints after a hard day in the garden, no clack, he downs the first one in one," Billy said.

Alan laughed at the face Billy pulled as he showed his shock at the speed John downed the first pint.

"A misspent youth," John said joking.

Alan had finished settling in that day and joined them for a drink, Billy told him to watch John as he drank his first drink, to emphasise that he wasn't joking. John didn't let him down, and drank it in one, then asked when Billy was going to buy the next round as he was thirsty. Billy indicated to the bar man that John wanted another pint, and a fresh pint appeared in front of John. Alan tried to explain to Billy what he did for a living, and how a computer helped because of the complicated and extensive numbers he needed to crunch. Unfortunately, it went over Billy's head he kept asking questions all the way through Alan's explanation, until Billy gave up none the wiser or so it seemed, until the following day, when Billy suggested that John get a computer for the case. It would help them, if only to store the information, John was shocked he didn't think Billy had understood, but evidently he had, and was just pretending that he didn't understand.

"John," there was some hesitance to Billy's word, "we are looking for a very intelligent scientific based person from the Manchester area, or am I jumping to conclusions?"

"Billy he's a very nice man, but he does fit the profile, the murderer will also be a very nice man, which is how he gets the women to go out of their safe zone with him. I know they want the money, but they are not stupid, and are careful with whom they go, to some degree. So our killer will also be a nice guy, charming even. I came to the same conclusion, but I am also afraid of frightening him off now that we have a decent lodger, without a good reason, and at the moment, all we have is a coincidence. I will watch, and if he goes missing when a woman disappears, then it is more than coincidence, until then I will just enjoy his company and use his brains; also we need facts, evidence. The work he does is linked in some way to what we understand as time travel, or that is the assumption; remember that programme Quantum Leap well he is working in Quantum Physics as well, another coincidence," John said as a question?

The next few weeks went as normal, Alan settled in well, he didn't join them very much for a drink, but usually about once a week he did. The vegetables were growing, and there was a green garden as the sprouting vegetables made for the sky, wicker canes in an inverted 'V' shape went up, with a top cane to support the peas and beans they had planted. The weather was being kind to them and hadn't rained much, which now brought its own problems in that John and Billy had to water the plants after finishing the weeding and tending. Lynda had visited and told John that his lodger was lovely and how lucky he was to have such a genuine person as a lodger, she had heard as he had, terrifying stories about lodgers.

Andrew also visited one weekend and again said how nice Alan was, this pleased John but also brought its own fear, that he was fitting the profile more and more. There hadn't been a missing woman reported, and he had been in his room most of the time working.

From what John could get out of him, the work was going according to plan, and he was making progress. They had successfully completed the first trial run, and now Alan would need to evaluate the results. If the results were as good as he expected, then he would need to complete another trial run.

Sandra still came with Jenny, to clean and cook meals for John and Billy. Billy stayed each day for his dinner, they usually had sandwiches for lunch, and Sandra or Jenny would tut jokingly, and then make the sandwiches for them. Lynda was having problems getting a judge to sign the exhumation order, which was now delaying them. John as pragmatic as usual, just said that what will be, will be, and they must find a way around the problem. John's contacts were all retired now as he was which meant that they would be of no use.

Andrew had lost most of his London contacts over the years whilst he was in Manchester, and the one's he had in Manchester would not be able to help, the new Chief Super was more interested in saving money than catching criminals John had commented sarcastically.

Six weeks after Alan had moved in, there was another missing person reported. She was found in nineteen thirty two, and went missing three days prior to John being told, again it was an old colleague who told him. The authorities were not interested in John's ideas or theories, so it was down to the people who still worked in the force, after John had retired, and they were now getting few, and far between, she had disappeared from Reading. William, an ex-colleague of Lynda's, sent the report to Lynda, after he had spoken to John, asking her to bring it down at the weekend, so that they could read it.

John was anxious now there had been a gap, which was unusual, unless the murderer had something else to do that stopped him from being active, but what worried John the most, was that the crime had been committed in a new town, why? Had he moved, was that why he had been inactive for the last few weeks? If so where was he now? John ever suspicious now began to wonder where Alan was that day; they had agreed that he fits the profile of the murderer, location, age, and his work. John would only find out if he could be the person they were looking for, when he got the file of the missing person, and the murder file, which was why he had asked William to contact Lynda to see if the file had now appeared, and to bring it with her when she came down at the weekend.

John fussed about all the next day, anxious to get his hands on the file; Lynda had rung him to confirm that there was now a file in records from nineteen thirty two, and it was the same woman who had gone missing from Reading. The date of her disappearance was on the Monday of that week, and reported on the Wednesday, William had rung John on Thursday, so John didn't have to wait too long before he could read the file for himself. The oddities picked up on, where in place at the present day, as John had expected, they no-longer played that important a role in the investigation now, because they already knew that the murderer was burying the bodies in time. Vague memories came to mind as he remembered his father talking to his mother about a woman who had been murdered, a cruel and vicious crime and that it had a sexual theme, at the time John didn't understand what he was talking about, but now he knew only too well what his father had been saying. As a sergeant in the force at the time of the murder, he would have been given details, so that he was alert to the situation, and he had made house to house calls during the investigation, but unsurprisingly it was to no avail, John knew why, neither the victim nor the murderer was alive then.

John had started early in the garden so that he would have time to study the new files when Lynda arrived, now he paced up and down like an expectant father waiting for her knock. Billy brought in a new pot of tea and asked if he wanted to go back into the garden, there was still some work they could be doing. John had said that he didn't, he couldn't concentrate on the work, and he was too worked up, why was it taking so long for Lynda to come?

"John it is only ten o'clock, she will just have left, she likes to lie in on her day off," he said.

"Not today she won't, she will be up and out by eight I bet you."

"Even so, it will be nearer eleven before she gets here, shall I make space on the boards for the new file pictures?"

"Yes you can if you like; did you see Alan on Monday night?"

"Yes, I have already told you that, I saw him at eight, nine thirty, and I could hear his music all the time, he was right here, he even came down and made us a cup of tea at about half eight, we left at nine thirty as usual for the pub, so I didn't see him after that."

"So, it can't be him then can it. I must say that I am pleased, I like the guy, and I am disappointed as well, if it were him, we would have got our man, but as you said, I saw him that night also."

"John you're wearing a hole in the carpet, sit down and have another cup of tea Lynda will arrive when she arrives."

"You're right of course, but I can't help it, I was never like this when I was in the force. I was as pragmatic as you are now; I seem to go from ill at ease to panic almost, where the hell is she?"

Billy handed John another cup of tea, he took it without looking and started to drink from the cup then put it down and started to pace again, his hand on his chin as he thought. Billy could only watch as he paced up and down chin in hand one moment and then staring out of the window as if that would make her appear, he knew it was illogical but couldn't help himself.

At last Billy heard Lynda's car pull up, he had decided to go outside, instead of watching John pace up and down. Lynda smiled at him, and Billy opened the back door of the house for her, and followed her. Just inside, she stopped and turned to Billy looked at his muddy boots and waited, till he realised that he had to take them off, her scowl said everything he needed to know, and obeyed.

In the lounge, where John was still pacing, but not as much, she handed him the files, and he quickly opened them, eager to read the file and find out about the missing woman. Lynda and Billy, who had joined him after they had made another pot of tea, sat and looked at John as he read the file.

"I agree Lynda it's our man again, but why new territory, that I find very odd, they like to feel safe, so tend to stay in one particular area to find their victims. He has moved a couple of hundred miles, totally new territory, very odd," John said shaking his head in wonderment.

"Yes Sir, I agree it's very odd, I believe he moved addresses, for some reason, a new job perhaps, and it took him a month or so to settle in and find the women he wanted, because he is being very specific about the age and colouring. A blonde has hurt him very much, and now that we have the missing person's files, we know their ages, most are within a year of the date either side, it is as if with each year, he advances the age of his victims. Someone born in nineteen fifty died in nineteen eighty, thirty years old, so in eighty one, his victim was thirty one."

"I had noticed that, so something happened to him when the girl, woman was a specific age, or he was, and it's on the anniversary, except he murders in between as well, so a weekly anniversary, no monthly, hum," John began to think, his hand on his chin again and pacing, "Lynda give me the dates of the missing women, is there a link there?"

"Yes, there is the tenth of each month, give or take a day or two, allowing for them not being reported on the day they went missing."

"Hum, interesting, and last Monday was the tenth, so we have until the tenth of next month, to find him, or another woman will fall victim to him," John said, as if to no-one in particular, as he continued to pace the length of the room.

"Sir I find it confusing, er, odd, how come he always has a victim on the tenth, what does he do, book them in advance, if so then he must be out of the property twice. Or, it has just struck me, why not go back in time, he buries the bodies in time, so why can't he go back in time or forward for that matter, he can go any time he wants, any day or night, and pick one up," Lynda said.

John stared at her, his eyes wide open; he hadn't thought of that, this was an all-new ball park. The day or time of day didn't matter, Alan was out of the house now, was he at work, or killing someone, how would they know? He stopped himself making an assumption that was wrong, he needed the evidence, something that convinced him that Alan was the killer, there must be several dozen men who fit the profile; Alan was convenient because of his close proximity.

Billy had been listening to them and watching John as the light dawned on the now seemingly impossible task; the time, the day, no-longer was important, the killer could carry out his deed whenever he chose. He could be at work and killing someone at the very same time, hundreds of miles apart. Billy shook his head as the impossibility dawned; he got up and said that he would make some sandwiches for their lunch and left John and Lynda.

The sun was out it was a warm April day and they decided to have lunch in the garden, John had more space to pace up and down as he tried to work out how on earth, they would ever catch the murderer. For every killing, he would have a solid alibi, one that was irrefutable; they would never be able to break him under questioning, in court he would be able to bring several genuine witnesses, to prove that he was not even in the town or county, when the crime happened. They discussed all the possibilities, all the probabilities, but even after two hours they were no closer to a way to prove, not only that a crime had been committed, but then that the person they had accused, was guilty.

Lynda's phone rang John looked confused as he heard music coming from her pocket.

"My mobile phone Sir, surely, no not out here in the sticks you won't have heard them."

"Mobile phones yes, we have heard about them, Steve has one, but they are very expensive to run aren't they?"

"Not now Sir, they are becoming more and more popular, smaller and the coverage is far better, I am surprised that I have reception here, however, excuse me. Hi Glynn what's the news,——, oh, that's good this morning great, when can you start,——, Monday and, oh great nineteen thirty two,——, oh,' Lynda said, she seemed disappointed, 'I see yes, I will discuss it with John, thanks anyway, even so it will be a help, bye."

"Well, what have we to discuss?"

"Glynn has received confirmation this morning that he can exhume the bodies he wanted for his thesis, and it includes our nineteen thirty two woman. The disappointment is that he will not be able to prove that she was not born in that era, because she could have been born in say France, in the south where the air was not as bad. There will not be the same chemicals in the victim's body that would have been found if she were from London or Manchester, but there may be other missing chemicals that he would expect to find in a woman of that area. It's not as conclusive as we had hoped, but I still think it is worth trying."

"I agree the chemicals in the bones of a person from the south of France at that time, would be different from a woman born in the north of England in the present day."

"Yes Sir they would, but that will not prove that she was buried in time, which is what we were hoping for, it will be another month before he has the results of his tests, he will have to do tests on several bodies to ensure that his findings are conclusive enough."

"Fine we will have to wait and hope for the best. There may be enough to convince a judge or Chief Super, that there is an on-going case that needs investigating."

John was awoken early a couple of weeks after the meeting with Lynda, to the sound of Alan vomiting, he got up to see if there was anything he could do to help, but Alan said it was just a stomach bug, and he would be alright in a day or so. John went back to his bedroom, deciding to get up, it was only seven in the morning, but the sun was up and promising to be a nice day after it had been raining all the previous day. He went down stairs and again heard Alan go to his bathroom, when Alan came down John asked if he needed the doctor, Alan said that he didn't; John looked at Alan, his usual bright eyes were deadened looking opaque and half shut.

"Are you sure you don't need a doctor, you look terrible, why not take the day off, go back to bed, I'll call the doctor for you," John had seen similar symptoms in Jane a few months before she had died and became anxious for Alan's well-being.

"Sure John thanks, but I have a lot on my mind at the moment at work, and I am pushing myself, so I will look rough, but honestly it's nothing just a bug, I'll be alright."

John let the subject drop and carried on eating his breakfast, but noting that Alan didn't eat, just a cup of coffee, and then he was off to work early. That evening John had prepared dinner for them both, he sometimes cooked an evening meal for them, but Alan again didn't want anything to eat, and just picked at the food out of courtesy to John for cooking the meal. John told him that he was not doing himself any favours, by working so hard. Then thought about the times he had missed meals, been late for dinner, or not arrived home till the early hours after watching someone they suspected, or interrogating a suspect. John told Billy of his concerns for Alan, Billy just said that he was old enough to decide for himself and for John not to worry.

After dinner John, Billy and Alan, who had eaten very little, went into the lounge John, and Billy had a coffee each, which Billy had made, Alan just had a glass of water.

"Alan, I have been watching Quantum Leap again, do you think time travel will ever be possible," Billy asked?

"Now there is a question, personally no I don't, but there are some who think it will, and good luck to them. Time Billy, is what we call an intangible, it doesn't exist as a physical item, like a chair, you can't get hold of it, but it obviously does exist. That is why we have days, hours and minutes. In prehistoric times they just had seasons, moons, so they would say that happened, last moon, or last quarter moon, for the last month. Thursday is named after the Roman god Thor, the Romans inventing if you like our current understanding of time and our calendar and the months named after Gods, also Emperors like July after Julius Caesar. Why is a chair, called a chair? It's just a name for an object, yet someone gave it that name for a reason, the reason probably lost in the annals of time."

"Oh, so if we can travel in time, can we see the future and find out what will happen?"

"No, the future hasn't happened yet, and may not happen, what if you died tonight, but this evening you travelled into tomorrow what would you see?"

"Good question I would be dead so I wouldn't see anything, yet I would be because at that point in time I wouldn't be dead, or would I?"

"See what I mean, there is a theory that if you did travel into the future, then you would only see what you expected to see, because you wouldn't be able to allow for the anomalies that happen the little twists of fate that affect all of us and create history."

"Hum, interesting, but we can, or some people think that we will be able to travel into the past, because that has already happened," John joined the topic.

"Yes," Alan said, but with a big question mark over the comment, he stood up and walked over to the window then turned back, "by going back in time, you would recreate history, what happened would not be the same, because you were not meant to be there at that point in time, and now you were, so there would be a change. Wouldn't it be great if we could go back in time and kill Hitler that would stop the Second World War wouldn't it? Now there's a question, would it, or would Goebbels or Himmler then be a different Hitler, and win the war. Who is to say that a different leader would be better, and if it wasn't Hitler then there would be a different leader wouldn't there? So by killing Hitler you have changed history, but would it be for the better? What if you went back in history and saved a great mind say like Madam Currie, you now know that radiation kills, so we go back in time and tell her, now what happens?"

"So we will never be able to go back in time then?"

"I wouldn't say that, but as a window into the past ok, but to physically go back and interfere with history, would be totally unacceptable, you could and would do untold damage to the time line, perhaps bring about the demise of mankind. There has to be serious discussions before anyone is allowed to go back in time. To have the means is one thing, but to, actually do it, is a totally different kettle of fish."

"Sorry you are confusing me, you believe in time that we will be able to go back in time, sorry that came out rather confusingly," Billy asked?

"I am sure of it, but whether it would be wise or not, is a different matter, but we will never be able to go forward, there is no history till it has happened. If you'll excuse me, I am feeling rather tired it's been a long, hard day today."

John and Billy said goodnight, and then left for the pub, John again expressed his concerns for Alan, and he said that his fatigue reminded John of Jane when she was ill. Billy couldn't disagree, but kept his council not wanting to upset John.

Sundays were special days for John, which was when he put the case to one side. Even when Lynda came down with work, a file or information for them, they kept, Sunday's for the garden, or selling their produce from their makeshift stall. Lynda usually cooked dinner for them; if she wasn't there, then it was to the pub for dinner. Alan had also joined in, in the Sunday ritual, helping in the garden far more enjoyable and healthy than down at the gym, as he used to do, he had said the first Sunday he had joined them. The Sunday following their discussion on time travel, Alan had, had to work, which was unusual, because he usually worked a five day week, with weekends off. Saturday he spent in his room on his computer, but Sunday he was with them.

Several points worried John about Alan, he obviously had a very good job, earning more than Jane, and he had, yet he drove an old car, and rented a room to live in, why when he could easily afford a house, and not a small house. With the salary, he would be getting he could afford a very nice house, three bedrooms, etcetera? His fatigue was another concern of John's, and recently he had been questioning the electricity bills, something he had never done before they were as always, ever since he had arrived, apart from the first bill, which as Alan had said would be excessive, after that Alan usually paid around fifteen pounds per quarter. Subtle but noticeable personality changes were taking place, he had never been slow in paying for a round, but recently he wavered, held back as if he were reluctant to spend the money.

Reading was an hour's drive or so away, John decided that seeing as the murderer had found a new hunting ground then so should he, and suggested to Billy that they survey the red light district, as they had done in Manchester, on Friday night. Billy agreed, but telling John that he needed to be careful, he didn't have any support in that town, and not to get arrested again, John laughed, but also realised that Billy was right, they would be alone on this one.

It was a bright evening, the moon and stars were all out, a nice, clear early summer's night. John toured round in his car, trying to find the area; he had made some enquiries from Lynda, who also didn't like the idea of him going into a red light district with Billy and no back up. But John was determined to catch the murderer, and this was his only chance seeing as the hunting ground had changed. It wasn't until ten thirty that they finally were happy that they were in the right area, and John found a parking place, and then they walked to the street. John used the missing woman as a starting point, and after buying time with two women, he showed them her photo. They told him that she was, or had been working that area and that his best option was to go to the phone box at the far end of the street and ask for Lucy, as long as she wasn't high, then she would be able to help them. John decided that seeing as one of the women was blonde, he would tell her to be extra careful, and the reason, stating that if she didn't believe him, fine, all he was doing was warning her to be extra careful when a man in his early forties, smart, probably good looking and well educated, approached her.

"Better, to be busy than dead," he said warning her.

They moved on, walking slowly, looking into the doorways and around the street lamps. John counted a dozen or so women, he wondered if it were a quiet night, with so many on the street, being late in the evening he expected them to be busier. They spoke to a few of the women as they passed, two of them told John that Lucy was her friend, and to speak to her. The telephone box was empty, no-one was stood by it, they decided to wait, and Billy lit his pipe and puffed on it, billows of smoke poured from the bowl as he got the pipe going.

"Waiting,—puff, puff,—long are we,—puff, puff," Billy asked?

"Good grief Billy they'll send the fire brigade in a minute seeing all that smoke, ahem," John coughed to emphasise the point.

"Typical of a non-smoker, always nagging, I like it, real taste this shag has."

"I don't care what you call it; I've seen steam engines produce less smoke than that."

"You need a woman, to stop your nagging, she'll do it all for you."

They laughed and settled in for a bit of a wait, John took the opportunity to ring Lynda who had decided to work a night shift. She was trying to get her paperwork up to date before the reviews, and keep tabs on a case that was reaching a conclusion.

"You are what!"

"We are standing near a telephone box, waiting for a woman, kinky isn't?"

"Kinky, that's a new word for you John, are you at last joining the twentieth century," Lynda said joking?

"No, dear Lynda, I am definitely not, but that word fits exactly how I feel, I have never waited to procure a woman before, and I find it disconcerting."

"Oh, what about Manchester then, how was that different?"

"I was conducting an investigation, now we are being ogled by the women, and the men who are driving past, and I can guess what they are thinking."

"I see," she laughed, "Well Sir, who but a dirty old man would wait for a particular woman, when there is a street full of them?"

"I'll remember that tomorrow when you arrive; oh that reminds me, any luck with your pathologist friend Glynn?"

"Yes, he has confirmed that she was not living around that time, either here, that is in Manchester, or London, nor was she living in any of the European countries, he found traces of a substance, or element, in her bones, that was not in the air at that particular point in time, anywhere. The substance was only found in the air following Windscale and other radiation leaks, the air is now higher in radiation than in those days, and that is what he found a higher than acceptable level of radiation for that period.

She lived in the fifties, and he would guess nearer to Sellafield, formally Windscale than Manchester or London. She would only have been a child and may have been brought up there. Here, goes nothing, she had a high level of Iodine one three one, so she was in or near Windscale, when the fire broke, out in nineteen fifty seven. Iodine one three one."

"Peep, peep, peep," the phone said, John fumbled for more change but had none and put the receiver down.

"She has some great news," John said excitedly to Billy.

"Oh yes, what is it?"

"I don't know, the pips went, and I didn't have any more change, and stupidly I didn't give her the phone number to ring back in that eventuality. Oh, I am kicking myself now for that. But something about radioactive Iodine, which was found, in the nineteen thirty two, woman's bone, to have that, she must have been, or lived near to Windscale when it caught fire, in nineteen fifty seven that makes her about forty three, just the age we would expect for the year she was murdered. That reminds me, I need a card for Alan, it's his birthday next week he is forty three."

"Look I've waited long enough, now piss off, I don't do old men."

The woman who spoke was about five six, medium build, with large breasts, which she used to their best, showing a cleavage John didn't think possible. A trim waist, not that John could see that much of it below her breasts, but above she had quite a pretty face, small round, chubby you might say, with blonde hair, hanging half way down her back, she was a natural blonde, that much was evident.

"Need a handkerchief," Billy offered to stop her constant sniffing?

"Look I'll call my man over if you don't bugger off, I'm expecting someone."

"Ok, we'll be quick, it's about your friend Alexandria, we believe that she has been murdered, I am an ex-policeman, and because, well it's too hard to explain here and now, but for reasons, I can't go into, the police won't investigate the case.

Let me show you a photo, there is that your friend," John said handing her a copy of the nineteen thirty two victim?

"Y, well the picture is old, and the light dim, it could be, but she had black hair, jet black and would never dye it blonde, just as I would never dye mine black. Now piss off, if you frighten him away being here, it'll cost you five hundred for the night, which is what he is giving me. He wanted me, but I was ill and Alexandria came instead, she rang to say he didn't show, and then she disappeared, that night, now you are pushing it, go on fuck off," she said now annoyed and waved her arms at them shooing them away.

"Hello, hello, what have we here," a male voice said behind them, "curb crawling are we, I have been watching you, and now you have upset our Lucy."

"You sound like an old TV cop, Dixon of Dock Green, and we are leaving, why," Billy said?

"It pays to have a sense of humour in this job, now I could book you two for soliciting, curb crawling, but I don't want to give you a bad name at your time of life, so why don't you just run along?"

"CID, or vice, I am investigating a series of disappearances, and a woman fitting the criteria disappeared from here, all I am after is information about the woman, she was working this street the night she disappeared, so a logical place to start don't you think," John said calmly?

"A private dick hey, we don't see many of them round here, a bit old for it aren't you, and what qualifications do you have?"

"My card, ex-Chief Inspector Alker of New Scotland Yard, murder squad, and the woman for your information is dead, but you will not investigate it as a murder, because there isn't a body, and there never will be. That woman, the one on cocaine, she is in grave danger, grave danger, she fits the profile of the victims to a 'T'. We can stop overnight and talk in the morning, or talk now, but it will take quite a long time, I am sure that I can now convince an officer say, but not the powers that be, there is no solid evidence of my theories."

"Why not now, I am off duty, and doing a favour for an old friend, you know her as well, Lynda Summers, something about burying bodies in time, it's a debt she called in, I don't really know what she was on about, except that very soon one of the prostitutes from this area will disappear, never to be seen again. So could I patrol the area for a couple of evenings till midnight say and look out for two silly old men acting strange, stupidly I agreed? Oh sorry DS Hammond, and yes I do work vice as well, which amused Lynda, tonight instead of arresting them, I am looking after them like a pimp, but without the money," he said laughing.

"Let's talk, I have in my car several photos, of missing women, including the one from here Alexandria Karlov, I believe, and a matching photograph of a dead woman from nineteen thirty two who you would swear was the same woman. The photos of the dead women go as far back as eighteen seventy two and beyond, but we stopped there. One or two, yes I agree could be looking a like, but ten all identical, never? I have also learned today, so I have nothing in writing at the moment, that Iodine one three one, a radioactive chemical has been found in the bones of our nineteen thirty two victim, that can only have come from when Windscale caught fire, in nineteen fifty seven, don't you think that it is very strange, to say the least, that something from the middle of the fifties, has been found in what was living tissue in the thirties?"

"Interesting, to say the least, shall we go then, it's almost time for me to go home anyway, I do need some sleep each night, to be on my best form at work tomorrow."

John led the way back to his car, he got in the front seat, and Billy sat next to him and Hammond in the back, next to John's brief case. John told Hammond to open it and look inside. He took the photos out and started to look at them, and then put them into pairs nodding his head all the time.

"Ok, you do have something here, an anomaly, it is very unusual to have so many women as victims who look exactly like the missing women, and you say that none of these women have been found?"

"No, not a one, plus as I said, there is now the Iodine one three one, which proves when and where she lived for a period. Dead bodies buried under six feet of earth, two hundred and fifty miles away, do not absorb radiation; it is absorbed through the Thyroid, soft tissue, which rots far more quickly than bone, and would from nineteen thirty two to nineteen fifty seven have rotted away."

"Ok, ok, I have to agree, what can I do?"

"Nothing, that is the problem, the body usually turns up before the missing person file, because of the wait before a missing adult is recognised as such. I need to have the missing person file as soon as they go missing, even their family can wait a day, before reporting it, so it will never happen. What I would say is keep an eye on blondes in particular, the woman that disappeared last month from here had black hair, so he dyed her hair blonde, he was stuck; he wanted Lucy. He had actually booked her, and she was ill, so she sent Alexandria; she was a year older than he would usually go for, Lucy is the right age, and colour, watch her in particular, he will be back on the tenth of next month."

"I will do my best, I will try and get some help, but I don't have much in the form of reason for a full investigation, I would need your file, and that report about the Iodine."

"I can't help you there, I don't have the report as yet, but I will get Lynda to fax it to you. Billy on Monday we are going to see Alexandria's mother and ask her if they ever lived by Windscale, just a bit more proof if they did, for when I go to see the Chief Super, or the Commissioner, I have to get it opened up as a murder enquiry, I now have some decent proof."

Lynda came down with the file and the report, John read it with interest, it was conclusive enough for him, but then he knew the whole story, and so it would seem conclusive. When he put his Chief Inspectors hat on, what he had to show, and there was doubt, enough, with cost constraints to stop a full enquiry.

"Dam, dam, dam, I was so sure that it would be conclusive, but with just one woman, it could be said that she was near a source of Iodine one three one, I need to be sure that the only source is from a manufactured radiation, or a by-product of processed plutonium, or uranium, whatever it is they make, dam, dam, dam."

"It is uranium fuel Sir," Lynda said calmly.

"Pardon?"

"Fuel for the reactor, Sir it is uranium, from that they make atomic bombs and fuel for nuclear reactors, I am no physicist, and don't know if Iodine one three one is a by-product or waste, or what, but that is where it comes from."

"Very good Lynda, so it is part of the process and would not be found naturally is that correct?"

"Hum, that, I can't honestly say, but perhaps you could bluff it, and say that it is. How well informed on enriching uranium do you think the Chief Super is, Sir?"

"You," John shook his head, "cheek, I think you have it all, as well as all the gall, and not as well informed as you appear to be. There is only one way to find out, on Monday in Manchester, can you get me her phone number so that I can ring ahead. We will go by train and stay one night, then on Wednesday I will find out whether, or not, he knows as much as you don't, won't I," John said with a grin.

Monday John and Billy left with Lynda for the train; she dropped them off at the station then carried on to work. She had rung Manchester and managed to con the officer to give her the phone number of Alexandria's mother. Lynda then rang her to arrange the meeting, saying that John was a private investigator and that he was looking into several cases of missing women. She said that he would like to visit her and ask her a few questions, to see if there was a link between the missing women. Alexandria's mother was pleased that her daughter had not been totally forgotten, unlike the police who seemed to be doing nothing, and grabbed at the chance to assist him.

From the train station, John and Billy took a taxi, once seated in Mrs Karlov's lounge with a cup of tea and some cake, John asked some basic, friendly questions, to ease into the one he really wanted to ask. Mrs Karlov looked surprised when he asked if they had ever lived near to Windscale.

"Well, yes, how did you know that, of course from the records I presume, been doing your homework," she said answering her own question.

John looked at her and wondered if she should know the truth, and decided against it.

"Where exactly did you live, why did you move, and when, if you don't mind me asking Mrs Karlov?'

"Oh let me see, there was that fire, and we didn't feel safe, Colin my husband set about trying to find work away from there, it took him several months, yes, it was the summer, no, Autumn, yes, November of nineteen fifty s, no, eight, that's right yes eight. Alexandria was nine, when we moved, and the house well it was right close to the reactor plant. Colin said that they were making bombs there, and if one went off then we would all be dead, so we moved away. Alexandria was offered a job in Reading six months ago and moved down there much to my disapproval."

"I don't think they made bombs there, just the uranium for atomic power stations, but it could be used for bombs I suppose," John said.

John and Billy left, happy in the knowledge that she had been living there when the fire started, and for a few months afterwards, which accounted for the Iodine one three one in Sadie's bones. John had his proof; it was worth the journey for that bit of information. He was sorry that he couldn't help Mrs Karlov and tell her the truth; she will never probably know what happened to her daughter.

Wednesday was another sunny day, and very warm, John hated the heat. Especially when he was driving, through London, he preferred to travel on the underground. He had decided to do as before, and park on the outskirts and then take the tube into the centre; his appointment with the new Chief Super wasn't until three in the afternoon, so he had plenty of time. He arrived at New Scotland Yard in plenty of time and took the opportunity to go and see Lynda; he was in luck in that she was in, and she told the officer on reception to send John up to her office. They chatted for a while, John told her about the visit to Manchester, a young officer, or so he looked to John came in and Lynda asked him to make a brew for them, John had his usual cup of tea.

"Made in the cup, ah well things change, and some not for the better," he commented.

"I know you insist on tea being made in the pot and allowed to brew etcetera, but I never realised that you could actually taste the difference till now?"

John smiled at her, "your colleague, was standing right behind you when he made it, fooled you."

"You definitely will not have a problem in the interview, you old con man," she said and laughed with him.

At two fifty five precisely, John made his way to the new Chief Super's office, and spoke to the secretary who told the Chief Super that John was here, and she showed him in.

"Mr Alker, what a pleasure it is to see you, now I'm sorry, but the balloon has gone up, and I am afraid that I am pushed for time; had I found out earlier, then I would have cancelled so can you please be concise?"

John looked at the balding, overweight man sat on the other side of the desk, and took an instant dislike to him, an arrogant, over bearing; ignorant, pompous, sod came to his mind.

"Of course thank you for seeing me, I appreciate that you are very busy, but I have a case that, well it will blow your mind to use the vernacular. We have a serial killer on the loose, he has killed somewhere between twenty and a hundred women over the last ten years or so, may be more. There are no bodies, and that is why he has never been hunted, but, I now have circumstantial and also conclusive proof, that he is, active now," John emphasised the 'now', "here are photos of."

"Mr Alker, Mr Alker," the Chief Super interrupted, ",please, out of respect for your exceptional service to the force, I agreed to see you, but I don't have time for niceties, there is no way I am going to open an enquiry on one man's say so, without conclusive proof, not circumstantial. I am sorry, but if that is all you have, then I will have to leave you as I said, I am very busy," the man said smiling inanely.

"Out of respect for your position, I will not call you names, but remind you that you said that you had five minutes, three of which you wasted, now if I may continue I expect you to honour our agreement. As I said, I do have conclusive proof as well," John paused and looked at the shock on the Super's face, no-one had spoken to him like that, "a pathologist, a well-respected pathologist writing a thesis on the effect of the atmosphere on bones, and therefore the human body, exhumed six bodies, one of which was a woman who had been murdered. He discovered that she had Iodine one three one, a radioactive material which is produced when either plutonium or uranium are processed, I am not sure which if not both. In nineteen fifty seven Windscale caught fire and released this toxic product into the atmosphere, it is not produced naturally, so the only way that it could have entered the body of the victim, was, if she were alive and living near Windscale at the time of the fire. The modus operandi was identical to the one I investigated in nineteen sixty two, both of these women had identical twins who disappeared after nineteen seventy eight, as did all the other thirteen victims that I have on file. The one with Iodine one three one was killed according to our files in nineteen thirty two, when it would have been impossible, for her to have come into contact with Iodine one three one. Now there is the proof, the Iodine, solid, conclusive, irrefutable, and the circumstantial proof are the photos of the thirteen look a likes I also have, right my time is almost up, now will you open a full investigation or not?"

"I find your attitude rather brisk and cheeky, to say the least, this is my office, and I will not be spoken to like that, no I will not open an enquiry."

"Then I will have to go higher, perhaps there is someone with brains, who is also a policeman, dedicated to protecting and serving the populace as the sign says. If one more woman dies then I will hold you responsible," John said and stood up collecting the photos, the Super hadn't even bothered to look at, and stormed out.

John almost knocked Lynda over as he rushed down the corridor.

"John, in here now," Lynda said sharply, seeing his fixed and angry face, "what the hell is going on, calm down he is an arrogant little sod and we have to put up with him, but don't give yourself a heart attack over him, he isn't worth it. Now what happened?"

"He didn't even listen to me, just looked at the pile of photos on his desk, not the photos, the pile, and said no, make me an appointment with the Commissioner, let's hope he will listen.

"John don't, listen to me, I have sent the file as you requested to Hammond in Reading, and he has asked to speak to their Chief Inspector over it. I think you will have more success at that level. Perhaps not a full enquiry, you would have listened and done something about it but would your Chief Super?"

John looked at her, shrugged his shoulders and sighed, I suppose you are right, I went too high; this is more grass roots work. I need to speak to the Chief Inspector in Manchester and Reading. I am so anxious; I know that, in ten days, another woman will die unless we can stop him. I know that she will be killed in Reading and dumped in London. I even know ok it's a guess, but my gut reaction is that it will be Lucy. Right age, sex, profession, and most importantly colouring; and I can't stop it that is what is getting to me."

John sat in the chair exhausted, the fight, the heat and the journey had all taken their toll on him, he was no-longer a spring chicken and should act his age, so he told himself, would he ever convince the powers that be of the crimes being committed under their noses?

"Here John have a cup of tea, it took a little longer this time, I brewed it in a pot for you," Lynda said handing him a mug of tea.

"Thank you, I need it, don't get yourself into trouble on account of me, I'm just an old fool."

"Hey stop that you hear me, you have more about you than most of the senior officers here, you have caught more criminals than any of them, you know what is happening and must fight it. Don't let me ever; catch you feeling sorry for yourself again. Once you give in, then he has won, don't allow that. I retire in a year, two at the most then I will be able to help you full time, you will have another lodger."

John smiled an ironic smile and looked at Lynda, "Two years my," he stopped himself, "five to ten, and if what I think is correct, I won't have a lodger much longer. He has terminal cancer, I am sure, I went through it with Jane, but he won't admit it, which one, I don't know. I have seen him vomit blood, and he is acting strange, he never argued about money, but recently he has. I don't know, tight, checking every penny, he was never like that, before. I wouldn't cheat him, he knows that, but I also understand that he should be careful and check every bill, but, ah well I suppose I had better make my way home to beat the rush hour traffic," John said wearily, and got up handing Lynda the empty mug.

John went home and rang Andy to see if he could get John an appointment, and to tell him about the Iodine, Andy said that there was no need, he would see Graham the Chief Inspector under Andy who had been made up to Super, that evening and tell him unofficially, he felt that was the best way to approach this, and would ring John the next day. John sighed as if a weight had been lifted from his shoulders. Billy noticed the sigh and told him to relax a bit, and Andy would get the deal done for him. John smiled at him and nodded his head, it had been a very long day and all he wanted now was a pint.

Next morning the sun was up again, it looked to be another nice day, John and Billy set about their work in the garden.

"Rain later on today, we need to get these seedlings in for the late crop John," Billy said.

"Rain, look at the sky, not a cloud in sight, it's going to be a lovely day, we can have a Bar-B-Que for dinner tonight."

"Since when have I been wrong and you right, hey, I am telling you, it'll rain later."

"Well if it does then I'll ring Reading and make an appointment with the Chief Inspector there, Hammond has already broken the ice for me."

Billy had worked on the land all his life and knew the signs, his gut reaction, as John would call it, and he had never been wrong. The first time John saw Billy's reactions working was the first summer, when he told John to keep the grass long because it was going to be a dry summer. John joked with him about it, but he did do as Billy had said, and sure enough, it was a very dry summer, when most of the short cut lawns were going brown, John's had stayed green, helped by throwing the washing up water on the lawn.

By lunchtime, the clouds were gathering Billy and John didn't stop, deciding to have lunch when it began to rain, Billy had said that it wouldn't be long before it rained, and he was right. By one o'clock, the clouds opened, and it poured down, they had just managed to get all the seedlings in, apart from the last row, which they planted in the rain. Soaked and sore from pushing to get all the seedlings in they went into the kitchen, John went upstairs showered and changed; whilst Billy used the main bathroom and put some clothes on that he kept there, for such an occasion. Back down stairs Billy made them some sandwiches, whilst John rang Reading.

Billy could hear John's side of the conversation, and deduced from that, that they would be going to Reading the following day for a meeting at ten thirty with the Chief Inspector.

John collected his evidence and put it in order, photocopying all his files, this took him a good three hours, even with Billy's help, but he now felt ready for the meeting, and they arranged to meet at John's at nine.

John double checked his briefcase, that everything was in order, and they left, John had also rung Hammond, and told him about the meeting. Hammond said that the Chief Inspector would be open to his case, from the little Hammond had been given the Chief Inspector had expressed interest, and if John hadn't rung then he would have got a call from the Chief Inspector.

John entered the Chief Inspector's office on time, having spoken to Hammond on his way down the corridor. It was what John would consider a normal office, not very big, a desk under the window two chairs for them to sit on, and the ubiquitous filling cabinets which filled one wall, John held out his hand and introduced Billy.

"What's this all about then Mr Alker," the Chief Inspector asked?

"John and Billy, please, in nineteen sixty two I was called to a murder," John began and reiterated the story, showing David Barlow the Chief Inspector the photos as he spoke.

"I must say that it is intriguing, and the evidence is somewhat weak, but by the same token convincing, I have never known of so many missing women and victims, who look alike, but then again I haven't gone so far back in the files, but also all with the same MO. Hammond said that you had more conclusive evidence than those coincidences?"

"Yes, indeed I do, here is a copy of the findings of a pathologist, it proves that the person would have to have lived near to Windscale, as it was known then, for the trace elements to be in her bones," John paused, "she died in nineteen thirty two, but her look alike lived near to Windscale as a child at the time of the fire. She would have had Iodine one three one in her bone, it wouldn't have killed her, it was only a trace amount, but it proves that she has to be the same woman. Iodine one three one is not found naturally."

"I can't argue with that, I don't know enough about radiation and its effects or what Iodine one three one is for that matter, but with a report like that I, well I can't authorise a full murder enquiry, sorry, but I can get my people to add it to their normal work as an addendum, that way it will be watched very closely, if another woman disappears and you can match her to an existing file, then I can go further."

"Thank you, what you are offering is a big step for us, but there won't be a file until the missing woman is dead. It is obvious now that I think about it, how can a file exist when there hasn't been a crime? By sending the body back in time, he creates a case, and it is investigated, so a file appears overnight as it were. Look now and there is nothing, look tomorrow morning and there; it is, worn from years of being there, yet a few hours old. I still can't get my head around that one."

During the conversation, Billy had sat quietly watching them at work, most of it went over his head, and he admitted that it wasn't his field of work, just as John had admitted to him that he didn't know what he was doing in the garden, and was taught by Billy, it was Billy's turn now to learn.

John was pleased with the way things had gone for him, and answered Billy's questions about the meeting. Billy was concerned why it couldn't be opened as a murder enquiry; John explained that the Chief Inspector was protecting his position. A full enquiry would mean that he had to justify the resources being used on a case that was apparently between thirty and one hundred and twenty years old. So by opening the case this way the officers on the street were aware of the murders, and actively looking for the murderer, without an actual case file being opened.

"Crafty sod, so that is why you are happy, as far as you are concerned the case is open."

"Exactly, I now have a force in the firing line, assuming that he has moved down here, and this is his new hunting ground, who are working to solve the case with me, great isn't it?"

"What about Lucy, will they watch her?"

"Not as much as I would like, they can't, it is an extra as the Chief Inspector said, so only if they are in the area will they check up on her, which will be down to us. The tenth is a week on Friday, and that is when we need to be here, watching her, it will be a long night."

"And if we are arrested for curb crawling, we have a friend at the nick," Billy said with a smile.

"Let us try and avoid being arrested, shall we?"

"It wasn't me that got us arrested you know, just so long as you realise that little fact."

"Yes Billy I do," John said, and they both laughed.

Chapter 17
Final Victim?

John and Billy met at seven for the drive up to Reading, it was a good hour's drive, and John decided that Lucy wouldn't be working before eight thirty, from what he had gleaned from his visit to thirty two Windsor Street. They parked in a side street near to the area the women worked, and walked the last bit. Entering the street at the far end and walking its length, noting the women, some of whom they hadn't seen when they last visited the area, and others that had talked to them. John stopped near enough to Lucy to be able to watch her, but not too close, he didn't want to frighten the assailant off or upset Lucy.

"Hello love, are you looking for a good time, I have a friend for your mate," a young woman asked them, she was about five six, auburn hair, and dressed in a waterproof which she allowed to fall open, showing the short skirt and blouse in white, that displayed her breasts, firm and unharnessed.

"No thank you, we are here to, well just to look as it were, having a rest and sheltering from the rain," John said caught off guard for a moment.

"Well this is my doorway so piss off then, unless you want to pay me for the use of it," she said forcefully.

"I don't think you can charge for the use of this doorway, I would suspect that it belongs to the owner of the shop, but we do not want to argue with you or distract what little trade there will be tonight, so we will move on," John said in his official tone.

"That's where you are wrong, mister know it all, I do own this shop, during the day I sell adult toys and other services, interested," she said haughtily, looking down her nose at them both.

"No thank you, good night," Billy said and made to move off.

"I don't see Lucy tonight, do you know where she is," John asked, guessing that she wouldn't admit to knowing and even if she did, she wouldn't say. What lose a potential customer for her never?

"She is ill a cold, I am free though, and I will look after you just a well, if not better, down stairs, I have a dungeon for naughty little boys."

"Thank you, we are not interested, just wanted to see Lucy, if she isn't coming then we will go home, thank you again," John said and nodded his head in a courteous manner.

Billy asked John if he believed the woman, John said that he didn't, but it was possible that she had taken more cocaine, and wasn't awake enough to come out. They moved around the street watching for Lucy. A gentleman stopped them and asked what they were doing, John asked him for his warrant card, which he showed them, and John told him who they were, what they were doing and why. He told them that he would be around that area all night, and would keep an eye out for Lucy. If she showed up, he would let them know in the morning. John thanked him, and they left earlier than they had expected. John received a phone call the following morning to tell him that she hadn't shown up and he guessed why, John agreed with him, and thanked him, then hung up.

When Billy arrived John told Billy about the phone call, and then they started work in the garden, it was a challenge for them, one and a half acres went with the house in the sale, and John had bought an extra half acre from a farmer whose field was attached to his garden. This was why they needed to spend so much time in the garden, and how come they were able to sell their excess vegetables from the stall at weekends.

It was Billy who heard the phone ringing; John went to answer it, "Hello."

"John there is a girl missing from Reading, one of the street women, Hammond rang me to tell me, she isn't blonde, and no file has shown up, but because of our interest in these women he decided to take a note of it and ring me. What would you like me to do about it," Lynda said?

"I am not sure, people do go missing, and that could be the case here, except for the specific interest we have in these women; there is no reason to suppose that she has been murdered. How far back did you check?"

"Way back and I found several back in the eighteen hundreds, all on the second year of the decade that fit our MO, but none that fit the description of this woman."

"It is difficult to say, I will go down to Reading tonight, and talk with the women, I can't ask Reading to do it, I don't want to antagonise this delicate situation, we have their co-operation let's keep it that way."

"I agree Sir, would you like me to come with you; I have a day off tomorrow so I am free?"

"That would be nice, I would appreciate your help, but what about your private life, would the boyfriend appreciate the fact of you going out with me," John joked.

"What boyfriend, I can't keep one, too busy with police work."

"You need a private life as well, don't allow your work to stop you from living, at forty nine you should be married my girl."

"Now you're sounding like my mum. I'll pick you up at eight; have a cup of coffee ready please."

"Make it seven thirty and I'll have dinner ready for you, we don't need to leave before eight thirty to nine."

Lynda thanked him and hung up, John went back to the garden and told Billy that Lynda was joining them; then they carried on working. Alan came home early, John looked at him and recognised the signs, he was now half the size he was when he first arrived, and looking very gaunt and tired.

"Alan it is none of my business, but you don't look well, have you been to the doctor?"

"Yes, and I am ill, but like you said it is none of your business, thank you for your concerns," Alan said and walked away to his room.

Alan had always been so polite and friendly, a charmer, this was unlike him, John began to get worried, Alan's character had changed, why, what was wrong with him. Alan had gone from an eleven stone man, fit and healthy, to a much weaker thinner man who didn't eat as much. John had also heard him cry out in the night, this made him realise what it was, and having gone through it with Jane, but as Alan had said it wasn't his concern, none the less, it still bothered John.

Lynda arrived early, and John put out the dinner then they washed up and got ready to leave. John read the file, what there was of it, in the car whilst Lynda drove. They parked in the same spot, John had the last time he went to Reading, and walked the length of the street. John's memory and his logical reasoning meant that he remembered where each of the women had stood, and soon spotted the vacant doorway. As they neared the telephone box end of the street, he was pleased to see that Lucy was still there sniffing, as usual, leaning on the phone box. They were lucky in that the rain of the last two days had stopped for a brief period, and the women were out in force. John spotted some new faces amongst the assembled women who made to approach him, but withdrew when they saw Lynda.

"Lucy, did you know this woman," John asked, showing her the photo of the missing woman?

"Yes she worked here why?"

"She has not been seen for a couple of days, do you know her well, is she ill or has she perhaps gone on holiday?"

"No, she was here last Friday, that was when I last saw her, then I was off ill with a cold I haven't seen her since. I didn't know her that well, but if you ask Janet over there, she was a good friend of hers, she'll probably know more."

"Thank you," John said and went over to the woman Lucy had pointed out.

John asked the same questions, she also didn't know what had happened to Beverly, and was getting worried. She asked initially what it had to do with him, and Lynda showed her, her warrant card, this had the desired effect, and she was more co-operative.

They stayed in the area watching for a couple of hours, then Lynda took them to the hotel John had booked earlier, they had a couple of drinks in the bar and then went to bed.

Next morning at John's suggestion they went to the local police station and spoke to Hammond, who was just about to go off duty, and they then spoke to Raymond.

"We had a chat with a couple of the women, I didn't want to ask you to because at the moment there is no case for you to investigate, and I didn't want to send you on a wild goose chase. We have done enough of that in this enquiry. All I can say is that she is a missing person. The hair colouring is wrong, that date is wrong, and apart from the fact that she is a street woman there is nothing to make us believe that she is another victim. Thank you for telling us, and if anything should show up then I will let you know," John told Raymond in his office over a welcome cup of tea.

"Thank you John, for not wasting our time, and we will keep you informed, it is just blondes that interests you is it?"

"That is hard to say, most of the women it has to be said were dyed blonde, whether or not it was post mortem we don't know. He has the time to drain their blood wash them and style their hair, a simple style just brushed, but even so all of that takes a lot of time, so we must assume that he has the time to dye their hair as well, if that is what is required to create the woman he wants to create."

"Ok, we will keep you informed, but there can be several women that are reported as missing arriving on Lynda's desk, I hope her Super won't object," Raymond said with a smile.

"I now have a fax machine so you can send then directly to me," John offered.

"I, well that would mean sending confidential files out of the office John, and you know what problems that could cause."

John had to accept the fact that he was no-longer a police officer and the files would have to be sent to Lynda for her to pass them on to him. It was a chance that she would have to take. He didn't like the idea of her taking the risk, but also knew that he had no option and that she was willing to take the risk, it was after all her idea, to photocopy the files originally and put them in the boot of his car.

On the way back home, John remembered that he hadn't bought a birthday card for Alan and that it was his birthday the following day, before they left Reading John went to a card shop and bought a card, in his usual style. He hated shopping and could never make his mind up as to which one to get, his one weakness as Jane had said many times. She used to select the card herself or ask his secretary to get any cards that were needed for the office. He just signed them, accepting that their choice would be far better than his. Again he was confused by the array of cards before him, Alan was a scientist, and didn't do any sports, yet of all the cards on display he picked up one with a golfer on the front. Back in the car he asked Lynda for a pen, she handed him one, and it didn't work.

"A serving officer with a pen that doesn't work, how on earth can you make notes," he chastised her, yet not?

"I noticed you said serving officer to get you off the hook, but I do have a red pen John, I'm sorry, but that is all I have."

"Well it isn't right, but I am in a fix, I need to give Alan this card tonight when we get back," John said.

He took the pen and wrote the card on his knee. He hated doing things like that, it was so unprofessional and sloppy in his mind, but the rush to get to Reading had messed up his plans and now it was more urgent, and so he had to live with the situation.

John wrote the card and put it in the envelope; Billy looked at him in an odd sort of way but said nothing. They drove home and then after eating dinner at the Bull, Lynda went home.

Alan seemed much better the following day, a good night's sleep seemed to have helped him, but John was fully aware of the good and bad days he would soon be going through, if John was correct in his diagnosis, and he was sure he was.

"Happy birthday Alan," John said cheerfully as he handed Alan the card.

"Well thank you, it must be six years or more since anyone bothered to send me a card, since my parents were killed in that car accident," Alan said and opened the card.

"I am hopeless at choosing cards, as my wife would say, my one true failing, so I hope it is alright?"

"I am so touched John, like I said I haven't received a card in so long, thank you."

John looked at Alan and watched as he went upstairs; putting the card in his room before leaving for work, there was something that niggled at the back of John's mind. Something wasn't right, but what?

The following Friday was the tenth of the month, and John asked Lynda if she could get a couple of days off and join them in Reading for the evening, watching for the murderer, John was convinced that he would turn up that night, but when and where? He also rang Hammond and told him of his thoughts, Hammond said that he was working, and would be able to keep popping down to help them, John thanked him.

It was two days later when Hammond rang John to tell him that, as part of an investigation, he was working on he had, had to interview a witness who happened to be a physicist, and had mentioned John's case to him. The Professor had suggested that John contact him and they meet, John agreed readily, and took the Professor's phone number down and rang him. They arranged to meet on Monday in the evening at John's hotel, John rang Lynda to tell her, and she said that she would drive down alone on Tuesday, because she was working on the Monday.

"Professor Weiss, thank you so much for offering your help," John said extending his hand in greeting when the Professor met him and Billy.

"My pleasure, from what Detective Hammond told me, you have a serial killer who is burying the bodies in time, very interesting. I am as interested in this as you must be, because of the technology, I wondered if it was possible and from what Detective Hammond said, it is," he said excited.

"That is the only assumption we can come up with, we have close on fifty bodies of unidentified women all blonde all killed in exactly the same way and some twenty or so females that are missing with photographs that match the dead women. Can there be another explanation," John said.

"How can I help you?"

"Tell me about time travel, what are the pit falls if any, what are the assumptions the scientists are making about time travel?"

"Well there are so many theories, like you can't have the same item in the same space and time; they would just cancel each other out. So your killer must know where he is when he goes back in time to avoid meeting himself. Every time you venture into another time you alter that time period just by being there. Like your women they were not meant to be there but now they are; that time period has altered. He commented on the files, again; an officer would be assigned to investigate the murder, yet he wasn't supposed to, so again the murderer has altered that time zone. One theory is that a crime, shall we say, because that is what we are discussing, will replace another crime. So the woman who should have been murdered may now not be, or just that the file has changed. Say an assault on a woman has now become a murder, then the victim would be recognised, we assume, whereas, in your case, they have not been, so the file will only appear once the crime has been committed, very complex. We presume that it will require a tremendous amount of energy and a vast piece of equipment, a warehouse full, but if as you say he is doing it alone, that theory must be incorrect, otherwise the authorities would know about it, it would be noticeable."

"As far as we know he is sending the bodies back in time, they are inanimate, because they are dead; excuse me, I am thinking as I speak, can a human go back in time that is to say living tissue?'

"I can see no reason why not, but that is interesting, yes, an item, an inanimate object, as opposed to a human, again it is an assumption that we can go back in time, but you have posed an interesting point there. What damage would or could it do to the humane body or mind, hum? There is one point, which perhaps you, haven't thought of, when is the crime committed? If we assume that he does go back in time, he can then say be with you in a pub at the time of the murder, and the following night go back in time and commit the crime knowing that he has a solid alibi."

"I must admit, I had thought of that point, yes why not, in that he could be with us at the Bull and at the same time be killing his next victim, so you can be in two places at the same time. We did consider that he may be from the future and travelling back in time to collect a victim then burying the body further back in time, but he has been leaving us clues, and he is active, and from this time period, we do know that much."

"John, are you thinking what I am thinking, I had a deja vu moment the other day, when you bought the card for Alan, I was sure that I had seen it before, but I put it down to a coincidence; that isn't the only card of its kind is it?"

"No Billy, it isn't, but I had the same feeling, and now I know where I, have seen it before, in the nineteen forty two file, battered from being blown up when that bomb landed wrecking the police station and the card falling into a puddle, then being collected and put back into an evidence box. The question still remains, how did it get there? The obvious answer is that my suspicions were correct, and Alan is our murderer, up until now I answered that possibility by reasoning that he was with us at the time of the murder, but now Professor Weiss has opened up a new box, in that he could have been, and commit the murder at the same time, this will take some getting used to."

"Let us assume that it is Alan, then how on earth are you going to prove it is him," Billy said.

"Good question and I don't have an answer."

The meeting broke up after another hour or so, whilst they discussed the pros and cons of getting the evidence to convict Alan or prove him innocent.

John and Billy wandered round Reading like a pair of sightseers, after lunch at a small cafe they went back to the hotel, Lynda was due about four she had told John, so they had a rest and then met in the bar at four to wait for Lynda. As John had expected she was on time, even after the journey from London and the afternoon traffic. John smiled at her as she entered the bar dead on four and gave her a surprised look.

"I know you John, I left early, and I have been in my room since three thirty so as not to be late," she told him.

"Nice to see I still have some power left over my colleagues."

"And I am proud to be called one, I have learned a lot from you over the last few years, thank you. Now what is all this about a Professor and time travel?"

John ordered a round of drinks and then explained to her the information they had gleaned from meeting the Professor, and the problems it has caused as well, adding that it also supported the theories proposed by Alan earlier.

"So he could come back in time and take her after we have seen her here all night, whoa, that doesn't make sense. Surely we would see her go with him?"

"No, if he comes tomorrow night, then we will know up until that point in time that she was there all night; but after he has taken her, as you say, then we will have a different memory of the evening, he is changing history. How that will affect us, I don't know, how can we have two memories of the same night? Will we, or will one overturn the other, I have no idea? The Professor seems to think that our memory of the evening will be factual, but the new memory will be as a sub-memory like deja vu. I could have sworn I saw her last night type of feeling, but I couldn't have, she is dead."

"That begs the question, is it worth us going out there tonight then, I mean if we are not going to see the murderer, be it Alan or not, what is the point?"

"Good question, but I think it is still worth the effort just in case, is it tonight or are we here when he comes back, or oh hell I am so confused, my brain just will not absorb this concept; why can't we have a good old fashioned murder where we can find and prosecute the murderer."

"You're confused, how do you think I feel, this is going way above my head, being in two places at once, I always understood that was impossible," Billy said looking as confused as he sounded.

"I agree Billy, but you have to remember that he isn't really; the events are as far as he is concerned a day apart, so, in fact, he isn't in two places at the same time, yet he is, sorry that didn't help did it," Lynda said confusing herself?

The evening had turned for the worse, and the rain expected during the afternoon waited until they were on the street. John walked the length as usual and saw a few of the women huddled in the doorways as he neared the telephone box he could see that it was empty, Lucy wasn't there. John turned and went to one of the ladies he had spoken to previously, and asked if she knew where Lucy was, suggesting to the woman that Lucy had another cold. The woman, was a tall, slim, anorexic looking woman, who told them that Lucy had an engagement that evening, and wouldn't be out, but offered her services instead, which John politely refused. He asked if she knew where they could find Lucy, she again said that she couldn't, they all now wondered if it was because she thought she stood a chance of getting their business by not telling them. Lynda produced her warrant card and asked again suggesting that they could always discuss her knowledge of Lucy's whereabouts down at the station. It was a gamble, but it had the desired effect, and she told them that she didn't, shaking her head as if to emphasise that she didn't know where Lucy was.

The trio split up and questioned all the women on the street about Lucy's whereabouts, but no-one knew she usually slept at one five seven Harbour View and had taken her men friends there, one told Billy, who now felt confident enough to question the women alone. He also found out that she had a booking for nine o'clock at another address, but she didn't know that address. Billy caught up with John and told him what he had found out quite excited, seeing as he, the only none copper there, was the only one to come up with anything decent. They waited, for Lynda to join them, and then John said that they needed to go to one five seven Harbour View.

"Where is a policeman when you need one, I am referring to Hammond of course, well, we'll just have to get a taxi, we would spend too long hunting for the address," John said agitated.

"No need, here comes Hammond, hi can you take us to this address it's where we expect to find Lucy," Lynda said?

"Sure it's only a couple of streets away, a lot of the women use that address, I'll come in with you, I would like to see inside, we have never had just cause to go inside yet, so it would be an advantage if I knew the layout of the house," Hammond replied.

Like Hammond had said it was just two streets beyond the telephone box where they turned, and then about half way down a semi-detached mid-fifties house with bow windows and a basement, with a small front garden and a side access to a gate with tyre track ruts from vehicles entering and leaving. Built in red brick with a bay window on the front and it had once been a professional or businessman's home, now nothing more than a brothel.

"Don't you think it looks threatening with four of us walking up the drive," John said?

"No, not really two old men, a woman, and me, what on earth could be threatening about that?"

"Numbers, that is all, I feel I would be better on my own," John said worried about the frontal assault, as he felt it looked like.

They all ignored him and the group stood in the open porch sheltering as best they could from the rain, Hammond knocked there was no reply, he knocked again, harder, no reply.

Hammond opened the letter box and shouted through it, "this is the police open or I will be forced to break the door down."

The door opened a little, and a woman's face appeared in the gap, "Yes, sorry I was in the bathroom."

"DC Hammond and Inspector Summers, we need to speak to you, may we come in?"

"I, I am not dressed, can you come back in half an hour or tomorrow would be better?"

"Madam I understand that you will not be dressed, I am not interested in that, I need to speak to Lucy, is she in, and if not, I will need to look round to convince myself that she isn't. So in either case I need you to open the door to allow me and my colleagues to enter. Or if you wish I could get a search warrant and bring a squad down here to search the premises for drugs, which I am sure, are on the premises, now how do we do this?"

"Ok, ok, but, please be discreet," she said and opened the door for them to enter.

The hallway was like thirty two Windsor Street, wide with a staircase to the left of the hallway facing them, to the right was a door into the front room, she showed them into that room and offered them a cup of coffee, trying to soothe them. John looked her up and down, and for her age, about fifty five, she was in good shape, and by no means undressed a full length skirt covered her legs with a white blouse and waist coat in black leather above the skirt. Black shiny leather boots covered her feet and her hair jet black and pulled back into a severe bun. She removed her leather gloves to reveal her nails, which were painted, in a deep red nail varnish, her make-up was also severe, yet put on with care bringing out her deep hazel eyes and full red lips, a school mistress of the early twentieth century Victorian or Edwardian in style.

"We will be happy to sit here for a few minutes if you wish, I presume you are busy," John said, realising that she had a client in her rooms from her appearance and what little he knew of domination.

"Thank you, that would be er, considerate of you," she replied and left them.

A few moments later they heard a car drive away and then she entered with a tray of tea for them.

"I am sorry to have disturbed you, but I am hunting a murderer, a serial killer, and I am convinced that Lucy will be his next victim. She is ideal; she is the right colour, right profession, and the right size, as well. She is small making her easier to control, with force if necessary, and her habit, will make his job even easier. So it is important that we find her, very important, and we believe she sleeps here and may be here at the moment," John said as a question?

"No she isn't, and yes you can look, all the rooms are empty now. If you know that she will be his next victim you must know who he is then, mustn't you?"

"No, we don't, but we do know that he is after a certain type of woman in a specific profession, and on certain days, of all the women we saw on the street to-night, and on the previous times we visited the street. Lucy is the only one that fits the bill perfectly, and he is on the prowl tonight. Please help us to protect Lucy?"

"I am sorry, she has gone out with a very nice gentleman, and we do assess our girl's clients before we allow them to go out with them; otherwise they must use these premises part of the care we take of the girls."

"She has already left with him, when," John asked now agitated?

"No, she has gone to meet him, the first time they come here, then if we agree that the girl is in safe hands, we allow them to go out together, they meet up at a pub and spend the night together, that is what they are doing tonight, Lucy will get five hundred for the night. Obviously they do not have to live by our rules and can go with anyone they choose, but most of them are wise enough to realise that what we do is in their own best interest."

"Plus your commission, or does that come out of the five hundred," Hammond asked?

"Lucy will get all of the five hundred, my, our commission her client has paid," she said taken aback at Hammonds effrontery.

"Do you know where she is, I can't stress how important this is, we only want to see that she is alright," John said trying to bring back the conversation to a more convivial and pertinent setting.

"Yes, but I can't tell you, that would be a breach of our confidentiality, and without that, we don't have a business, besides he was a very nice gentleman," she replied.

"I will go alone, and I will not speak to her, I don't want to ask her anything, just see, as in visual from a window, or another table if they are dining," John was pleading now, something he had never had to do in the past, and it felt unnerving to him.

"I, well, I will tell you the place, but you must promise not to speak to her, I," she stopped when the door opened then slammed shut.

"The fucking creep never turned up, I'm off to bed," Lucy shouted angrily from the hallway.

They heard her feet thumping up the stairs in temper.

"It seems that you needn't bother, she is here, see, fine."

"We are sorry to have troubled you, and thank you for the tea," John said getting up, indicating that they were leaving, "If he should ring and apologise asking her to join him please ring me at this number, and ask for room two one five."

Lynda stood up and handed the woman a card with her mobile number on it and said that it would be easier if she rang her, as she could be reached at any time. The woman took the card and said that she would do.

They all left the following morning after saying goodbye to Hammond at the hotel; he joined them for breakfast then went into the office when they left. John was quiet on the journey home Billy knew that he was deep in thought, wondering how they had made such a mistake, they both knew that last night was when the murder would take place, they both knew that Lucy was the prime victim, yet she was safe and sound why? Had he retired was it Alan, who now, because of his illness was no-longer able to commit murder? What had gone wrong?

That night Lynda had stayed with John and they ate at the pub then returned to John's house and sat in the lounge, John hadn't said much all day pondering the events of the previous evening.

Why had they left the house when told that Lucy was out with a nice gentleman? Knowing that it was Alan, and she was about to be murdered? Why had he taken the woman's word for it; that was so unlike him, he always wanted concrete proof; so why had they left? Lynda's phone rang, she answered it.

"Yes, Inspector Summer speaking,——-, sorry you say that Lucy didn't return last night and hasn't been seen since,——-, yes thank you for letting us know," she said and hung up.

Lynda's face was a mixture of annoyance, confusion, anger, and worry, "Sir, didn't we hear Lucy come in last night, or was I dreaming that part, if so, why did we leave when we knew who she was with and that she was to be his next victim?"

"Lynda we all did, now it begins to make sense, we did hear her come back, but he has just gone back in time to last night, so we now feel that it was a dream, but our time has moved on, so has his, but Lucy's hasn't, we know she was there, we heard her, but because he has changed history it becomes a distant, a false memory, where is Alan now," John demanded?

"In his room, isn't he," Lynda said?

"I can hear his music, so I presume that he is, shall I go and knock," Billy asked?

"Yes, go and offer him a cup of tea, expect an answer, if you don't get one, ask again, until you do, or get me and I will use my key, in case he has had an accident, that is perfectly legal."

Billy went upstairs and knocked on Alan's door, he replied that he didn't want a coffee and thanked Billy for the offer.

"I'll get an arrest warrant and search warrant for that room John," Lynda said.

"On what grounds, because he has just gone back in time, they'll laugh at you, but there has to be a way to get him, we now know it is him. Yet we can do little or nothing, it is too late to save Lucy, so we have a month in which to find a way. Let's not rush it and spoil a good arrest, let me think for a day or so," John said standing up and pacing the room hand on chin as he dredged his memory for a suitable reason for a search warrant.

The phone rang on the following Friday, John answered it; "John I'm coming down tomorrow, I did a stupid thing and tried to get a search warrant and arrest warrant. You were right, the Super asked me if I was feeling alright, and, if the job stressed me too much, being a woman, and all that, the 'B', I'll have him. What can I do, he more or less asked me for my resignation, a time machine indeed?"

"Do exactly that, come down and we will get it sorted, Alan is very ill now, this last week he has gone worse, I don't think he has much longer."

Lynda arrived on the Friday evening, straight from work and flopped in an arm chair from being upset more than tiredness, she had, had a stressful week after her request it seemed that everything she did was now checked to see that it was right.

John and Billy came in from the garden, and Billy offered them a cup of tea, Lynda said that she would love one, John also said he would and to offer Alan one, as well. Billy went upstairs and asked Alan, who moaned in pain. Billy rushed down and told them that Alan wasn't well and needed to go to hospital, would they call an ambulance immediately?

John rushed upstairs to Alan's room and found him on the floor in serious pain. By conditioning and training John took in the room, he hadn't been in since Alan had taken the room, it had changed on the outside wall was an enormous machine with an opening in the middle about six foot high and three feet wide. Whilst he was taking in the room, he knelt down by Alan's side.

"Lynda is calling an ambulance Alan, where is the pain?"

"All, argh, all, argh over, my head is about, argh, explode, argh," he yelled rolling around clutching his head and doubled over in serious pain.

"What have you been taking is there any around for me to dose you with?"

"Morphine and I can't take any more, it could kill me, and besides I have run out, argh."

"Morphine, how, oh, never mind, it doesn't matter now, I feel useless, all I can do is wait here with you till the ambulance arrives."

Chapter 18
Death Bed Confession

It took a few minutes for the ambulance to arrive and take Alan away; John went with him in the ambulance to the hospital. It was hard on John, he had seen it all before, and the memory of the pain and anguish Jane had suffered, came flooding back to him, making him want to weep.

John spent the night with Alan at the hospital, and when he was sedated fully, the following morning, John went home to have a shave and change his clothes. Billy was there he had slept on the settee in case John had needed him, and asked how Alan was. John told him saying that he had a few hours to live in his opinion, the pain was so sever, and that Alan was drugged all the time now.

"John I almost forgot, I have brought this file to complete the set, I am sure it will be the last one, it is Lucy, I found it way back in the oldest files, before I left I decided to check for myself, eighteen twenty, before Sir Robert Peel founded the police force as such; it was a report from a newspaper that had been put in the files, even the photo from the paper I knew it was her. I feel very stupid about going to the Super now you were right, I suppose that has ended my chances of ever getting any higher in the force, I did fancy following in Andy's footsteps, but I have fucked that up haven't I?"

"May be, let's see what happens, I am hopeful that he will give me a death bed confession, have you got a tape recorder?"

"Yes, now that you ask, I have in the car, do you want it?"

"Yes, please, I want a record of this interview, but I am not sure what I will do about it. What I would like you to do is to clear, er, my office, I am convinced that he is our murderer, but he is dying and won't make it through the night, so you will never get him to court, and the file will stay open, because we will never be able to convict him, but I want that,' John paused to find the right word, "cretin, to know the truth, if not for my own sake but for yours."

'What if it isn't him?' Lynda said.

"My gut reaction tells me that it is him, and it's never been wrong before. What I want you to do if you will please is clear the office and destroy all those files, they are only copies anyway, but if I am right then my case is solved."

"And if you're wrong, as I said before?"

"I am too old now to carry on, you will have to investigate it for me, if you so desire?"

"You know I will, and report back if I solve it for you, I can still come and visit you can't I?"

"Yes of course, you will have to keep me informed anyway," John said with a smile, he leaned over and kissed her on the cheek, "Thank you for all your help and support."

John left for the hospital and went to Alan's bedside; he took hold of Alan's hand and held on to it as a wave of pain swept through Alan. Alan opened his eyes after it had passed and looked at John.

"You know don't you," he said, in almost a whisper?

"Yes Alan I do," John said with empathy, "but we need to clean things up quite a bit don't we, you need to confess, to tell me why and how."

"I was fourteen at the time, and a bitch and that is the only name I can give her, she ruined my life, she made my family ashamed of me. She made the teachers dislike me, and instead of encouraging me at school as they had always done, they left me. I had to get to where I am alone. She showed me that all blondes were evil, and had to have the evil removed, I did that by removing their blood, the only thing that goes throughout the body, carrying their evilness within it, I made them pure.

She said that I was the father of her child, I wasn't, I hadn't even had sex; I was still a virgin when she accused me. Argh," he cried as another pain swept through him, "what I had to do was meet the women, and assess them to see if they were evil, they were. Then I made arrangements to meet them and didn't turn up. I argh, I went back in time the next day to meet them, and then take them forward in time two seconds, that was all it took two seconds. Now because, they were not in their time period, they were limp, outside their time as it were beyond it. Then it was easy to tie their ankles and pull them up, remember, I was in my time period so it didn't affect me, and cut their throats to allow the evil to escape into the sewers where it belonged.

I then washed them and made sure that none of their outer evil appearance, like nail polish and argh," Alan stopped allowing his body to recover from the pain, "on them. Then laid them out in the vortex, when it is working it looks like a vortex, a swirling mess of time I dialled the exact time I wanted. A different decade, but the very day she accused me the tenth of the month, January nineteen sixty two was the actual day; and sent them back down the annals of time, to that time, when they landed. I could see them, and if necessary join them to adjust their position, but I never needed. Death was swift, I saw to that, with the two second time difference they never woke up once I had taken them forward. I have a lab in a disused warehouse in Manchester that is where I took them. It would have ended soon because it is going to be pulled down in a few months, and I am ill I knew it was terminal so I wasn't worried about being caught, what could they do, kill me," Alan laughed at the senselessness of the idea killing a dying man, "I once said to you that a time machine was a dangerous thing, my dying wish is that you go back and destroy it." Another wave of pain swept through Alan, and his voice was weaker, when the pain had subsided, John moved even closer to him, to hear what he was saying. "I have destroyed the one in Manchester, and I was destroying the secondary one in your house when I collapsed. Please don't think too badly of me, it had to be done. When my parents died still thinking that I had made her pregnant; they were proud of my achievements don't get me wrong, but they never really got over that shame, now it is common place, but then, there was still a stigma to making a girl pregnant, they are all evil." He stopped to allow another wave of pain then went on, "it is powered by a radioactive isotope, this is deep inside the machine, and it is that, that has caused the brain tumour, and it spread, or the poisoning caused other cancers, going backwards and forwards in time inside that machine. I didn't realise that I would be exposed to it, but as you pass through the opening once it is on, you are in direct contact with the radiation, when I discovered this it was too late, I was already ill; even so I corrected the fault, and you can now travel safely. John, I did remedy it by enclosing it in more lead," he stopped again for another wave of pain, this time it was more severe than before and didn't go away, John called the doctor who gave Alan another injection of morphine.

"I can't increase the dose anymore John, if I do I will kill him," John's doctor friend said.

"Would it make any difference now or in a few minutes in agony, he won't last much longer," John said a tear in his eye as he went through the same misery and pain of watching Jane suffer towards the end of her life.

Even though, John despised Alan for what he had done, he didn't want to watch him suffer like this; he didn't want to go through it again.

"A good question, ethically yes, in principle I don't think so, but I am bound by ethics," he said shrugged his shoulders and walked away sullenly, knowing that John's pain was as much if in a different way to Alan's pain.

John sat there holding onto Alan's hand; he wanted to kill him for what he had done, but not like this. He wanted to see him locked in prison for his crime, but that wasn't going to happen. At that moment in time there was a little boy, lying in the bed, crying in pain, and John couldn't take away his pain. Jane had suffered the same, but she was a woman. Alan hadn't got over the shame and so, was it really his fault? Was he totally to blame for his actions? That the girl had turned a brilliant scientific mind into a psychopathic killer, schizoid, a brilliant Professor and a killer, which was he speaking to now, Doctor Jekyll or Mister Hyde, from what he was saying it was a mixture of both perhaps now Doctor Jekyll the powerful one acknowledging Mr Hyde's actions.

"Alan, I will go back and destroy the machine, where is the warehouse, give me that address please so that I can destroy that as well, is there anything there that can help them build another machine?"

"The address is in my diary, I never went there after I had bought it, I used the time machine if I needed to go so that if seen then I had several friends to confirm that it wasn't me, they saw, like when I cleaned the women, I," he paused as a minor pain wave passed, John assumed that it was as intense as the others, but now controlled by the morphine, "went back in time, you have known for a bit haven't you, I could see it in your eyes, the same look that my parents had, shame. A few days ago you gave me my birthday card, I rushed upstairs I had an idea, you see I knew that you knew but needed proof, so I sent the card back in time and placed it under the woman's body for them to find. The red ink gave me the idea that was not you, it was all wrong for you, so I told you that it was me. I destroyed the machine at the warehouse, and was destroying the one in your house when the pain became too much, you have to destroy it, see I changed history twice, once by leaving the body then by leaving the evidence for you."

"Yes Alan I have, but it was never shame, just wonderment, why such a brilliant mind had got so twisted, and how on earth, I could catch you, and then get you to court with evidence. I have a great deal of admiration for you, and yes, I also despise you, it's a funny conflict of emotions. Alan if the file only appears when you send the person back, how come I got the card your proof that it was you?"

"Easy John, when I received it, I went back in time, and left it under her body, I remembered leaving the room at that point so managed to get in and leave it so that when I sent the body back the file appeared with the card, cleaver of me don't you think. To give you the one true clue to my identity before we even met. Fate is a funny thing, even when you can twist it as I did, argh," Alan went silent as the pain swept through his body, then went on, "at least you are honest, I understand, Thank you John," Alan squeezed John's hand so hard it hurt, then the alarm went off and his hand relaxed.

The doctor rushed in with the nurses, he looked at John, that same look as he gave him when Jane had died. He checked for a pulse, and heartbeat, then looked at John again.

"DNR, he didn't tell you that, he just told me, why go through more pain than I have done,' he said to me, 'Do Not Resuscitate," John lied and left the room.

John entered the house and Lynda told him that all the files and paper work were now in the boot of her car ready for the shredder back at the office. John didn't speak he just went up to his room and closed the door and cried, relieving himself of the anguish inside. He couldn't go through that again, twice in one life time, that was too much for anyone to bear.

Although Lynda had said that she would be leaving that evening she didn't, and stayed on till morning, Billy had gone home because Lynda was there in case John needed anybody. John had breakfast with them; it was a quiet breakfast as John pondered his next step.

"I have a story to tell you both, it's about a brilliant young lad in his early teens who was cheated, and shamed, so much so that it turned his mind. There is a fine line between genius and insanity, and he was pushed over that line. I have decided that he was a victim, just as much as the women were, but in a different way. Yes Alan was the serial killer; I got a deathbed confession from him. That sounds bad, I didn't have to question him, he gave me one freely, and he got it off his chest. The files will have to stay open, we can tell all those involved the truth, but no-one else will believe us, I am going to fulfil his dying wish and destroy the time machine. Lynda destroy those files please, and Billy and I will destroy the time machine, you can tell the Super from me that it is over, we have found our killer, and I was right all along as were you and Andy, I will ring Andy and tell him, will you also ring Hammond and tell him for me please?"

"Yes Sir, are you sure we could close the case, if we showed the time machine?"

"Yes, and create a monster even bigger than the one upstairs. No Lynda this will die with us."

John and Billy had lunch at the pub, they were just in time before he closed the dining room, and John had commented that it was no wonder he was so hungry, it was well after their usual lunch time.

After lunch, Billy went out to the shed, to get the tools John had asked for, a pick an axe, a sledge hammer, anything big and hefty that he could use to break it up into manageable pieces, whilst John rang Andy and told him the outcome. When Billy came back with the barrow loaded with the tools he helped Billy take them up into the room, Billy gazed in wonderment at the machine.

"Billy I now want you to build a bomb fire, I don't want anything left to help the scientists to build another one of these, and we will melt and burn everything we can."

Once Billy had left the room he picked up the only book Lynda had left of the case, his note book that he had put in a drawer in the lounge; he had forgotten to give it to her. He opened it and looked through the pages at all the names and addresses of the victims and their families, he wondered if he should tell them, give them some kind of ending to their grief, their loss, not knowing if their loved ones would ever return or not? He decided against it, they would not believe him and then call him an idiot, a silly old fool, so it would be pointless.

"By the time, everything was ready it was dinner time, and we went to the pub it was now eight in the evening. We were both very tired so decided to leave the machine till morning. I asked John if he wanted me to sleep there that night, I was showing concern for a dear friend; John declined my offer saying that he was alright."

"I went home, and then there was this whoosh, about ten o'clock it was, I looked out of the window and saw the house with a gaping big hole in it, I have no idea what John had done, but he is somewhere in the distant past I presume. Too far-fetched for you, I am telling you the truth honestly," Billy said to Tony.

"Billy that is the only explanation I can believe I am convinced that it is the truth, but as you say no-one will ever believe it. I am sorry, I can't print it as a news story, I will be laughed out of the profession, but as a story, then it has legs. Look out for, no, when I have written it, I will send you the novel. I will need to change the names etcetera, but you will know the truth, as I do, thank you so much for telling me. As I told you before the truth is stranger than fiction, if you wish, there will be a book for Lynda and Andy, as well.

The next morning Tony packed his bags and left the village returning six months later with three books in his hand, which he handed, to Billy. He also handed Billy a cheque made out to the local village hospital, in honour of John, for a substantial sum.

Made in the USA
Monee, IL
27 May 2022

Paradox

John Eric Poulson

ISBN: 1-4776-9653-9
ISBN-13: 9781477696538